D1161964

A MAN CALLED CERVANTES

OTHER BOOKS BY BRUNO FRANK

AVAILABLE IN ENGLISH

DRAMA

TWELVE THOUSAND

FICTION

TRENCK

THE PERSIANS ARE COMING

THE DAYS OF THE KING

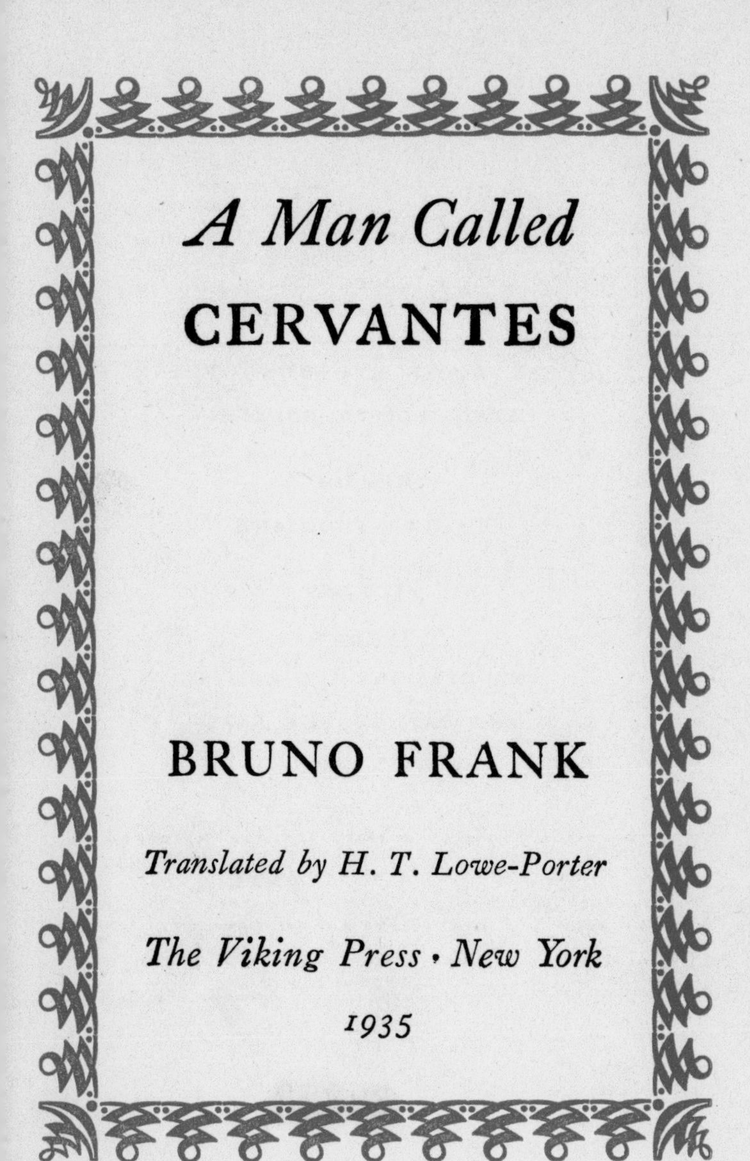

A Man Called CERVANTES

BRUNO FRANK

Translated by H. T. Lowe-Porter

The Viking Press • New York

1935

FIRST PUBLISHED MARCH 1935

PRINTED IN U. S. A. BY THE HADDON CRAFTSMEN, INC.

DISTRIBUTED IN CANADA BY THE MACMILLAN COMPANY
OF CANADA, LTD.

F O R E W O R D

"A certain strong man," says Thomas Carlyle, "fought stoutly at Lepanto, worked stoutly as an Algerine slave; with stout cheerfulness endured famine and nakedness and the world's ingratitude; and sitting in gaol, with one hand left him, wrote our joyfullest, and all but our deepest, modern book, and named it *Don Quijote.*"

A certain strong man. Those are the right words. An outsider, a failure, unknown, he remained for almost the whole of his life "a certain Cervantes." He was fifty-three when the artist Francisco published a collection of the portraits and biographies of Spain's famous men. Of Cervantes there was no portrait, and no word.

His life is known to us only in part. Shakespeare, his contemporary—they died the same year and month—knew fame earlier, yet Shakespeare's life is as obscure. Today we have scholars who write dissertations on Goethe's wine-cellars and the keenness of his vision. Then things were different. We have no letter of Cervantes preserved, no manuscript. A few legal documents, appeals, notes of hand, residuum of his continual poverty. Scarce any evidence from men who knew him.

And yet the most unlikely and improbable epochs of his life, like the Algerian period, are vouched for beyond possibility of error. Then follow years of complete obscurity. There is not enough to build up a biography without gaps. There is only a frame, upon which we may weave a fabric. Yet it would be impossible to deceive oneself upon the man's inmost nature, though there were only his own immortal book to go upon.

This immortality of *Don Quixote* has a special character. Its creator, from being "a certain Cervantes," has mounted to the height of another and different anonymity. The peoples in the lands that are not Spain scarcely know his name. But they know what *Don Quixote* is. They connect the name with something at once absurd and touchingly noble. People who never read a book may speak of Dulcinea, Sancho Panza, even Rosinante, without knowing that these are characters in a book. Not Achilles and not Hamlet have got so far as this. For which there is probably good reason.

CONTENTS

PART ONE

A MAN CALLED CERVANTES

Part One

CHAPTER ONE

Audience

There were no coaches in Madrid. The Cardinal-Legate had to ride to his audience. They had routed out a white mule for him; he rode side-saddle like a woman, his brilliant robe swelling down about him. A fine, icy rain was falling on his flat purple hat. Old Fabio Fumagalli, Canon of Saint Peter, led his animal by the rein. Beside and behind him his attendants trudged in the dirt, three minor clerics and several servants, all of them looking gloomily down upon their stockings, splashed to mid-leg with filth. The gentlemen of the cloth held up their skirts with both hands, like peasant women, and thought of the well-paved Roman promenades.

This was a strange capital city to which they had been sent: A market town, no more and no other, had this King picked out for his residence. If it sheltered fifteen thousand Christian souls it was doing well. The houses were nearly all one-story clay huts, so low that the Cardinal, sitting on his mule, might easily have touched their roofs. This was the capital of half the world. From this little hole were governed Spain, Burgundy, Lorraine, Brabant and Flanders, and the fabulous El Dorado beyond the sea. Orders issuing hence were received by Spanish viceroys in Naples, Sicily and Milan. The King of France, the Venetian Republic and the Papal State—these still maintained themselves, if with difficulty, against the ruler whom it pleased to reside in this spot. In clothes and customs Spanish was the vogue—and this its source and fount.

The few folk abroad in that November rain bent the knee before the rider in the princely robe. Looking at his face they stared in surprise—it was a boy who rode there: a pale, thin, sickly visage showed beneath the purple hat-brim.

Cardinal Giulio Acquaviva was twenty-two years old. The Pope had sent him hither to convey his condolences upon the death of Don Carlos, heir to the Spanish throne—a mission of some singularity, since few doubted that the father had helped the son to his death.

The delegation had been almost a month on the way from Rome to Madrid. The sea had been stormy, and the barks of Barbary pirates crossed it from every side. The spiritual dignitaries reached land more dead than alive. A sojourn devoid of comfort awaited them. The Cardinal Nuncio spent the night sitting upright and coughing in his damp, hard bed in the papal embassy at Madrid.

During the frightful and prolonged sea voyage a new and even gloomier meaning had been added to his mission. For he might now condole over the death of the Queen as well. The beautiful, gentle Elizabeth of France had only reached the age of twenty-five. Following the deaths of the Maries of Portugal and of England, hers had been the third in Philip's marriage bed. Whatever his hand touched, that withered and died.

Pretext enough, then, for the journey. For its actual and

private purport was something else. Discord reigned between the Vatican and this Most Catholic King, Defender of the Faith, Scourge of heretics. The son of Charles the Fifth abased himself to the dust before God and the True Faith—but not at all before the Pope. "For Spain there is no Pope": these words the President of his Council had spoken in a public sitting. The ailing, twenty-two-year-old youth was the bearer of most serious communications.

For the permanent Nuncio had made no headway at all. Audiences had been seldom vouchsafed him; he had continually been asked to write instead. King Philip loved the written word. He dwelt silently and pertinaciously among papers. Sparingly he spoke; by the same token the more copiously and methodically he chose to write. Documents and prayer—these were his life.

Through his bearer of condolences the Pope hoped for success where the permanent official had failed. The youth would come before the King under peculiar and tragical circumstances; he might find the way to the man's emotions and to his heavy-laden soul. Acquaviva was loved in Rome. Even Pius loved him, uncompromising old Dominican that he was, under his triple crown. Perhaps Philip might love him too.

The permanent Nuncio was haughty. The first thing he did was to give the ailing man bad entertainment in his own house; no man troubled himself as to Acquaviva's state and his attendants even lacked food.

At last the Canon, Fumagalli, acted. He was a white-bearded peasant from the Romagna, built for strength, more like a soldier than a priest; since early youth he had been a retainer of the house of Acquaviva. He too loved the delicate, saintly, consecrated youth. He went to the master of the house and there was a brief, entirely respectful interview. After it, matters greatly improved.

But it gratified the Nuncio's spite to observe how the visit of his uninvited guest lingered on. He had been here now for three weeks. A deferential inquiry as to when a visit of condolence would be agreeable got no reply at all for many days; at length a communication from the Chancellery stated that the sympathy might be tendered in writing. In writing: the universal word—but to a Prince of the Church, who had spent a month travelling hither with his train, a scarcely endurable insult. Yet there had been nothing for it but to ask again. It was inconceivable that he should return to Rome and inform the successor of Saint Peter that his ambassador had been denied the house. When in the end an audience was vouchsafed the delicate balance had been already thrown out of gear. Whereas the whole purpose——

The Cardinal's train had reached the palace. But it could not find the entrance. Across the fortresslike, nookshotten façade of the Alcazar stretched a scaffolding where workmen hammered in the falling rain. Philip's abodes were always being rebuilt.

They went right round the whole rugged pile. At a rear door the legate dismounted. Pikesmen were on guard there, in vast hats, yellow jerkins and orange trunks. They understood not a single word spoken to them—being Germans. At last the servants shouted and a man in a soutane came down the steep stair and explained in Latin. There was no access to the royal apartments from here. Once more they mounted and circled back to the front and the scaffolding.

The attendants stopped in a guard-room on the ground floor. It was cold, and even now at midday scarcely any light came through the tiny windows obstructed by beams. "And this is what they call travelling for pleasure!" said Fumagalli, holding the Cardinal's streaming red hat on his knees. "We shall lose His Eminence yet, on this expedition."

The Cardinal passed—slowly, with a stitch in his side—up the dark stair. There was an evil odour about this medieval palace-fortress. A courtier went on before, sidewise; they mounted higher. "The King of Spain must be receiving me on the roof," Acquaviva thought; he had a merry soul beneath his purple robe, and was a blithe, sweet-natured lad in all his piety and wisdom.

They turned aside at the topmost story and crossed first an open, battlemented corridor; blown upon by the biting north wind and seeing below them the whole poverty-stricken, dirty little clay village and the barren, melancholy heights of Castile beyond. Then they passed through rooms, long and low-ceilinged, sparsely furnished with a few coffers. Clerics were everywhere, in soutane or habit, talking in groups or merely idle. They gained a square chamber, full of armed men; their officer saluted, with a ring of arms. In the room beyond, a perfectly bare corridor, the courtier left the Cardinal while he announced him to the King.

Directly above Acquaviva's head a bell rang out the midday hour, loud and echoless. The door opened. A chamberlain ushered him in.

The room was bright. From lofty windows left and right a flat, chalky light converged upon the writing-table behind which King Philip was at work. He laid his tools aside and looked toward Acquaviva as he entered with great, deep-set, namelessly tranquil eyes. The other made an obeisance, then waited, courtierlike, to be addressed. But nothing came. Thus he had leisure to observe the most-talked-of gentleman of the Christian world.

What he saw amazed him; and he gave himself pains to account for the fact.

Philip sat bareheaded; he appeared thus in none of his many portraits and one was unused to thinking of him so. The Cardinal could see how blond he was: very fair the waved and silken hair, only a shade darker the beard which framed his large and sensitively modelled mouth. His nose was fine and delicately shaped, his skin like translucent porcelain; the preponderant impression was of well-kept elegance. Only the heavy, prominent brow introduced a vaguely threatening note into the pleasing whole.

He was clad in black velvet. In these days of mourning even the ruff had disappeared. The Order of the Golden Fleece hung round his neck on a chain of dark-coloured stones and sparkled faintly on his breast.

"Should I begin myself?" Acquaviva thought, and noted uncomfortably that his face and hands were hot with discomfort. His gaze roved helplessly round the royal chamber, where there was indeed not much to see. Tapestries covered the walls; the few pieces of furniture were simple and heavy. A small table stood on one side near Philip's chair, with a little crucifix and two silver reliquaries.

"His Holiness sends me a youthful priest," came a rather low voice then, courteous and utterly vacant, speaking in laborious Italian. "Execute your commission."

"Your Majesty, Holy Father greets you and sends you his apostolic blessing. It is my task to express the profound and sincere sympathy which His Holiness feels for the death of the Infante Don Carlos, and to assure you that the departed is the object of his daily and unwearying prayers."

"That is a great deal of honour for the prince in question," said the colourless voice.

Acquaviva was struck dumb. It was an entirely unexpected turn. All the courts in Christendom might, without mincing words, discuss the sad and thrilling event; but the King himself, surely it went without saying that he would drape the affair in a few folds of formal phrase! He had good ground to.

The Prince had been a cripple, and half a madman. Heir to half the world, the whole world knew his every step from childhood up. They knew of the nurses whose breasts had been so bitten that they died; of the animals that the lad burned at the stake; the attendants whom he had ordered to be castrated; they knew of his attacks of rage, his bursts of hysteria, epileptic seizures. The half-human creature did not even make exception of his own father. That he had sworn to kill him was the least. The Christmas before there had been rumours that he schemed to run away to Flanders, there to put himself at the head of the heretics. With uncanny swiftness the information reached Rome, where it threw the Pope into a state of great disturbance. He was reassured. The Prince was already held a prisoner in Madrid. He died. It was on the score of such a death that Acquaviva was conveying the papal condolences.

"His Holiness," he said with an effort, "ordered a memorial mass to be held in Saint Peter's on the fifth of September. His Holiness was present in person to do honour to the heir of so mighty a kingdom. Your Majesty will be aware that it was an honour up till now vouchsafed only to kings."

"Only to kings," repeated the King, in harsh, abrupt Latin. "I thank the Holy Father. God has laid upon me the task of preserving the true faith inviolate, of keeping justice and peace, and, after the few years of my pilgrimage, of leaving behind me in good order the realms entrusted to my charge. Everything depended upon the person of my successor. But it pleased God, in punishment of my sins, to weigh down the prince Don Carlos with such manifold and heavy defects that he was quite incapable of reigning. For him to inherit the kingdom was to imperil it. It was impossible he should live. Sit down."

The last words were uttered in precisely the same tone as what went before. The young Cardinal did not quite grasp them, bewildered as he was by all this unexpected and piercing candour.

"Sit down," repeated the King.

There was only one chair in the room, a low armless stool. Acquaviva pulled it forward. As he sat down it eased his nerves to hear the silken rustle of his own garments.

"Majesty, I obey. But what I have further to say should not be delivered sitting. Holy Father himself could not have told me to say it, but I know that his heart speaks to me across the sea. God has also taken from you to Himself in the past few weeks Her Majesty, the Queen: the best, the noblest, the most pious soul—and thus——"

"Very good, Cardinal. Was there something else?"

The polite voice vibrated with an unspoken recoil. For the King had loved this sweet-natured, cheerful and charming Frenchwoman.

"There are questions pending, Your Majesty."

"Questions. Certainly. The Pope keeps a permanent legate at my court."

Acquaviva had a perfectly round spot on either cheek, red as his robe.

"The permanent Nuncio has been a long time out of personal touch with the Holy Father. His Holiness begs that my words be taken as issuing from his very mouth."

"I will listen attentively," Philip said. A gust of wind made the rain rattle on the pane. Both paused as they heard it. When quiet ensued the King added, slowly and with precision:

"His Holiness knows, and nothing can alter it, that I will rather resign my crown than allow to be torn from me that which my Father the King and Emperor held before me."

"Resign my crown!" That was the Latin of Cæsar: every member a square block. There was no phrase-making here. The same man had once said: "If my son became a heretic, I would fetch wood myself to burn him." He had had no son when he said that. But from this slow, difficult, uncompromising soul any extreme might be expected. The will of God came not through Rome, but direct, upon him who had been invested with power and authority. To be Spanish and to be orthodox were to him the same thing. He was God's heavy-laden steward; his earthly majesty, in all its immeasurable fullness of power, was but a narrow forecourt of eternity, whereon his eye was fixedly, unchangingly directed. Out on the desolate foothills of the Sierra rose that enormous living tomb, the Escorial: granite vision of his religious faith, it sprawled there meaningless and naked in a naked landscape, a citadel, a barracks of orthodoxy and a sepulchre where he thought to mingle the bones of all his race. He was forty years old, a handsome and elegant figure; but already, down to the last detail, he had arranged for the thirty thousand masses with which the whole ban and arrière-ban of Spanish priesthood were one day to make secure his road to everlasting bliss.

No pope of all the past could have better matched this King than the old man who now sat upon the throne of Saint Peter: the ascetic monk, the one-time Grand Inquisitor, Philip's dark and gloomy counterpart across the sea. And with him he was at odds.

No little was in the balance. Dissolution threatened, a Spanish State Church loomed up. All the signs were there.

Giulio Acquaviva began to speak. He sat with the sickly head in its scarlet cap bent to one side, his gaze directed upon the figure of an animal in the carpet; and erected to the gaze of the Most Catholic Sovereign the structure of the grievances felt by the Vatican. He began mildly, with the venial, the less significant; and passed on with skilfully mounting effect through stages of dismay, estrangement and indignation. No period was without its deferential compliment to the King: his merit was exalted higher and higher, that the succeeding complaint and accusation might be proportionately weighty. He gathered together all his wit, his religious faith, his fervency, yes, unconsciously all the moving charm of his ailing youth—any other man listening to him must have thought of what a frail and priceless vessel the True Faith here availed itself! Everything was in the balance. The moment was decisive. Doubtful indeed whether another such would come. Giulio was also speaking Latin, perfect Latin, out of courtesy toward the King, who had just used it.

The occasions were so many. With all his soul the Pope desired to see them lightened. He loved and honoured the King, upon whom rested all his hopes of conquering the heresies which everywhere so horrifyingly lifted their heads. With what Christian joy had he not lately learned that Count Egmont, head of the Flemish heretics, had been publicly executed at Brussels, despite the services and triumphs he had previously done and won! He was fain to think that all the encroachments and affronts were the work of subordinates, that His Majesty would not countenance them.

Intolerable, for instance, had been the attitude of the Duke of Alcalá, Spanish Viceroy at Naples. He made a mock of authority, letting bishops and delegates from the Vatican wait for days in the filthiest antechambers. Finally admitted, he received them in bed—report went, not even alone.

Philip made no answer, gazing into space with his lower lip hanging.

In this country it was no better. A year before, the Pope had prohibited bull-fighting; those promoting it were threatened with excommunication, those slain forbidden consecrated burial. But they had received it. The bishops did not effectuate the ban. The concourse and pomp were greater than ever. And this happened under the eye of the King.

Acquaviva raised his eyes and made a respectful pause for reply.

And Philip answered. Only a few words indeed. But it was very singular: Acquaviva did not understand. Something in the King's speech sounded strange and harsh; it escaped him. "Have I fever?" Acquaviva thought. "I feel clear-headed enough." He could not ask. He went on.

Those were minor matters. But, indeed, did the apostolic writ run anywhere in Spain? And what about finances? Did not the King tax the clergy at will and draw vast sums for the benefit of the finances of the Spanish state instead of the chief treasury of Catholic Christianity? God knew, and the King knew too, that nothing was further from the Holy Father than self-interest. The vicegerent of Christ lived like a mendicant friar, taking a bread soup at midday with half a glass of wine, at evening a little fruit. His clothing was so poor as to give rise to scandal. But he needed money for the administration of the mighty kingdom of human souls entrusted to him. He begged his great and beloved son to take cognizance of the fact.

The King gave answer in another few sentences. Again the Cardinal did not understand. Straining to hear, he held his mouth open until it was parched. Tears came in his gentle eyes, tears of mortification, anger, helplessness. And this time the other perceived that he was not understood. Acquaviva thought he saw a gleam like a faint smile flit across the King's well-cared-for features. He might be wrong. But, by all the saints, what and how was this King speaking? Surely a strange kind of Latin—for Italian it was not, though it had a note of it now and again, and even single words came out clearly—well, at any rate, the Cardinal could not sit there and puzzle over it. He had to fight on, across ground that quaked and gave way beneath him. The good young Acquaviva—how inexpressibly he yearned just then for his rooms in the Vatican, his little twilit chapel that was always so cosily warm, where he was wont to pray with such fervour before a beautiful Perugino Madonna! Blessed hours! The Holy Father had laid it upon him to walk through purgatory—well, then, onward, through the flames!

He drew himself up. His voice took on a metallic timbre.

He cited an exemplary and cardinal case, which clamoured for settlement. It dealt with the unhappy Archbishop of Toledo, Bartolomé Carranza, Primate of Spain, who had been cited before the Spanish Inquisition on grounds of a leaning towards Lutheranism. But before the Spanish Inquisition alone, Acquaviva emphasized the fact. Rome had never believed in the guilt of this highly estimable man. The Pope, strictest of the strict, found no guilt in him. Were it a matter only for the Curia, the good old man would long since have been freed. But the Spanish judges opposed—and by direct order from the King. Meanwhile the bishopric of Toledo, the first and richest of Spain, stood empty, and the State drew the whole of its immense revenues. Not the Holy Father, and not he, his legate, but far too probably the general opinion of the world would see herein the true ground for the Royal hardness of heart.

Let that be as it might—Acquaviva got up, for it seemed to him the right moment—this would no longer be tolerated. The Holy Father had laid it upon him to be extremely clear on this point. They were arrived at the decisive struggle between Spanish and Roman theology. The question was whether the Most Catholic Sovereign, Defender of the Faith and Scourge of heretics, would honourably submit, or whether he would disregard the authority of the Pope, and decide for the Spanish State Church—in short, for apostasy. The Pope wished it to be stated unequivocally that he would stop at nothing—not even the Interdict.

Silence. Silence. No start from the King, not the smallest gesture, not a twitching of the white features. A courteously listening mien, a gaze which passed over the Cardinal to rest upon the tapestried wall.

"The Apostolic Seat," Acquaviva said formally, "decides against the Inquisition. The Archbishop returns to Toledo. The Pope demands his rehabilitation. Carranza deserves it. And"—with an extraordinary effect of sudden mildness and warmth—"not only the Christian, the dutiful Catholic, but also the son must willingly grant it, since the Emperor and King, his sovereign and father, died in Cloister Yuste in the arms of this very selfsame Bishop Carranza."

It was out. Acquaviva drew a deep breath into his narrow lungs. He had begun well, mounted well to his climax, expressed the uttermost, threatened with excommunication—and closed upon a note of the sheerest humanity. He must be answered. Here was no longer a subject for chancelleries, it gave no opening for consideration "in writing." The Cardinal waited.

The King waited too. Then, without lifting his eyes he began with measured voice to speak. And Acquaviva did not understand. Philip began, indeed: "*Imperator et rex, dominus meus et pater,*" but there the idiom changed again. Where had his ears been? Philip was speaking Spanish to him, a curious sort of Spanish at least, he vaguely felt. He was right. Slowly and by degrees the Spaniard warped his pronunciation, he assimilated linguals and palatals, gave u-colour to his o's and thus produced a sort of mocking, bastard Latin, the meaning of which the other thought at times to grasp, but which for ever eluded his sense. It was a masterly performance.

Giulio was very near to tears. How was it he had come here, without knowing the language? But who could have thought it necessary? For Italian was still the tongue of the elegant world, and Latin common to all the sons of the Church. Both together equipped one for any mission in Europe. But not against this one man.

There came into his mind something which the French Ambassador had whispered to him only the evening before: how the King had watched for many hours, through an opening in the dungeon wall, his son's long agony: with an unmoved heart, not making his presence known. Yesterday he had not credited a syllable of what M. Fourquevaux said; now he believed it.

Philip went on talking. He spoke at large, with fine modulations of his voice; softly, but in elegant, effective cadences, with quiet but obvious enjoyment. He had time. He gave himself time. It seemed to the unhappy lad in the red robe that he would go on until nightfall. The sounds hissed and steamed about him, now and then a half-familiar word thrust up through the foam; he swayed on his stool, he almost sank backwards—for was he not ill in any case? Then the courteous voice said in Italian, by way of period:

"That is all that I can say, Cardinal. I will not longer detain you."

He had made no perceptible movement, but may have set a bell in motion, for the door stood open with a chamberlain on the threshold.

The rain had ceased; a pallid, almost wintry sun was shining. Old Fumagalli led the mule by the rein. He looked up in concern at his master and nursling, swaying exhausted and pale in the saddle.

"Thou lookest so worn, my dear son," he said softly. In good and in very evil hours he addressed him still like a beloved child.

"And worn I am," the other said from the height of his mount.

"Thou must away from this country, Giulio. It is no climate for thee."

"I will go, so soon as they call me."

"What wouldst thou more? What wilt thou still in Spain?"

"Learn Spanish. Find me a master."

CHAPTER TWO

The Spanish Master

"The whole antechamber is full, Eminence," said Fumagalli, coming back from outside. "A dozen poor chaps are sitting there, all very hungry and wretched to look at."

"A dozen language masters! Where do they come from?"

"From the humanistic schools. There are six or seven in this dung-heap. I sent notes to all of them."

"Very practical," said Acquaviva.

"But I should dearly like to know why you want to learn Spanish at this late day."

The Cardinal looked at him. "Late? You say 'late,' my Fabio. You do not give me many more years, is that it?"

"I mean now, as a grown man and Prince of the Church," Fumagalli cried out aghast.

"Let me tell you a story. Listen! On the evening when Socrates was to die, a friend came into the prison and saw that the music-master was there, playing to Socrates on the lute. 'How then?' cried the friend. 'You are to die tomorrow and learn a new song today upon the lute?' And Socrates said: 'But when else shall I learn it then, my friend?' "

"Who talks of dying? The little cough is nothing. Are you warm enough?"

Acquaviva sat well covered in a reclining-chair; close beside him stood the glowing brazier, large and round and resting upon three legs ending in lions' paws of the finest workmanship. Fumagalli had brought it with his own hands from the sleeping-chamber of the apostolic nuncio, not asking any leave.

"It is beautifully warm here," said Acquaviva. "But about the Spanish: another audience is not out of the question, and it would be charming for me to surprise the King with a few phrases."

Fabio narrowed his eyes. The Cardinal always spoke with such suspicious lightness of this King! He had said no word. But after the audience he had been more poorly than ever.

"Another audience! I doubt it. He is up at the Escorial, watching his workpeople."

"All one. Without Spanish one cannot get on. It is important for the Vatican correspondence too. The Holy Father will realize that."

"As Your Eminence thinks. Then I will let in a couple of the birds."

"But one at a time, Fabio."

The antechamber was full of the odours of bodies. The number of candidates had doubled. They were mostly young, badly nourished, and not better washed. Wrapped in their student mantles of coarse dark cloth, they sat in a row on the velvet-covered bench, turned their caps in their hands and looked at each other grudgingly. Who was to draw the prize?

Fumagalli's eye paused inevitably upon one figure which

stood out of all this array of ill-kept youth. He went up to the man, who rose and towered before him in a dark, flowing silken mantle, with a high biretta on the grey, beardless head.

"Is Your Honour not here in error?" he asked courteously, for the man's costume seemed to betray scholarly rank. "Those who are here today have been commanded for a certain purpose."

"The purpose is known to me, Your Worship, and I am here designedly."

Fumagalli made a gesture of invitation and ushered him to the door. But with the scholar another had risen too, a slim, agile student, with lively eyes; dressed like the others, but possibly cleaner. He hesitatingly made as though to follow the first.

"Stop here for the present," said the man in the gown. "You would only spoil everything."

The other obediently subsided to his place, the fact that he was protected earning him sundry scornful glances from the rest of the company.

"Your Eminence," Fumagalli announced formally at the door, "among those waiting was also this gentleman. I thought fitting to bring him to you the first."

The scholar introduced himself. He was Don Juan López de Hoyos, a well-known name, he added; Doctor of the University of Valladolid and head of one of the grammar and art schools—the best in all Spain, he made no bones of saying.

"Your visit honours me," Acquaviva said, pointing to a chair. "I know how to prize it. But I cannot believe that a man of your rank is prepared to give a beginner Spanish lessons."

"It was to be expected, Your Eminence, that many candidates would present themselves. So I chose to accompany my pupil hither, in the hope to serve him by my recommendation. Fortune is so blind," he added, seeing or thinking he saw a slight frown gather on the Cardinal's brow, "it may be permitted me to open her eyes a little."

"It is my eyes, to speak without metaphor, that you would wish to open, is it not? But my sight is very good." And Acquaviva laughed.

The humanist decided to laugh with him. "The young man whom I have brought is very shy, he would not know how to let his light shine. Let anyone praise him, he will disclaim the virtue. He could not have recommended himself to Your Eminence. And since he is gifted——"

"He only needs to know Spanish."

"Know Spanish! Precisely. But only he knows Spanish who knows Latin. And how he knows Latin! I have brought proof with me."

He fetched out two little quarto pamphlets from the skirts of his gown, and proffered them to the Cardinal with his black-gloved hands.

"What is it?" Acquaviva asked, not taking them. He felt a distaste for the model Latin pupil that was being foisted upon him.

"One notebook," answered Hoyos, "contains a printed poem with which my pupil won the prize at the last open poetry contest—the first prize, Eminence, although in our country this is almost always given according to rank and patronage. The second——"

"Let us stop with the first. Perhaps Your Honour would be pleased to read the verses aloud."

"Certainly, with pleasure," answered the humanist. "We are dealing here, of course, with a gloss, or commentary."

"A gloss?"

Hoyos evinced surprise at such ignorance. "In our competitions," he explained a little condescendingly, "a theme in verse form is set the candidate; upon which it is his task to comment upon the spot, in faultless strophes. That is the contest. The lines of the theme are given first." And he read:

> " 'If the past I might regain,
> Could I once more happy be,
> If my hopes might bloom again
> As of yore, what bliss for me.' "

"Transitoriness is the theme then?"

"And this is the gloss," Hoyos went on:

> " 'All in life, alas, must fade,
> So my joy hath vanished quite;
> Fortune is a fickle jade,
> Spreads her wings and flees from sight.
>
> " 'Though in dust and ashes lying
> Writhes my heart before her throne,
> Though for endless ages sighing,
> Yet no peace I call my own.
> Joyful were I once again
> If the past I might regain.' "

"Awful," commented Fumagalli, also in Latin. The humanist whirled round, cut to the heart. Behind him Acquaviva gave his friend a warning look.

"I only mean," explained the Canon, "that there seem to be certain contradictions. Fortune is *either* a bird, has wings and flies through the air, *or* it is a princess and sits on a throne. But both of them——"

"But by no means, my dear sir, is that contradictory to art. For art changes its theme and produces it every moment in new and vari-coloured light. That is an elementary law," he said pityingly. "Your Eminence will permit me to proceed."

"Pray do."

" 'Other joys I do not covet,
Splendour, victory, fame and power,
Not the greatest riches' glamour,
Nor the glory of an hour.
Only sweet content be mine,
Wrapped in whose celestial light
As the sun at dawn doth shine,
Gilding all with radiant hue,
Joy again I might renew.' "

"That is enough," said the Cardinal. "I see."

"But it rounds itself off in the last two strophes."

"They will be of the same calibre, Master Hoyos. But how can I tell that this skilful Latinist will be an equally skilful Spanish teacher?"

"This second notebook contains the proof." And he held it out so insistently to Acquaviva that the Cardinal could not but take it.

It was printed on better paper, and had a vignette on the cover: a stately catafalque, studded with arms, emblems, figures and inscriptions, surrounded by torches and flapping standards.

"What Your Eminence has in his hands is the official report of the obsequies of the late Queen. It appeared only yesterday. The funeral oration, chosen by the most capable judges, has as its author this very young man whom I am recommending to you, and whose verses have just been called awful by this gentleman."

"Do not take that too tragically. Forget it. But as for the Ode——"

"It is in Spanish, Eminence, so you could not read it. Rely upon my authority, when I tell you it is composed in the finest, highest, most florid Castilian, full of similes and elegant figures, as far as possible from the Spanish of our daily speech."

"Aha!"

"His origins dispose my pupil to good breeding. He is of good family, noble, an hidalgo . . ."

The Rector looked round at Fumagalli, who was gazing inattentively out at the window, bent forward in his chair and murmured: "He bears the name and is a near relative of——" He whispered.

"Really?" said Acquaviva. "That is interesting, and pleases me."

"Then may I call him?"

"Pray do, Master Hoyos."

The humanist left the room, dismissed by Acquaviva with a gesture that held the mean between farewell and blessing.

"Miguel"—his voice was heard in the outer room—"His Eminence awaits you." Then the sound of his departure through the opposite door.

The youth with the lively eyes entered the room. When, after a very deep obeisance, he straightened himself, it was comic to see the look of astonishment upon his face. Obviously he had expected a grey old patriarch and discovered a contemporary. His mouth remained open, and the shining eyes on either side the hooked nose went very round. The nose too, like an eagle's beak, had a comic effect, as though it were the only thing finished in the unfledged face, and all the rest were to follow after.

"Come closer," said the Cardinal, and felt laughter in his throat. "You have an enthusiastic intercessor in your Rector."

"Master Hoyos is very good to me, Your Eminence; he knows that I am poor and he would help me."

The voice was mature—not deep but ringing, and with a virile warmth.

"You are a poet, it seems." Acquaviva lifted the pamphlet with the catafalque on the cover.

"Just that it is makes me doubt, Your Eminence, whether I should be a proper schoolmaster. When one has been very strictly drilled to write Spanish and Latin verse on every subject in the world one must in the end lose spontaneity. Literature and daily intercourse are two different things."

"So you think then that I should not choose a student for a teacher?"

He reddened. "While I was waiting outside I was wondering if any ordinary goldsmith or armourer would not be better for Your Grace."

"But sit down a little," the Cardinal suggested. The lad took a seat. "You speak as though you did not want the place."

"I desire it ardently, Your Eminence; it would be incomparable good fortune. But I am frightened at the idea of disappointing you."

"But you have advantages to offer too. An armourer or such a person would speak the language of the folk. But you are of a famous house, nobility——"

"How so?"

"Well, your Rector will not have erred. You are an hidalgo."

"Ah, *Dios!*"

"What does the word mean? It has a proud sound."

"*Filius de aliquo*—son of somebody—it does sound proud, indeed. But means absolutely nothing. Every second person is an hidalgo. For instance, everybody who lives in the King's capital is so by decree."

"Your armourer would be too?"

"Would be too, Your Eminence."

Fumagalli in his corner wagged his bearded head; he was won over, and unseen made a significant little grimace at the Cardinal. But Acquaviva gave no sign.

Young as he was, his rank had brought him in contact with too much self-interest, too much courtierlike finesse. The lad seemed ingenuous—that might be method.

"If we should come to an understanding," he said seriously, "you would have before long to leave your native land. I would not conceal from you that your place in my household would be a modest one. You would be no more than page or chamberlain. It would be best to have no illusions."

"I should be happy to go to Rome, Eminence."

"Even the rank of your relatives would give you no exceptional position there. You probably cannot conceive the number of bishops' relations there are in Rome. The city is full of them."

"I do not understand to what Your Grace refers."

"Do not pretend," Acquaviva said, an impatient furrow on his brow. "Your master told me that you are a nephew of the Archbishop."

"What archbishop?"

"The Archbishop of Tarragona, Gaspar Cervantes."

"But surely I should know that, Your Eminence."

"Then it is not true?"

"I do not know him. I know nothing of him."

The sceptical expression was gone from Acquaviva's face. He exchanged a look with the Canon. The latter left his place, opened the door into the antechamber and called out:

"The place is filled, gentlemen. His Eminence expresses his regrets."

There was a noise of shuffling feet, a murmur. They departed, leaving behind a thick atmosphere of envy and body exhalations. Fumagalli flung open the windows.

CHAPTER THREE

Dear and Honoured Parents

To Don Rodrigo de Cervantes Saavedra and his consort Doña Leonor of the family of Cortinas, Alcalá de Henares, in the house next the Posada de la Sangre de Cristo:

DEAR AND HONOURED PARENTS,

It is scarcely three months ago that you gave me your blessing at my departure, but already it seems to me as though years had passed since then. Your child has in the interval seen and experienced so much that is new, that this letter of mine can give you only a quite inadequate account of it all. Daily I give thanks to God, that He has so graciously revealed to me, in my young years, His world so full of wonders, of which so little time ago I should even have not dared to dream.

A captain of the Swiss Papal Guard, travelling to Spain, has taken charge of this letter. He seems to be a good and honourable man, therefore I have entrusted him at the same time with exchange of over forty *reales*, which the Spanish bank of account at Madrid shall pay out to you in cash. As that is but three hours' ride distant from you, someone can surely go over soon and claim the money. The sum is not large and I beg that you will consider it only as an earnest. Perchance God may so order it that I may become rich and can make an end to your need. One meets here daily people of far less education than your son, who yet have achieved well-to-do positions.

Do you likewise, I beg, seek an opportunity to send news and the renewal of your blessing upon me. Give me knowledge as well of the state of my sisters Andrea and Luisa and my dearly loved brother Rodrigo, and tell me particularly if he has in the meantime achieved his hope of serving as a soldier of the King. I would wish that it might be the case, for the proverb we have at home seems to me to put it well when it says:

> Church or sea or courts of Kings,
> One of these good fortune brings.

But when you ask whither you shall direct your budget of news in order that it may reach me in the mighty city of Rome, my answer sounds majestic enough, for I am to be addressed at the Palace of the Vatican. Yes, it is the solemn truth: your son dwells in the same house and under one roof with the successor of Saint Peter—though about the roof you must not take me too literally. For the Vatican has many roofs, and very likely more than a thousand rooms. It is a town in itself and no small one; grown up through extended periods of time and enlarged without any particular plan: so that one even after living in it some time can easily have trouble in finding his way about. But of the thousand rooms I certainly occupy one of the very least; it is high up in a tower said to have been erected by Pope Paschal and contains more rats than comforts. There is always talk of pulling it down and putting something more beautiful in its place, but then bad times come again and there is too little money, and everything stops as it is. Thus it is even with the church of Saint Peter, whereon there has been but little work done since the death of Messer Buonarroti five years ago. A great cupola is to be erected over the high altar, but as yet naught is there save a huge mass of scaffolding, where workmen are seldom seen at work, and the laths rot and sometimes fall about.

What you will most certainly want to hear above all things is whether I have seen the Pope and can describe him to you. Up till now this has happened twice. Once he was pointed me out from a window, as he strolled in the gardens below with two of the clergy. Of pomp or splendour of attire there was naught to be seen. He wore a white cloak, not even quite clean, was bareheaded and leaned upon a stick. He is an old man of perhaps sixty-five years, entirely bald, with long snow-white beard, strikingly thin and of awe-inspiring mien. One sees at once that where he is concerned there can be no joking and that with him the defence of our Holy Faith is in good hands. He never fails a sitting of the Inquisition, the dungeons are too few for the many heretics, and, in the past year only, two have been strangled and four burned alive. I saw the Pope for the second time when he said mass in Saint Peter's. He did not say it before the high altar—that happens only four times in the year—but seven great golden candelabra were burning and the walls were hung with purple. The Pope administered the Sacrament himself and his manner was in striking contrast to that of most of the prelates present, who sat round very free and easy, with covered heads and talked as though they were somewhere else. I had arrived early and could observe every small detail. The sacramental vessels seemed quite the usual ones, only the chalice struck me as having a curious arrangement consisting of three little golden pipes. I was told later, very solemnly, that it was intended to protect the Pope from being poisoned. He himself gave the Sacrament to only a few privileged persons; with him and after him officiated the Cardinals Saraceni, Serbelloni, Madruzzo and my dear lord, Cardinal Acquaviva.

This was one of the rare times when my lord has left his room. His health is bad, it has suffered from the hardships of the sea voyage and the rigours of the Madrid winter. We are given only a few months, at best a year; he himself speaks with the greatest freedom of his near and certain death. He has an indescribable mildness and friendly good cheer, and when the end comes he will, beyond doubt, enter into heavenly bliss without much hindrance on the way. He sits in his easy chair and unweariedly dispatches the business of his office, to which an especial honour has of late been added: he has been entrusted with the Great Seal, and no brief issues from the palace that is not ratified by his hand. He does not find so much time as I could wish for the Spanish studies which are the cause of my being here; often for days together I am quite free and can go where it pleases me. Then I seem useless to myself, one of the huge army of do-nothings and loungers who people the Vatican and the household of the Cardinal, wearing a mysterious air of being indispensable!

I myself see quite clearly how little need the Cardinal had of me here in Rome. For if he had looked for a Spanish master he could have found fifty. The city is full of Spanish, Spanish priests, Spanish monks, Spanish travellers in astonishing numbers; our dress is very common, being worn more and more by the Romans themselves; many beggars, even, beg in Spanish.

You may imagine that I employ my ample leisure in seeing all of the city that I can. Rome is large, of course; but it is plain that it must once have been vastly larger, for inside the thousand-year-old city wall, still standing, is much space still unbuilt or else covered with ruins. Magnificent palaces alternate with the wretched hovels of the very poor. Strange to see the watch-towers of the Christian knights built into the theatres and temples of the Cæsars, so that all the centuries jostle one another. On every hand one sees evidence that this has been a bloody battleground throughout the ages. Many ancient buildings possess no steps—this for purposes of defence; people let themselves down from the window by ropes. Even today there is no great security. It is thought foolhardy to leave the protection of the city; pilgrims making the prescribed pilgrimage to the seven churches outside the walls are accompanied by armed escorts.

The Church is all in all at Rome; indeed one must honestly confess that there exists no other occupation. Even in Madrid, so much smaller and less pretentious, there is more trade and business life. That is so lacking here that one asks oneself in wonderment how all these human beings supply their needs. The scene is the same on weekdays and Sundays, the chief occupation of the Roman seems to be an aimless sauntering. Amazing to me is the number of carriages, in which people of position drive slowly about. Some of them have a sort of *œil-de-bœuf* enabling the occupants to see out better and look at the pretty women in the windows. But then come quarters which are wholly rural; between San Angelo and the Vatican cattle graze, and yesterday in the square before Saint Peter's I saw a black sow delivered of five lively little piglings.

Everyone in Rome speaks of how much the life here has changed, how much more blithe and splendid it once was. Since the Fathers assembled in Trent and promulgated their stern edicts, and especially under the present Pope, all has become more religious and more simple. Even the Carnival festivities, which used once to last several weeks, have been confined to a few days. All that I saw of them seemed childish to me, consisting chiefly of races, of somewhat extraordinary character. The contestants run about wholly naked, spurred on by the mob. There was a children's race, then one of quite old men, lastly of Jews with long beards, who were the source of great merriment.

But it is easy to understand that the Holy Father does not care to see reckless behaviour and noisy pleasure in these serious times. His cares on the subject of our Holy Faith are far too heavy. One hears that the Sultan is preparing another attack, and that his next objective is the island of Cyprus, which belongs to the Venetians and is the last bulwark of Christianity in that part of the sea. Horrible tales are told of cruelties practised by the infidels upon Christian prisoners that fall into their hands. The Holy Father hopes greatly for an alliance against the Sultan, in which all the Catholic kings and even Russia shall take part. The negotiations seem to stick. But war is in the air, every week one sees in the streets of Rome more men of bold and military carriage—they are streaming hither. If things come to such a pass, then may our Rodrigo too play a part in these meritorious efforts—and sometimes I could find it in my heart to envy the lot which he has chosen.

I have written this letter at night, not without haste, for the Swiss captain leaves at early dawn. Forgive me that I have huddled together matters important and trifling without much discrimination. With all my heart I wish you good health and freedom from care, and pray God fervently that He may have you in His gracious protection. In gratitude and filial love I kiss your hands.

Your son,

MIGUEL DE CERVANTES SAAVEDRA.

Rome, the third day after mid-Lent. Sunday, 1569.

If any one of you goes to Madrid to seek the money, will he look in on the bookseller Pablo de Leon in the Calle Francos, and inquire after the success of my pastoral poem *Filena*, whose sale he undertook? You know that many connoisseurs have praised it.

MIGUEL.

CHAPTER FOUR

The Venetian

He went about in the black of his native land, and its cut easily assimilated itself to the clerical. "So, my child," Fumagalli had said to him, "we shall soon have you acquiring a little tonsure and a little benefice. After all, what are you here for?" And gave him good-natured counsel. Though certainly he himself was not such a model of clerical deportment. He had a tread that thundered even in sandals, and his priest's gown hung upon him like a soldier's cloak.

Churchly belief and pious devotions were like breathing to young Miguel. On his way about the city he often stopped to pray in a church—and there was no lack of them of all ages, sizes and degrees of beauty, on every corner. But before long he found the particular one which drew him.

It was Santa Maria ad Martyres, called Santa Maria Rotonda by the common folk. In early times it had had still other names. The square it stood in was not very large nor especially beautiful; wretched little houses lined it, on one side built against the church itself; in fifteen hundred years the level of the square had lifted until now one had to descend a shabby flight of stairs to enter the building.

Yet even the portico, with its massive grey granite pillars, gave him an extraordinary sense of refreshment; the vast rotunda he never entered without a thrill. He would stand for long, drawing great deep breaths, in the centre space, before turning to one of the altar alcoves to pray.

"Yes, yes, the Pantheon," said Fumagalli, looking at him with quizzical eyes. "So that is what you have picked out, is it, little one?"

They were sitting together in the Canon's room, a large chamber adorned with four Gobelins depicting the passage of the Alps by Hannibal and his troops. The windows looked down upon one of the Vatican's fountained courts.

"I do not know, Venerable Father, what happens to me there. For in the House of God one feels of course a sense of reverence and grace; but one must call upon this boon for it to come; must sink one's own personality, and let priest and music work upon the spirit. But there! Without a word, without a sound, the great space itself summons one to prayer. In no other place am I so heavenly happy and blithe and free of spirit—I feel as though I could fare straight up to heaven, straight into the light that streams in through the glorious opening above. And the mighty round, so complete, so without blemish, so solid—it is like the Everlasting Law. Law and freedom, both are present. In what other place in the world could I find what I find there?"

"Yes, yes, little Miguel, the Pantheon. But from what I hear, God is just as present in the poorest and meanest village church as in thy great round dome with the pillars and the eye of Olympus."

"Of course," Miguel said.

"Of course! And that is all he can say. But tell me: was

it for this they deposited the bones of twenty-eight wagon-loads of martyrs in that heathen temple, that you might feel such well-being in the place? Freedom and law, and the blue ether, and upwards into the light—and have you no misgivings at all about yourself? I should say that even the twenty-eight wagon-loads of bones have not been enough to oust the ancient owners of the place."

He laughed, got up and strode to and fro in the room with his soldierly, sandalled tread, among his Hannibal hangings. Miguel, somewhat abashed, followed him with his eyes.

But he found no reason to give up his preference. After all, Santa Maria ad Martyres was a highly consecrated place: the feast of All Saints originated indeed in the translation of these holy relics. There could be nothing to say against it, the Canon was only chaffing him. Nevertheless, he spent less time hereafter beneath the dome's great eye and turned a little sooner to his devotions.

There were no prayer-stools before the altar: one knelt upon the ancient porphyry and marble pavement.

One day as he got up to go, a woman, whose presence he had not noted, turned her head towards him: a broad, blond, sensuous face looked up at his, with an expression at once defiant and provocative. He made haste to go. But at precisely the same hour next day he was there. She was kneeling on the selfsame spot.

At home in Spain he had known no women, he had really seen none. Spanish women did not show themselves. Looking at one from afar off, she seemed completely packed into her high-necked, wired and stiffened and wadded costume; the hair always covered, the ears hidden in the ruff.

But here in this spiritual capital, crowded with youth, all

was different. The ascetic Pope might preach through his priests and promulgate rules for morals and costumes; much of the one-time gaiety still remained. Spanish might be the mode; but the Roman women turned the Spanish garb into something loose, light and feminine. They wore bright, clinging silks that outlined the figure; and instead of a ruff an open lace fan set off a head of hair that waved with natural charm and could not be too blond to please. They were generous: displayed the throat freely, even as far as the cleft between the breasts.

He was resolved to follow his fair one. At the church door, under the columns, his courage failed. She vanished in the maze of alleys leading to the river.

On the third day he was at the church before his time. His prayers were shallow. He rose and walked up and down in the temple; he could not be quiet. He disturbed other worshippers, who turned distraught eyes upon him. She did not come. Nor on the next day. She came no more. It was like a barb in his flesh. That broad face with the flat nose, so seductively blond, seemed to him more ideally lovely with every night that passed.

In the autumn he went again to the banker who had arranged the Spanish exchange for him. This was for the fourth time; his ailing master, though he had scarce employed him further, had on one pretext or another increased his hire, and this time he was joyfully carrying a whole ten *thaler* to the money-changer. It was a considerable sum, for which his people at home would receive fully eighty *reales,* enough to keep a modest family months long in rustic Alcalá.

He crossed the bridge of San Angelo on winged feet, and after a few paces turned off into the Via di Tor Sanguigna.

It was here his Sienese banker dwelt, in a delightful old house, only three windows broad, with two pretty columns guarding the door and at the upper story a gay little loggia. The office was in the court; Miguel had to pass through a dark ground floor to reach it. Sacks and bales lay about, for the Sienese was not only a banker but a merchant. Miguel light-heartedly transacted his business within, folded the receipt and left.

The court was vacant and still. He looked up at close range at the inner façades—and stopped stock-still. Above, in a second story, he saw her; she had on a pale-green robe and stood at one of the open windows. It might be the banker's house, and she his wife. He could not turn away his eyes, indeed in his excitement he strained them so that they blurred. Her shimmering, uncertain outline was like a mirage. He had to lean against the entry wall. But then he pulled himself together, shook his head over his own plight and got himself out into the street.

And again she was there; having passed from the court to the front of the house. She stood in the loggia, leaning over and supporting herself with her hands on the stone coping, so that the wide green sleeves fell forward; she looked deliberately down at him, and her bright face was lighted with a smile.

Before he could form a connected thought, he felt his sleeve touched. Beside him stood a middle-aged woman, dressed like a servant. In plain words, as though the affair were the most natural in the world, she invited him to follow her. Her mistress awaited him.

On the dark stair he stumbled, the woman had to steady him. Then she disappeared; and in a small, windowless antechamber, where two tiny lamps burned, he came face to face with his fellow-worshipper of the Pantheon.

"I have often noticed you," she said with a smile and an accent not of Rome, which straightway enthralled him. "It was time that we made acquaintance." And she ushered him by a gesture into the larger chamber through the curtained doorway.

Here it was bright daylight. There were two arm-chairs, a toilet table, and in the middle of the room the bed, ample and magnificent, with a white silk cover embroidered in gold.

Young Miguel had never been in a Roman house before, had never exchanged a word with a Roman lady—at most one or two with maids and shop-keepers. He spent his life in the priestly atmosphere of the Vatican. All power of comparison or judgment was lacking in him.

The woman was conscious of something unusual. She was puzzled.

"You are a priest?" she questioned, when they sat opposite each other in the two arm-chairs; and made a vague gesture towards his clothing.

Miguel explained at once, eagerly, as though he were being examined. And the sound of his voice gave him courage. He talked very well, the words came easily and flowingly, being informed with feeling. He would scarcely, he said, have dared to follow her, conscious of the gulf between them, but now the leading was too clear; she, whom he had known to be unique, whom he had admired, lost and sought everywhere, she had been found in the only house in all Rome he ever entered!

Now he was launched. He described them meeting in

Santa Maria Rotonda, kneeling on the ancient pavement beneath the eye of Heaven; his inability to think of his prayers once he had seen her; the moment when she had escaped him in the maze of streets near the river; his despair when she did not return. And now—now! What incredible providence, what infinite bliss!

His head whirled as he spoke. For a fragrance came from her, from her soft, thinly clad form, that overpowered him as incense cannot do: an exhalation from her young and blooming flesh, mingled with a breath of some pungent perfume.

Abruptly she stood up, saying that he must go. "And not come back?" he asked, his voice nearly failing him.

She considered, looked sharply at him. And then an unexpected burst of laughter drew the lids closer over the pale eyes, the tempting mouth widened still more, the white throat pulsed, she seized both his hands firmly in hers.

Oh, yes, she cried, he might come back, but only at definite hours, forenoons, only forenoons, and only on Tuesdays, all other times were unsafe. She ushered him out, murmuring vague sentences, whose import he only pieced together and grasped when he was once more at home in his tower at the Vatican. She seemed to have said that she was the widow of a merchant, living in retirement, in expectation of a new and advantageous connexion which was shaping itself and must under no circumstances be endangered.

When he arrived on the hour, the following Tuesday, he found his blonde in a bad temper. Perhaps she had not slept. She scarcely concealed her regret at having begun the little affair, and made sour faces while he sought to please her. Then, quite abruptly, she closed the conversation by standing up; threw herself upon the bed and motioned him to her, with impatient and fretful gestures which were the reverse of inviting. The fine silk coverlet had been taken off and lay carefully folded across a chair.

Young Miguel was inexperienced. She endured his caresses, a smile lurked in the drooping corners of her mouth. He was too dazed to mark anything at all, else it might have sobered him. But then her laughter died away.

He was a novice. But born for passion. Unerring instinct showed him the way to mutual joy. There came a moment when she braced her hands against his shoulders, looked at him large-eyed as though for the first time, and smiled.

But when he rested with his head on her arm she continued to look at him. "You are a most amazing little schoolmaster," she said with respect.

The face beside her had turned beautiful at one stroke. It was no more a boy, no more an unfledged priest who lay there, but a man, firm-lipped, with lightnings in his eyes. The nostrils dilated, powerfully, slowly. The abundant chestnut hair lay in soft disorder across the brow.

That was the beginning. Miguel lived now only from one embrace to the next. Heart and nerves were penetrated with bliss. He could have stopped the peasants' carts in the streets and hugged the little donkeys that drew them. He overflowed with affection. He sought to quell his overwhelming energies by long, endless marches through the streets of Rome. And he roved about the melancholy, romantic *campagna*, quite unmindful of lurking vagabonds. Whoever shook hands with him felt as though he had received an electric shock.

"What has come to you, my son?" asked Fumagalli. "A

future priest must be milder in his motions—you rush down the sacred stair as though you were in a dance-hall!"

He was in a bad mood, and scolded. The Holy Father's latest idea was an interdict upon beards for the priesthood. Fumagalli still wore his, like a peasant, the only one in the Chapter of Saint Peter. He had no idea of submitting, so he said to everybody who would listen—he would rather jump out of his cassock. To change the look of his face at sixty—no, thanks! As far as he could see, the Pope himself wore a beard. It was a little too much.

Miguel soothed and pacified him; he had abundance of sweetness and warmth to pour out. It would not come to that, he said with conviction. The threat had only been made to frighten people—he had it on the best authority. At the end of a month it would be forgotten.

"You are a good lad," the Canon muttered. "You know how to say the comforting thing. But it is a crazy shame, the things a man has to put up with. One would rather have been created something else on this earth." He did not specify what.

Gina was a Venetian. After weeks young Miguel knew hardly more of her than this—and the name. She talked little; their morning hour together was a raging fire—naught else. He had managed, without much difficulty, to arrange to come to her twice in the week, Friday as well as Tuesday. Several times he found her still asleep, in a disorderly room, and disinclined for love. He chided the indolent sleeper; she answered with an odd and spiteful look. But his fire kindled and caught her up; soon she would lie on his breast no less panting than he. He would put anxious questions, for he feared that the looming marriage would come and carry off his bliss. Dreadful to think upon, it was—dreadful too the wrong he did that unsuspecting wooer. He did not dare confess his sins, for he knew it was vain to vow he would repent and sin no more. But God was merciful, He would not condemn him for a fire whose flames he was powerless to put out.

She never answered, Gina. She drew him to her white breast and smothered his questions. Was it not better so? For were the light of actual day to be let in upon their wild and fantastic relation, what could he himself have said? What could he tell her, what promises make for his own future? True, he was sometimes filled with formless, boundless hopes, he dreamed in his tower of honour and glory which she should share—as poet, as soldier, even as discoverer; never, of course, as priest. Certainly he could never give her up, give up the odour of her body, her voice, her laugh. Before he knew her, he had not lived.

But perhaps she too was waiting? Waiting for a word, which should make her burst every bond. Perhaps she was nursing anger in her heart because he did not speak, because he was silent? Her dumbness, her taciturnity, seemed dangerous. Perhaps he was losing all, by not speaking?

But when he took his resolve, and opened his mouth and spoke, spoke of the future and their common life—the word marriage, though barely uttered, produced a horrific result. For Gina burst into laughter such as yet he had never heard from her. It had no mirth, it was harsh and glassy and venomous, not to be stilled.

"Marry me, little priest?" she burst out at last, her voice cracking. "Live with me in your tower, on water and rats' meat? Whoever heard such folly?" The talk ended like all the others, in passion and panting kisses.

No, he knew nothing of her. She waxed eloquent upon one subject, and one alone: Venice. Her home. She was religious enough, Miguel knew that, and gave God all His due. But she hated Rome, its stiffness and formality; the innumerable priests and dirty monks; the processions of penitents scourging themselves as they sang; the chilly streets where trade did not thrive, the never-ceasing din of bells, the ruins on every hand. And she described Venice, her native city. The crowded, bustling capital in its web of living waters, the dazzling piazza where all the world took its evening promenade, the little squares and streets bathed in tenderest light. Hither streamed from all quarters the elegant world, fashionably dressed travellers who came not to pray and do penance, but to pleasure themselves in pleasant company and to spend money for value received. How eloquent she was when she spoke of the throngs on the Rialto, the gaily decorated gondolas with women in gala dress leaning back proudly among the cushions! "Every gondolier is a handsome fellow, however poor," she cried, "and I would give all your cardinals' robes for the scarlet hose that he wears." Then the Carnival: the whole city one great festival weeks on end, everybody masked day and night, everybody laughing and whirling in the giddy rout of pleasure, the Piazza San Marco one endless ball, every little courtyard a private box. Gaiety everywhere, carefree, friendly, live and let live. And the head of all this was not a zealot and beggar monk, but a government that looked upon joy with benevolent eye, and never interfered—and the most long-suffering police. . . .

"Why are you always talking of the police?" he asked, for it was not the first time that the word had come up in her talk. "What have you to do with the police? What have the Roman ones done to you?"

She gave him a strange look and fell silent and morose.

This was on Tuesday. When he returned on Friday with a packet of silk which he had brought as a present, no one opened. He knocked; first with his hand, then with the brazen knocker. All was still. When he stood again in the corridor, full of dire misgiving, unable to go away, her maid passed him in the half-darkness. He had never seen her since that day when she had fetched him in from the street. He stopped her. Where was her mistress?

"Gone," she said viciously. "Cannot you see for yourself?"

"Where?" he managed to ask. "To her betrothed?"

She looked him up and down as though he were some strange animal. "Probably. She is marrying. A prince is marrying her."

"Don't talk nonsense. Tell me the truth." He took out money. "Where does she live? Can I see her?"

"Oh, yes, you can see her; it is quite easy. Do you know the Arco Portogallo?"

He shook his head.

"Then ask where it is. You're sure to find her there."

"When?"

"Evenings, of course. Late." And she went on up the stair.

"Which house?" he called after her.

"You will see."

The afternoon would not pass. And his evil star would have it that on this very evening he was summoned for a lesson. It seldom happened now. Acquaviva was more likely to employ him as secretary, giving him writing and copying to do. The Spanish lessons, when he gave them, consisted of reading together. So tonight he took his place opposite his master's reclining-chair and they began to read from two copies a work of the Spaniard, Lope de Rueda. It was the famous *Armelinda,* a play which the young Miguel had always considered a masterpiece—it had even kindled in him the ambition to write for the theatre some time himself.

But today it all seemed to him artificial and crude. What were these magic draughts and love potions compared to the fiery juices that burned in his veins? No one could write like that who had ever felt. His thoughts wandered, he became unable to correct the Cardinal's pronunciation and accent, though both might have been improved.

"You are absent, Don Miguel," said Acquaviva gently, and closed his book. "And you look unwell. Is something the matter?"

Miguel excused himself. The coming on of cold weather always affected him, he said. It would pass.

"Yet it is milder in Rome than in your Madrid. But perhaps your quarters are not comfortable. Can your tower be heated?"

All that was perfectly satisfactory, Miguel answered, touched by his ailing master's concern. At last the Cardinal let him go.

It was the tenth hour. Another piece of ill luck. All the gates would be closed and guarded. For some little time now, anyone who wished to leave the papal citadel had been required to have permission in writing. Miguel tried to parley in two places, but the Swiss Guard turned him away in guttural German. He cast here and there, up stairs and down corridors, through gardens, galleries, courts and forecourts; at last he found the distant little Porta Porsterula unguarded and unbolted. It led into a clayey desert beyond.

He made a wide detour round the huge complex of buildings, crossing ditches and hedges on his way, and by the empty lanes of the Borgo reached the Ponte San Angelo. Once across he ran on along the river; the unpaved road was without any light, and no moon shone in the mild, damp December night. He passed the port of the Tiber, where a few poor barks lay at anchor with a green light at the masthead. A dog on one of them tuned up at sound of his footsteps.

Following his directions, he turned a little away from the river, where a long, straight street ran in, the Ripetta. Suddenly he stumbled and fell, hurting himself. He got up, and saw on what he had fallen: four great sections of a ruined obelisk lay there in ruins in the middle of the street. He knew, from the instructions he had been given, that he was now near his goal.

On his right there rose an extraordinary circular structure. He knew what that was too: the mausoleum of Augustus. Trees nodded out of it into the darkness, and a web of little lanes and alleys wove itself round the colossus. This must be the place.

It was the quarter of the poor foreigners, and the streets were named accordingly: Via dei Schiavoni, Corte dei Greci, Arco Portogallo. Unsavoury forms moved about; he accosted them for his direction and got foul-mouthed replies. In any case it did not matter, for how could she have taken lodgment in such a quarter? He stood still.

The Arco Portogallo was an ancient brick ruin, with two new wooden doors, which were now open, giving a view into a crooked alley.

There was light here from torches stuck into the walls of the one-storied houses to right and left. It illumined a fantastic scene of nocturnal activity. Miguel moved towards it as in a dream. Groups of women stood there, dozens of them, very variously clad, for some were fine, others wore cheap grey mantles. They chattered and quarrelled, they accosted the men who moved furtively about among them, testing and trying. Above were many lighted windows; noises of laughter and brawling came down.

Suddenly he came face to face with her. The torchlight gleamed in smears like blood on the broad white surface of her face. She saw him, beckoned and screamed out:

"Look, look, there comes one—he wants to marry me! He is a priest, but he wants to marry me. Good, then, Signor Miguel, only don't be backward! Here you can marry me day and night. But it costs more in the seraglio than in the town: every wedding a *scudo* down!"

And she went ahead of him towards her own door close by, strutting somewhat with pride at the laughter her speech had evoked.

He shrunk back as far as he could get. He could not turn away his eyes. A man staggered out of one of the doors and fell heavily against him. Miguel found an opening between two of the houses, got through it he knew not how, and stood in the open, on a windy meadow. It was as though he had seen death itself.

CHAPTER FIVE

Fever

He had had the document in his own hands.

It was natural that a zealot like Pope Pius should hate the lax morals of his capital. In every frailty he saw a deadly sin, he was accessible to no plea, had no resort save pitiless severity. At the beginning of his pontificate he had made adultery punishable with death. He was forced to soften this to whipping and lifelong imprisonment; against which neither rank nor merit was a shield.

He was resolved to get rid of the courtesans, root and branch. The time had long since passed by, of course, when women of free life held sway over Roman society; when cardinals, ambassadors and artists foregathered in their salons; when the household of an Imperia was like a prince's court and admission to it harder to get than a papal audience.

But the cosmopolitan character of this ecclesiastical capital and the unmarried state of its ruling class kept up the numbers of purchasable women even in the sombre times upon which it had fallen. They still lived in the best quarters, among prelates and high officials, bankers and rich dilettanti: on the Via Giulia, the Via Sistina, the Canale di

Ponte. They lived respected—and but for them the merchants of Rome could not have lived at all.

For Pius they were the devil's brood. He would have preferred to burn them all at the stake. He did not long hold his hand. A summary edict of banishment was promulgated. Within six days they were to be out of Rome, within twelve out of the Papal State. Thus was the capital of Christendom to be purged, the commandment satisfied, and peace ensured.

But there was no peace. There was uproar. Merchants and dealers were in despair. Tradespeople who had extended credit to the women declared themselves ruined. The tax-farmers in council announced that the revenues of the state would be less to the tune of twenty thousand ducats a year, such would be the falling-off in the importation of luxuries. Rome, it was said, would be depopulated. The least one could expect would be a decrease of twenty-five per cent. And why? And why? But nobody ventured to speak out against the edict. The Curia waited, and listened.

A delegation of forty decent citizens had audience with the Pope. They were most eloquent—in vain. Either they, said the monk, or else he. Holy Rome, where the blood of martyrs had been poured out, where rested the relics of so many saints, where religion had its centre and the successor of Saint Peter his holy seat, was no place for whores. Either they or he; he would remove his residence to some spot less corrupt, rather than suffer this state of things to go on. They must listen to reason.

They did nothing of the sort. Petition followed on petition. Cardinals of more moderate views intervened in vain. The Florentine and Portuguese legates, yes, even the

Spanish, let themselves be put forward—and were sternly admonished.

The exodus began. Property-owners and tradesmen wrung their hands. The women set out: the rich ones in coaches and litters, the others on mule and donkey back. Some were bound for Genoa, some for Naples, many for Venice. They took their possessions with them. But they did not get far. The Papal State, even the near vicinity of the capital, was full of banditti. On either side the wretched roads they lay boldly in wait, and the police did not seriously hamper their operations. As the women went their melancholy ways, they were attacked and plundered in large numbers, some even murdered. The survivors helplessly and hopelessly turned back to Rome.

The result was that those who had not yet left were suffered to remain. But all the better quarters of the city, where respectable citizens dwelt, were purged of them. A ghetto was prescribed, in the remote and abandoned neighbourhood near the mausoleum of Augustus. Elegant *hetæræ*, who read their Catullus and conversed in four languages, were penned up with common prostitutes. No one might leave the seraglio by night or day, on pain of whipping.

All this had happened three years before. Nobody but the Pope cared much for this law; the officials shut their eyes; the order was disobeyed, evaded, forgotten. It was not long before the seraglio held only the grosser sort; the others, protected by their admirers, were scattered again throughout the city. The old situation obtained—but less obtrusively. One saw the courtesans only at their windows, they left their dwellings only to go to church. Church-going atoned for much.

But now, this winter, a new denunciation roused the Dominican to a fresh outburst of anger. He demanded a report on the state of things; saw how they stood—and attacked afresh.

Lists were prepared. The police would proceed under orders to certain houses, seize the unsuspecting women and drive them in shoals. Whatever householder should in future venture to harbour them was threatened with a dungeon for life. The ghetto round the tomb of Augustus was to be fenced in. Thus Pius drew a cordon round the plague of fleshly lust.

Young Miguel Cervantes had had the list in his own hands; he tendered it to his Cardinal for the latter to affix the seal. He had not paid attention to the list; what was it to him? But now he saw it again before him, in characters shockingly engrossed, and every flourish of the scribe's pen. "The prostitutes Panada, Toffoli, Scappi, Zucchi, Zoppio . . ." Regina Toffoli, that was she.

His nature strove to parry the frightful onslaught of shame and anguish; it gave way, he fell ill. Once, as a little boy at home in Alcalá, the like had happened to him. Two larger and stronger lads had fallen upon him, tied his hands and beaten him, defenceless. He had nearly died then, as now, of a high fever with paralysis of important functions. Subjectively the thing had been quite endurable, for there was no pain, and a low delirium deprived him of all sense of reality.

So now. He lay on his uncomfortable bed in his tower chamber. No one came near him. A dull-witted Cistercian monk twice brought him stale food to eat; seeing it remained untouched he brought no more. On the fifth day Fumagalli missed his protégé. He started back to see him in his straw, with burning head and glittering eyes, beside him a pail of doubtfully clean drinking water. The chamber was ice-cold, the wind blew through it from four windows.

The Canon wrapped the sick man in the woollen bedcover, picked him up like a babe and carried him up and down stairs and through echoing corridors into his own room. Cervantes lay now on a comfortable bed, his eyes shielded from the light, among the Hannibal tapestries.

The physician came, Dr. Ippolito Benvoglienti, a solemn man with a lofty brow, arrayed in finest black cloth. He looked and tested, tapped and listened. It took a long time.

"A high fever," he said after a while.

"I thought it was childbed," the Canon said scathingly.

The learned man prescribed and withdrew in high dudgeon.

Fumagalli set up a truckle bed. He did not leave his nursling for an hour. He bathed him and put on lukewarm bandages. He administered a clyster, the abdomen being hard and swollen, of oil, camomile and aniseed; it had its effect. The third-day headache came on. Fumagalli laid mastic poultices on Miguel's temples. On the fourth day the fever declined, on the fifth it was gone.

Fumagalli himself went to the kitchen and tasted the soup. He approved not at all, smashed two plates and made the kitchen ring.

Once, when he came back with the steaming broth, he found Miguel in tears. He set it down by the fire and let him weep. After a while he said:

"Eat now. Stop brooding. It is all behind you. The world is wide." He had asked not a single question.

A bell near by rang the hour of twelve. "I must go," Fumagalli said. "Read mass. I've had a blowing-up."

"Then make haste, Father. *Ne fiat missa serius quam una hora post meridiem,*" quoted Miguel with a weak smile.

"But afterwards *we* shall read," cried Fumagalli as he went out, "and that will be another matter."

This other matter was Fumagalli's favourite book: Cæsar's *Commentaries.*

Miguel knew the work—but the Canon knew it almost by heart. He read aloud, slowly, in his bass voice. Cervantes lay and listened. His heart-beat slackened to the measured tread of the legions in Gaul. From the Gobelins on the wall the head of the Punic hero rose among the rocks and looked him boldly in the face.

He recovered his strength, he wanted to get up. Fumagalli would not allow it. Taking care of him made the old man happy.

They talked of war, and the march of events. Fumagalli brought the news: about the Turks, about Cyprus and the Mediterranean.

The Christian states came but slowly to a composition. They were all devout, they were all of martial mind; but also they were all obstinate and crafty, and exceedingly close-fisted. France withdrew completely; the Emperor in Vienna had misgivings; among the others—Philip, the Pope, and Venice—bargaining ensued over the equipment of every galley and every consignment of grain. Philip was the most businesslike among them: he put off, demurred, and hesitated. His every assistance to the godly enterprise he sold at the highest price, and dickered over every galley-slave's every ship's biscuit.

But things grew more serious with every week that slipped away. Nicosia on the island of Cyprus fell, and the capital, Famagosta, was hopelessly endangered. Crete, Corfu and Ragusa were in peril from the Turks.

Finally they settled that the Pope should bear one-sixth of the cost of the war, Venice two-sixths, Spain the remaining three.

When the Canon talked of these matters and inveighed against the stinginess and shilly-shallying, Miguel scarce heard what he said. Such dry and dingy realities had no meaning for him. His inner nature revolted against them. Faith and heroism, unshattered and glorious—these were his realities. And the warlike peasant in the cassock was not the man to chide him for that.

In these days it was that a long-awaited letter came from the parental home in Alcalá. First came blessings and good counsel, and then news of his brother Rodrigo. Rodrigo had indeed become a soldier. In the battles with the last of the Spanish Moors in the wild mountains south of Granada, he had achieved a reputation, and was now to follow his Captain-General, with the fleet, to fight a decisive war against the Sultan.

Who was this leader of his? Don John of Austria. A glorious name, but for Miguel only an empty sound as yet. He asked the priest, who knew. It was amazing what he knew, this priest; he knew everything.

"He is a son of the Emperor Charles, my lad," he said eagerly. "Quite young yet, not a day older than you. Half-brother of that Philip of yours—and you may keep him too for all I care. The mother was a German. He is supposed to be as beautiful as a god and to dream of nothing but victories. Your Philip wanted to make a cardinal of him, of course. But he is Grand Admiral now, and going to attack the Turks, and, if our Supreme Head here in the house gets his way, we shall have a crusade and Don John will conquer the Holy Sepulchre."

Young Miguel's spirit was like a field ripe for the sowing. Every word sprouted. Such was his power of fantasy, of sensuous imagination, that he could see the young prince before him, in shining white; his beautiful features became one with those of the Punic hero who looked down upon his cot from the wall, under a Renaissance helmet with a waving plume. Would he could leave this city and follow that standard! Rome was hateful, after what had happened. And he was not made for a priest—as little as he who had declined the Cardinal's hat. Day by day he grew strong—and pondered.

Then Fumagalli told him details he had learned of the fall of Nicosia. A safe retreat had been granted to the defenders of the Venetian stronghold. But the Turks broke the agreement, and twenty thousand unarmed men fell victims to their lust for slaughter.

That was horrible. The Christian and the man of feeling in Miguel were alike on fire. He pondered no more, he asked no questions. He thought not at all of the cruelties practised by his own Spain on men of other faiths: of the tortures, banishments and slaughter of human beings up to the hundreds of thousands, of the rage against Jews and Moors since the time of Ferdinand and Isabella. That was the command of God, and doubt was sin. The murder of Christians was something else.

And now for the first time he was allowed to leave his bed. But Fumagalli had told too many stories. He was dismayed when he saw their effect: renewed fever, a serious relapse. The sick man tossed and cried out. Fumagalli had to hold him in bed with both hands.

"You must not believe all you hear," the old man said, when the attack was over. "There are many liars in the world."

But it was much too late.

CHAPTER SIX

Review of the Fleet

The Captain-General did not come. The Venetian and the papal ships had been lying for two months off Messina. Some Spanish galleys were there too, awaiting the main contingent. They anchored to one side, to avoid trouble. Whenever the soldiers of the different groups met each other, in the alleys and taverns of that lively port, cracked crowns were the result. It was said that the Spanish King had withdrawn from the enterprise; that Don John would not set out; that they were all to moulder here while the Turks rode up the Adriatic. The Venetians saw them already on the Piazza. It was the end of August. Don John and his ships came not. It was plain that he would not come.

But he was on the way. He moved very slowly with his galleys. He had time. And he liked being fêted. First, four weeks in Genoa, where he kept brilliant court in the Palazzo Doria. All the women were in love with the Grand Admiral. Then a month in Spanish Naples, where the fun was even more furious. Balls and tourneys alternated with feasts of the Church. The field-marshal's baton was conferred, and the standard of the Holy League was blessed. That took time, and much preparation. Even to work out the order of precedence in the seating of Santa Chiara took three days.

Reports of all this came to the papal commander, Colonna, at Messina, and to the grey-bearded Venetian who commanded the ships of the Republic. The men themselves knew nothing. They grumbled. They had service, hard service, and nobody was used to that. Why the gun practice and the sword drill? They all knew what it was to cut and thrust; everybody knew what a sea fight was like: you drew alongside the enemy's ship, threw over landing-bridges and laid the infidels low. That was no art. Anyhow, as usual, they were not getting their pay, and could not have their fun ashore. And there was always something to do to the boats; they had to caulk and pitch, and tear their hands with tackle till they bled. And Don John did not come.

The *Marquesa* was a particularly old, bad ship. Every two days she drew water, the pails were always going. Her Captain, Diego de Urbina, a full-blooded man with a good-natured face under his iron helmet, was popular with his men. He prefaced every command with "Soldiers and gentlemen"—but he gave too many commands. Perhaps he wanted to tire out the men, to prevent mischief.

They lived packed like sardines in the tiny ship. A hundred and fifty soldiers slept together in a low-ceilinged space where one could not stand up and breathing was difficult. And as rumours were always going round that the plague was in the port, they drank the popular antidote: brandy with garlic. Very likely they enjoyed it, but the stench never left their quarters.

Here abode Miguel de Cervantes—and was in the highest spirits. One would scarcely have recognized the little priestling of the Roman days. He was broader, with a rosy face beneath his helmet; he wore moustaches and a chin-beard, which he trimmed every week himself with the scissors.

He had spent a long time with his company at Naples—and it had not been good. His more delicately organized nature made him shrink from his fellow-soldiers; they were a rabble for the most part, delinquents who had taken shelter under the flag to protect themselves from the law. He had daily to defend himself; dealt out good blows and got better in return; learned by the power of his imagination and intuition to speak their very language; could tell good stories and good jokes; was always ready to lend a hand; was not ridden by ambition. Here before Messina there was one final row. Young Miguel, that is, had something about him which the others without exception found matter for laughter: he read. He always kept four or five printed books tucked under his coverlet. One day he found one of them open and defiled—the *Commentaries,* which Fumagalli had presented to him when he left, a fine copy, with a fine dedication. *Si fractus illabitur orbis, impavidum ferient ruinae* stood on the title-page, now besmirched: a good pagan dedication, certainly, for a cleric to write! It was evening; they were all going to bed, huddled together, by the light from an oil lamp.

"Who did that?" asked Cervantes. Laughter answered him; for they all knew of the deed, which the perpetrator had committed openly and which they all considered a capital joke.

The man stood up, half-naked, with shaggy breast, and advanced upon the injured party. He was a colossus, a peasant from Galicia in northern Spain, stupid and brutish.

"You fouled it, now you can lick it off," Cervantes said. He was still dressed, in a leather jerkin with black sleeves. For all answer the other spat at his feet. There was silence and tension all about.

"You don't want to, but you must!" and with all his strength he struck him across the mouth with the defiled classic, twice, three times. The book went to rags. The other was already upon him, they knelt on one of the oars in the half-darkness; the four-square figure nearly obliterated the slender Cervantes.

"We shall see a corpse soon," someone said in pleasant anticipation.

But Cervantes had luck. He hauled off and caught the peasant on the chin, on that spot a little underneath and to one side, which every skilled fighter knows and aims at. It was luck—but most effective. The Gallego lay with limp arms and eyes rolling in his head. An approving roar went up. Miguel shoved the dishonoured volume under the fallen man's head for a pillow, washed himself in the pail and went to bed.

Next morning they heard that the Captain-General was come—had arrived from Naples in the night. The whole rich city was awake. She was famous for her fêtes: the Emperor Charles himself—and certainly he knew—avowed that never elsewhere had he been so received as in Messina. The harbour was decorated in a trice, from palace to palace purple velvet was spanned. A whole forest of flags blazed in the sunny sky. Many-voiced bells pealed out; salutes were fired, without ceasing, from the citadel.

But no one got shore leave. There was to be a review of the fleet in the afternoon; everything was scoured and polished, ships, arms, one's own person.

Don John of Austria had come with forty-nine galleys. They lay outside in the straits, scarcely visible. But the flagship anchored close in, about the middle of the harbour. A great golden cross was erected in the stern-sheets, before the poop; beside it on the high mast was the banner of the League, presented by the Viceroy in Naples and dedicated in Santa Chiara. All the soldiers, Cervantes among them, often stopped scrubbing to gaze across like children and discuss every detail of the marvel. The standard was of stiff blue satin damask. Above, in the centre, of colossal size, was the Saviour on the Cross. At His feet the embroidered arms, the Pope's in the centre, of Spain and Venice to right and left. Golden chains wound from emblem to emblem, and a fourth device hung heavy and massive from the knot: it displayed the arms of the Emperor's son, the Grand Admiral of the Fleet.

They had to look. It was in a way a command. They stood aligned upon their decks about four in the afternoon, all sails set, the long oars banked, while to the roaring of cannon the flagship moved slowly past them; and every one of these rough, callous mercenaries beheld, and every one drank in, in that radiant figure of dynastic and martial glory, the perfect epitome of all the warrior elegance of the epoch.

And it was done on their account: this was the picture they were to take with them, it was payment in advance for hardship, wounds and death. They should die with this picture in their hearts. Whoever survived and returned to his home would evoke it in hours beside the hearth, before an audience squatting round him, open-mouthed. Cervantes too would never forget it. When he was old and wise—and Don John was dead, untimely removed by poison out of the world—even with him the picture would still live, he would speak of it, and paint it in high colours even while he smiled.

Only the rowers could not see. Deep down in the ship's hold, that gave no glimpse out across the sea, they squatted naked to the waist, chained to the oar in groups of three: criminals, prisoners of war and heretics, not much more than animals now, nothing before their eyes day and night save the back of the man in front. The overseer went among them with the lash and laid about as he pleased. Among them were old men with white beards. They had been sitting here since the now ancient galley was new. They alone saw nothing at all.

Don John stood beside the Cross, near the blue standard, on the high curved poop of his flagship. Beside and a little behind him were, on his right, Colonna the Roman commander, with a bald head like an egg, in dark harness from throat to heel; on his left, the dignitary Sebastiano Venier, in the gold-embroidered mantle of a Venetian Captain-General. They, like Don John, were bareheaded.

He was fair, with fine features and a white skin. His soft hair was tossed back to float about his young head; his moustaches turned pertly upwards. But what ravished everybody, perforce, what must have taken weeks to design and execute, were his clothes. Each soldier felt at once that he was looking on their like for the first and last time in his haphazard career. The cuirass itself was a marvel: a full-dress cuirass made of highly polished silver, brought up to a sharp ridge in the middle, upon which the sun of Sicily glittered with blinding effect. A faultlessly fluted, brilliant white ruff rose out of the hauberk and caressed the shaven chin. He wore sleeves of light silk, defining the shape of his arms and strewn with golden rosettes. But it was particularly as to his nether limbs that Don John was glorious to behold. His tights of silken tricot, almost terrifyingly taut and wrinkleless, came up nearly to his hips, where they were met by the fashionable short trunkhose of red satin and gold brocade, padded and stuffed, slashed and puffed and fretted, not unlike a woman's petticoat. This exquisite creature carried in his hand the consecrated field-marshal's baton, and over his armour the Golden Fleece. He smiled and he did not move, he stood like a coloured plaster statue; certainly for the effect, but also because movement would have endangered the set of his gorgeous state costume. It must have been a strain to stand like that.

The rude soldiery stared entranced. It was a ritual, it assuaged all doubts and fears. Moreover, the outlay was in honour of the generality. It was not the fleet that was here reviewed, but the other way about. This was the eve of battle; they would proceed to it under the ægis of an elegant demigod.

But there was still plenty of time. They remained in port. Reinforcements were expected, there were more drills and gun practice, more caulking and patching up of ships, more mending of sails, while the Admiral enjoyed his balls and banquets and adventures in Messina. It was the middle of September, and many people thought the year now too far advanced.

Then it was suddenly announced that there would be Mass said for the fleet. Every soldier received the Sacrament from the flocks of Capuchins and Jesuits who accompanied the ships. So now things were serious.

Two days later they lay along the coast of Albania, opposite Corfu. More inaction. Discord among the admirals. When the idea came to Don John that he would now review the fleet in earnest, the others refused, under various pretexts. Venier, a hot-blooded man despite his years, and rendered extremely fretful by the airs and graces of the Emperor's son, had a couple of mutinous Spaniards strung up out of hand. Don John saw in the act an encroachment upon his authority, and summoned the Venetian general before a court martial. The Venetians revolted. They menaced Don John's flagship with their galleys; the ceremony at Messina was entirely forgotten. The Roman, Colonna, intervened. The excitement calmed down. September passed into October.

On the fourth of the month a post brought the news of the fall of Famagosta. Cyprus belonged to the Turks. It was known that their united fleet, in battle array, lay in the Gulf of Corinth, not much farther south. A decision was taken.

The leaders received their instructions. Each assembled his men.

The hundred and fifty soldiers on the rickety old *Marquesa* were mustered on deck. Captain Urbina began. "Soldiers and gentlemen," he said. His good-natured face was even redder than usual beneath his helmet. Making speeches was not easy; luckily, the facts spoke for themselves.

Cyprus, then, was in the hands of pagans, the Crescent reigned in that quarter of the sea, the way to the cities of Christendom lay open to the Sultan. This Selim was a drunken tyrant, he swilled down his forbidden wine mingled with Christian blood. The stout defenders of Famagosta had been shamelessly massacred, women mutilated, hosts of children dashed to pieces against walls before their mothers' eyes. It was a foretaste of what Venice, what Rome and the cities of Spain would know, if there were no accord between them.

The Captain rose to a final climax, with the story of the heroic Bragadino, known and hated of the Turks, heart and soul of the Venetian resistance. For him they reserved a choice, an unheard-of martyrdom. The unhappy man was skinned alive. His skin was stuffed, dressed in his official robes, bound to the back of a cow and dragged through the streets of Famagosta. The powerful physique of the martyred man kept him alive for a day—he was privileged to see himself ride by.

"Such, my friends," concluded Urbina, "are your foes. Meet them, strike them down! The battle is joined. For God and Our Lady!"

The monstrous tale, whether true or not, had its effect. The dullest were worked into a frenzy.

Miguel staggered away when they were dismissed. He leaned over the ship's side and vomited.

It was near nightfall. He groped down the ladder and threw himself on his bed. He was trembling. He closed his eyes and made a violent effort to shut out of his consciousness what he had heard. His teeth chattered. In despair he felt the fever flare up in his blood. Curses sounded from the banks of oars above his head, the whip cracked. Then silence.

When the others came to sleep, they found him unconscious. He tossed and heaved, raved and shrieked. His power of imagination made palpable the horrors he dreamed. "To arms!" he cried. "The vengeance of God!"

No one could sleep. At last they carried his pallet forward to a corner under the hatchway, five feet long and three wide. A hatch stood open; fresher air came in.

Thus he went into battle.

CHAPTER SEVEN

Lepanto

He opened his eyes, for the sun shone full in his face. He did not know where he was. It was all quite still, the ship was not moving. The fever had gone, but left him too weak to clench his fist.

Painfully he lifted himself, got to his knees and put his head through the hatch. Then all became suddenly, blindingly clear.

They had advanced to engage. Two fleets lay opposed, each neatly divided into squadrons. And everything was so still, so soundless—like a painted scene. Could this be reality, that was like the pieces in a game, drawn out and coloured and mirrored in a glassy sea, under a glassy blue sky? Nature herself held her breath and watched.

He stared with eyes that ached from the sunlight. The order of battle was as simple and clear as though a child had devised it. His station was in the prow, and the *Marquesa* lay near the centre, so that he could see as from an opera box.

That must be the Turkish fleet over there. Their battle order was a half-moon, with the curve outwards. And, in a circle exactly corresponding, the Christian armada lay opposed, their galleys closely aligned, beaks facing the foe. On his left were the Venetians; he saw the lion standard and the thinner oars. But in front of them, broadside on to the Turks, lay a closed rank of vessels of a different type—the six galliasses of the Republic of Saint Mark, the much-talked-of great fighting ships, fifty metres long, powerfully manned and furnished with thirty cast-iron cannon each. It took seven slaves to man every oar of these ships. Miguel had seen these clumsy monstrosities before Corfu, and had heard that the Grand Admiral laughed at them. They could not turn, could not manœuvre, he was reported to have said; it was a crime to bring up such floating fortresses; and what became of the glory and honour of the Christian hosts, when instead of valiant combats hand to hand, there were a hundred and eighty cannon belching shot? Miguel well understood what Don John meant. Certainly these galliasses had little to do with honour and Spanish chivalry. But there they were, waiting to utter death.

The troops were all on deck as for parade. Helmet stood by helmet, shield and harness shone, the light was refracted upon swords and lances, and all was ready as for a battle on land. The sails were reefed, and flags hoisted on the mastheads. And everybody gazed steadfastly at the foe, lying so close, near enough to hate, near enough to grapple.

The enemy vessels were not different in build from the Western ones. But the whole fleet had a garish barbaric splendour. The great triple bow lanterns were gilded; the sayings of the Prophet, in their mysterious script, glittered gold and silver on the walls; and the whole armada was hung with a forest of striped and starry banners, in the high colours of the Orient. The Crescent stood out in the lambent air from the top of every lantern and flag-pole.

The warriors were massed as in the Christian fleet, in turban and tarboosh and loose, bright-coloured garments; armed with scimitars, spears, small axes and metal-bound maces; many with bow and arrows.

But foremost, in the centre of the line, with a space of clear water round her, lay the Admiral's ship. Cervantes, blinking, observed its every detail. The old man beneath the banner of the prophets, in the silver robe and green turban, a moon-tipped staff in his right hand, must be the Chief, Kapudan Pasha. He appeared to be staring straight before him, at the flagship of the Christian fleet: to where Don John of Austria must indeed be standing, in dazzling array.

Miguel's neck began to ache from the strain, his eyes from the light. His mind wandered.

This was the Gulf of Corinth. Their station had been well known. Here the decisive blow would be struck. What a place for a battle! The land visible hardly a mile away on the right was the Peloponnesus; Delphi could be only a few hours' journey away to the left. He thought thus—and must have been the only man to do so among thousands. He went on musing. . . . Actium lay in these waters. They must have passed it during his fevered night. Now, as then, the struggle was for control of the world. . . . Octavius brought up the Western powers, Antony those of the East, here came the crisis, here they measured their strength. But Cleopatra fled and Antony after her, burying his empire in the Egyptian's lap. And here again today would be fought out the conflict between East and West, between the Crescent and the Cross.

He let himself fall back, deadly tired. Certainly in either fleet he was the only one to think these thoughts. And certainly also the only one, in that decisive hour, who lay as useless as a woman on his cot, unable to put out his hand to take the helmet and shield which lay there beside him. Truly God had smitten him—with these attacks of illness, the latest of which had now destroyed the meaning of his whole existence. He was ruined for a fighter as he had been ruined for a priest; he was a poor, miserable wretch, not found worthy by Heaven to achieve merit and enter as God's warrior into glory.

And as if in confirmation he heard a voice penetrating the thin boards of the deck, the voice of a priest. Cervantes heard every word. General absolution was granted, the deck shook as they all knelt down. At that very moment, on board two hundred ships, forty thousand fighters knelt, and listened to the message that promised forgiveness for sins and opened wide the gates of bliss to all who should fall today in the battle for the true faith. Cervantes lay with his weak hands folded, while tears of impotent longing and anger welled from beneath his closed lids. The priest spoke first in Latin, then in Spanish. Then silence. He heard them rising from their knees. Now a cannon thundered—the flagship gave the signal. A storm of shouts arose from all the ships at once: "Victory, victory! *Viva Cristo!*" The galleys moved off. It had begun.

Howls, shrieks, creakings as of a world in dissolution came down to him where he lay. Thousands of voices yelled the *Allah-il-Allah,* mingled with simultaneous thunder from a hundred ordnance. That was the galliasses. He heard the splintering of oars, the ringing and trampling of men above his head, commands and shouts of encouragement. Powder-smoke drove into the hatchway. The little ship staggered, heeled to one side and righted herself.

He turned on his face, closed his ears with his hands. But he could not bear it, he must again to the hatchway. The toylike alignment he had seen before was gone; he gazed into the furious mêlée of the battle. And then he saw in front of him, on his left, the Venetian flagship.

It was seeking to pierce a way through the squadrons to the centre of the foe. The old man standing under the lion standard unfurled on the poop, that was the Captain-General, that was Venier. Cervantes' gaze hung upon him, his eyes grew large and staring. But he did not see the man's commanding forehead, the mighty brows, nor how extraordinarily his white beard shook as he shouted commands. He did not see his face, but only his clothing: the gold-embroidered mantle over the cuirass, the flat beret on his head. It was not Venier, the Captain-General, but the tortured and martyred Bragadino whom he saw. That was his costume, the Venetian official garb. It was not a ship that passed—it was a cow, jogging absurdly along with the eyeless, stuffed-out skin atop, as they had driven it past the dying man in yelling procession.

A mighty wave of horror, pity and lust of vengeance swept through his veins. Surely his heart would cease to function under that oppression? But it throbbed the harder, his sinews grew tense, he was no more a weakling, no more rejected, no longer impotent in the face of battle. He raised himself to his knees, stuck on his helmet, seized his short sword and shield, and rushed on deck.

The *Marquesa* was not yet engaged. The full ranks of troops, ready for battle, stood peering out between the rowing slaves. The space was small, the whole ship scarce five paces wide; they stood on the runway between the banks, on the banks themselves, on the little roof at the peak, on the network woven over the poop. Captain Urbina was stationed there. Cervantes pressed his way through. Urbina's honest face was turning blue, his helmet sat awry. "What are you doing here?" he cried to the tardy comer. "You are sick—go home to your mother!"

A deafening crash drowned his words. Oars shattered. Hull drove against hull. The *Marquesa* was grappled. Turbans rose up over the edge of the foreship. The first boarders were already on deck. They fought their way forward, they trod on the hands of the bellowing slaves. The attackers fell into the sea. Man wrestled with man among the waves; there was no thought of rescue or of flight. Cervantes saw one, swimming on his back, pushing with his feet, take aim at himself; the arrow whirred, a man beside him fell pierced through the eye. Then an oar hit the archer and crushed him. The *Marquesa* was free again.

All round about was destruction and tumult—no plan, no method. Wanton, raging murder. Five hundred ships were firing: cannons, mortars, arquebuses, blunderbusses. Ship after ship was boarded; one five times, one ten. The smoke from the six galliasses darkened the sky. Chivalrous or not, they made tremendous havoc. Midday was like night. Showers of sparks flew from the crash of swords and shields, maces and partisans and daggers—they looked like lightning flashes. No one any longer distinguished friend from foe. The flag of the Redeemer flew from a Turkish mast, an Egyptian was in command of a Roman galley. The raging sea was spotted with bloody foam.

Many ships were already on fire, others sinking; oars plied over wreckage and corpses and men locked together in the death struggle. Roars of "Allah!" and "Cristo!"—agonized shrieks, the crack of the whip across the backs of slaves, the insistent shrilling of arrows, the braying of trumpets. . . .

The *Marquesa* had got into clearer water, with only the inferior sort of vessel buzzing about her—feluccas and tartans, which she could easily keep off. And there was a view into the heart of the battle.

The decision was at hand. The two flagships were locked, their generals were at grips. The ships were high-decked, hard to mount. But they were mounted, over and over again. The troops of Kapudan Pasha were the Sultan's Guard, janissaries, familiar by reason of their unusual head-gear. Their scimitars did deadly work. Don John's picked men were arquebusiers. But that elaborately served arm was not much use to them, they took to cold steel instead. The Admiral, in his silver armour, was fighting in their midst. He still wore the splendid bush on his helm, but not the silken tricots—they would have split. He hewed and thrust, on fire with fury—no longer a Captain-General but a slaughter-mad youth. Cervantes saw him; he could see everything.

Then came a mighty shouting—the *Marquesa* attacked. Urbina had lost his head, for what could he do against that floating fortress? It was the Alexandrian flagship they were for, the high, gilded galley with the purple standard at the bow—he meant to grapple it! But the *Marquesa* was so low in the water that scarcely were the boards across than her decks swarmed with Turks. The fight was on—what a fight! A savage uproar, Cervantes in the mêlée, blindly swinging his sword. Suddenly beside him bobbed up the head of the Gallego he had punished at Messina—he was laughing, his teeth glittered in his lust of slaughter. He shouted at Cervantes: some friendly indecency, the gist of which was that here was a glorious scrimmage, just after his own heart. Cervantes was glad that the brute recognized him, and ashamed that he was glad. The combat was merciless. "Holy Mother of God!" groaned a wounded man. "God has no mother, thou foul dog," shrieked the Moslem, and gave him the quietus. Summary theology, thought Cervantes. Then he felt a shooting pain, his shield fell from his hand, his left hand; it was shattered by a bullet and hung down like a bloody rag. He had no time to think of it. His own were over there.

The flagship had been boarded by stratagem in another place; he followed, dripping blood, his sword in his right hand. He felt nothing. Naked barbarians pressed round the armed men; the rowers' chains were cast off, arms given to them; with the promise of freedom they staggered upwards to death.

Men wrestled hand to hand. When weapons were broken, they killed with the naked fist. Turks fell into the sea in rows, their purple standard was torn from the staff and brandished by a Spaniard amid jeers. A dagger caught him in the throat and others seized the blood-stained banner. "Victory!" they yelled. *"Vence Cristo!"* The ship was theirs.

"Vengeance is done upon the flayers!" Miguel said out loud, leaning against the Turkish hull. A raging fire burned in his hand, he had a rag wrapped round it. But he was free, he was light and vacant inside. Shots still whistled round him, he heeded them not . . . then almost simultaneously two bullets struck his breast. The first was nothing, it was spent and scarcely pierced the doublet. But the second forced its way through. He knew enough to know that it was not the heart. He fell against the wall; but a rousing shout of victory made him open his eyes once more. There in the distance, stuck upon a lance, was a gory head with a beard: they had got him, it was the head of Kapudan Pasha. Don John had him. All was over.

Such was the battle in the Gulf of Corinth, called after the place Lepanto, known to the ancients as Naupaktos. It had lasted three hours. Ten thousand Osmanli fell, eight thousand were taken prisoner, a hundred galleys captured, fifty destroyed. There was rich plunder of cannon and banners. Twelve thousand Christian galley-slaves were freed from their Turkish chains. It was a decisive victory.

In the Vatican the Pope shed tears of joy, he had visions of a Christian Jerusalem. Venice was liberated from a nightmare, to dream of redoubling her conquests. Only King Philip remained unmoved. Turkish blood was not heretic blood—and Don John's triumph had been too great.

The prestige of the Crescent was departed, its power almost destroyed, its empire lay a ready prey. But nothing was done. The League crumbled. Lepanto had no results.

CHAPTER EIGHT

At the "Black Hat"

They cured his chest and hand in the barracks at Messina and Reggio. For the former the surgeons needed to do little—it was already healing. But when they had done their bungling best for Cervantes' left hand it remained a helpless and paralysed stump.

There was no means then of deadening pain. In severe operations they made the patient dead drunk. Cervantes scorned the idea, and looked on as the knife bored into his flesh. It was a wonder that he escaped tetanus. About him his comrades died like flies.

The convalescence took months. Behind the hospital in Reggio was a little orangery; he sat there in the sun and read. The cure of souls at the hospital, a Jesuit priest, had lent him a Thucydides and a Plutarch, in Latin translations. Here he was in his element and among his own kind. The day of the battle had been decisive: it had given shape to the profoundest elements of his being, that fever out of which he had torn himself would never more return. His soul was tranquil and strong. He had stood so near to death, had seen it raging beside him in a thousand forms—it had no longer any power to fright him. So incredible was it that he still lived, that he felt life as a gift;

and with it out of that drunken carnage he had saved something else: an abiding, steady serenity, apparent to all.

Captain Urbina came several times to his bedside, and by commission from the Field-Marshal brought him honorariums in money: once fifteen, then twenty, then ten ducats. Cervantes suspected that Don John knew nothing about these gifts. Urbina was the youngest son of a scholarly and cultured family, who had put him into the army. It appeared that he had taken a fancy to Cervantes. He had wanted to keep him from the battle, and the triumph of the young man's fighting spirit over his flesh had greatly impressed him. "I have told the Field-Marshal," he announced. "I have several times related the tale. He will soon be coming to see you in person." But Don John came not, being more brilliantly employed. "He will write you a recommendation," said Urbina. "He has promised me. I have told him of your deeds."

"Which deeds, then, Don Diego?"

"Don't talk nonsense! We both know. The letter will go to the King. You will carry it back to Spain, and the King will make you a captain and give you a company."

That would be good fortune indeed. Captaincies were well paid: father, mother, brothers and sisters could live on it.

News from home was vague and rather disquieting. One of the sisters, indeed, was finally provided for: she had taken the veil. Miguel tried to visualize her as a *cordelière*—but the picture escaped him. He did not know where Brother Rodrigo was fighting. Rumour kept busy with the life of the elder sister, Andrea: she seemed to live with one man after another, no longer in the parents' house. There was no parents' house. The little property in Alcalá had been sold; Miguel suspected that it was auctioned for debt. He had letters from Madrid, Seville, Valladolid. The father had been a law-student in his youth; he seemed now to be roving about, trying his luck as a sort of counsel or unlicensed attorney. It could not be very easy for him, since every letter complained of his increasing deafness. The mother wrote not at all. Cervantes was tortured by his inability to give his ageing parents a life free from care.

At last they dismissed him as cured. He looked like a piece of brown granite; the stump of arm hung down plain to see, but not repulsive. What a blessing that it was the left! For the shield was always bound fast to the arm. There were rumours of fresh hostilities against the Turks. Perhaps some new and brilliant action would enable him to clutch fortune by the forelock.

But the time for martial success was past, for him and for Don John. The operations in the Mediterranean were pursued at random, under an unlucky star, wastefully, yet with insufficient means. Several times the fist was upraised for the blow and did not crash down. Again it would strike but not follow up the blow; the enemy rose again, scarcely incommoded. The Mohammedan fleet had long since been replaced. There had been a chance to seize and destroy it in Navarino Bay; but lack of accord paralysed every resolve, and the Christian armada returned empty-handed.

The Captain-General's ambitions hounded him about. He took Tunis. Took it for himself, as his kingdom, and conveyed his wishes to Philip through the Vatican. Philip was alarmed. He was himself not martial, and looked with misgiving upon this adventurer of only half-rightful blood. As a precautionary measure he instructed his chancellery to address Don John not as "Highness" but for the present as "Excellence" only. Then he gradually withdrew his support in gold and reserves. The following year Tunis was lost again, this time permanently.

Don John cast his eye about him. He wanted to rule. He had asked the Venetian Republic to give him in return for services rendered some part of their island possessions as a principality. The answer came that Venice was making peace with the Porte. The Turkish strength was growing. The Berber pirate states more and more arrogantly dominated the Mediterranean. Their corsairs skirted every coast, burned the port cities, descended upon the ships and carried back men and booty to their African lairs.

The King's troops seldom got their pay. They were troublesome guests in the rich cities of Italy. When no enterprise was on foot, the regimental discipline was relaxed and the men left to their own resources. They moved in troops through the peninsula, with martial bearing, honour always on their lips, but swaggering, dissolute, threatening, without regard for life or property. They were most unpopular.

There came a day when King Philip recalled his generalissimo from the southern seas. Some vague operation in Lombardy was in view; the time left uncertain, but Genoa named as the place where the troops should assemble. The Figueroa regiment, to which Cervantes had now been transferred, was to be among them.

Cervantes had no wish to move with the troops; and it was not hard for him to get permission to make his way alone from Naples to Genoa. Every mouth less to feed meant something to the hard-pressed commissariat.

A mount was quickly found. A Neapolitan oil merchant, going to Rome, felt himself lucky to have military escort. Mounted on a good black horse, Cervantes jogged beside or behind him along the Via Appia Antica. On the fourth day, at noon, they traversed the high causeway above the blue haze of the Pontine marshes. Buffaloes lifted their shaggy heads here and there out of the pest-infected grass. But towards evening the hills and domes of Rome rose up in the golden summer air.

He surrendered his mount to its owner—and set out to run across the city of Rome. His heart beat fast. Only now he knew how much he longed to see once more the Canon Fumagalli, and the gracious Acquaviva. Probably it was for that he had persisted in travelling independently.

All the gates at the Vatican stood open. No one troubled about the foreign soldier, no one challenged him. Under the present Pope there seemed to be freedom of motion. He cocked his helmet upon his brow, shoved his dagger to the front of his girdle and rushed up the familiar stair, bent on looking as soldierly as possible when he rushed into the arms of the soldierly Canon. Clerics whom he passed on the stairs looked round at him and shrugged their shoulders.

Here was the door. He pushed it open and stood still. A foreign priest, young, with a skin like parchment, rose indignantly from his *prie-Dieu* and coldly asked what Cervantes desired. Cervantes stammered. His gaze flew round the room. The Hannibal tapestries still hung in their place.

The priest knew nothing. An official of the Index had

been his predecessor in these rooms. He had never heard the name of the Canon.

Then Cervantes stood before Acquaviva's apartments. He knocked timidly at the antechamber door; no one answered. Within was emptiness, the doors stood open. All was in order and utterly lifeless.

At last a porter enlightened him. They were all dead. Fumagalli had died but ten days after the austere Pope, ten days before the Cardinal. He was buried in the Lateran.

The porter searched in his desk. "I must still have the notice somewhere," he said sympathetically, "the one they gave out after his death. But you could not read it, it was in Latin."

"Give it to me anyhow," Cervantes said.

By the little oil lamp he read, dim-eyed: *"Vix credi potest quanto cum moerore totius urbis decesserit, tantum sibi benevolentiam et gratiam ab omnibus comparaverit, morum suavitate ac vitae innocentia."*

"Mild he was, and free from guile," he said, and handed back the notice. "He is certain of bliss."

"Amen," said the porter.

He strode through galleries and darkening courts and sought the tower where he had dwelt. He saw a shattered remnant; they were tearing it down. He looked at it long: it reminded him, in the dusk, of a huge broken column of some antique monument.

There seemed to be unhindered exit everywhere, but he went out by the little Porta Posterula, that gave on to a clayey desolation. Then he skirted the whole complex of the palace, encountering hedges and ditches on his way, and went through the silent Borgo to San Angelo. . . .

At the nearest inn he took a room and threw himself on his bed without making a light.

Next morning early he continued his way northwards on foot. He travelled light, with a little leather knapsack across his shoulders, his helmet dangling like a cook-pot beside it. He carried only pistol and dagger, having left his sword and shield behind with the baggage-train. A knotted kerchief protected his head from the sun, and he cut himself a stick for a staff.

He made no great haste. He saw Viterbo with its beautiful fountains, Bolsena on its rocks by the lake, Siena the fair and chaste. By the tenth day he stood at a cross-roads in Tuscany; on his right lay Florence only five hours away. But that was not his route. He rested a while in the shade of a plane-tree and deliberated; then took up sack and staff, got himself ferried across the Arno and went down slantwise towards the sea.

A charming, tranquil scene spread out before him in the evening light: low, rolling hills, clad in mulberry- and chestnut-trees; vineyards on every slope and like gardens all the level ground. Peaceful farms and villas lay scattered through the landscape, everything witnessed that here for long no devastating war had raged. His road stretched up hill and down dale in the moonlit night; a sudden weariness overtook the solitary wanderer. Then quite unexpectedly he stood before a wall with a gate. A forest waved above the battlements; no house, no tower was to be seen. But in front of the gate soldiers sat round a table, casting dice in the light of a torch. From their uniform Cervantes recognized them as German foot-soldiers.

They waved him away indifferently, pointing to his

garb by way of explanation: he understood that there was no admission here for foreign soldiers. It was hard to arrive at an understanding; at last he took his pistol from his belt and with a gesture of exaggerated helplessness aimed at the wall. They saw the point, laughed and let him in.

The inner wall was planted thick with trees; this was the forest which had hid the towers from sight. He passed on, by narrow, cleanly paved streets, meeting no one. He crossed a canal and stood again at the city's edge.

Light came from under the blinds on the ground floor of a little house standing somewhat apart; above the door he saw by the moonlight a freshly varnished inn sign, a wrought-iron arm supporting a black hat.

He knocked. He had to do so four times before the door was opened, and the hostess stood before him with a candle in her hand—a plump young female with a frightened face. He asked for lodgment.

"So late, Messer Soldier!" she said timorously.

"Just so—so late that I must find a bed."

Still hesitatingly she led him in and showed him up the stair. "Will you send me up some bread and a glass of wine?" he asked, when they had gained his sleeping-chamber.

She nodded. "You are a Spaniard?" she asked, at the door.

"You do not like them, it seems?"

"We do not know them. They do not come here. One only in the past year. But he was quite different from you."

"How so?"

"Altogether different."

He had meant to move on next morning; but he stopped.

Not for long had he slept so well as in the clean, soft bed. In none other of the inns where he had been was there glass in the windows, or ever a wash-basin.

When he went downstairs he saw that the "Black Hat" stood almost against the city wall. There was only a small garden between it and the tree-studded inner wall; in the garden were two stone tables fixed in the earth, with stone benches. Cervantes was given his breakfast there.

"You are too close to the foe," he told his hostess, as she sat opposite to him. "When he comes he can jump straight down into your garden."

"Oh, they won't come. We are protected by the Emperor in Vienna."

"Let us hope so."

"And we have our charters too," she said proudly. "The Inquisition cannot run here."

That walled-in settlement upon which Cervantes had lighted was the city of Lucca. A peaceful, self-governing community, a sort of republic or a duchy without a duke, under the protection of the Roman Emperor. They were his soldiers who had sat dicing before the gate.

Two children had come up, a girl of eight or nine, a boy perhaps two years younger. They were pretty, neat little things, and looked like the housewife.

"You can tell at once who suckled them," Cervantes said. "They speak for themselves."

"But you are wrong, Messer Soldier. Only the boy is mine. The girl"—she leaned forward and whispered—

"belonged to my sister, over in Massa; she died four years gone."

"Ah!"

"It is the best are taken the soonest. I had such a good true man."

"A widow, then—so young."

"I was wed at seventeen. He never saw his son. Now I am four-and-twenty. And life is over for me." She gave a pious sigh.

"Surely not. At four-and-twenty—what cannot happen still!"

She smiled uncertainly. Something uncommonly good-natured and confiding exhaled from her whole little person. It was still early in the day, but she was dressed with care, and her waving, red-brown hair was tastefully dressed.

The boy had clambered on to the bench. Standing beside his mother, he peeped into Cervantes' left sleeve.

"What is the matter with it?" he asked, at once frightened and fascinated, pointing at the gnarled stump. "Isn't there a hand, or what?"

The mother went fiery red. "One must not ask such questions, Domenico," she cried in vexation.

"Let him alone. . . . Your two little paws are prettier," he said to the child, enclosing them gently in his own right.

"What all you must have lived through. Tell us about it."

"Tales of blood and slaughter."

"Perhaps tonight—if you are still here?"

"I shall still be here," Cervantes said.

And even by the third and fourth day he was still there. The easy, cheery life, filled with peaceful occupation, cast its spell upon him.

"You are a confiding soul, my lady hostess," he said once. "How do you know that I can pay?"

"When your money is gone I will take your dagger and pistol."

"Then I could not leave at all!"

"Stay, then," she said softly.

After all living was cheap at the sign of the "Black Hat." A glass of the light refreshing wine cost but a *soldo*. Business was good, the taproom always full. But in the evening quiet the neighbours sat round Cervantes and lent an ear to his tale.

"He knows how to spin a yarn, Mistress Angelina," Dinucci the wheelwright said, when Cervantes was not by. "You can take hold of what he says, you can fairly taste it, if you know what I mean. Quite different from the Spaniard who was here last year——"

"Don't remind me of him, Messer Dinucci! I still feel sore on account of the money. He wanted a chicken every day, sometimes two—then he was off and left me a pair of torn stockings in the chest for all payment."

"I can see him sitting here in your garden with his ribbons and chains! If you were to believe him, there is no town from here to Peru that he did not know, he had been in all the battles and killed more infidels with one hand than the whole of Africa can hold. His every third word was I, I, I, it sounded as though he would say 'I, your King.' Have you ever heard Don Miguel say I? I doubt if he knows what it is in Italian."

"Drink a glass to his health," said Angelina gratefully. "It costs you nothing"—and she filled it to the brim.

Cervantes' stories could not be wild or high-coloured enough for these simple folk, who never saw a word of print. Their fancy was most taken by tales of the Algerian pirates. What a blessing that the coast hereabouts was inhospitable and poor! None ever came hither.

Cervantes told them of the corsair ships, little and light, with powerful sails. In a calm they could row, swift as the lightning. The slaves fell dead of fatigue at the oar and were thrown overboard. They voyaged by night, without light or sound, and on a sudden they were there—like death itself. They carried off vast booty. On their feluccas and galleons the masts were hollow, and stored full of sequins and doubloons—Christian blood turned into minted gold. Cervantes knew the most feared and famous names by heart: Jaffer of Dieppe, Hassan-Veneziano, Dali-Mami. Most renowned of all was Haireddin-Barbarossa, Beylierbey and lord over Africa.

But there was merriment and endless laughter when he described the janissaries, the Sultan's Guard, fierce and intrepid folk, strange in habit and dress.

"They live together in their barracks, which are almost like cloisters. No woman may enter. They cook for themselves and have their housekeeping in common. Eating must be the most important thing in life to them, for all their dignities and orders are regulated by it. What we should call a Colonel is among them Head Cook; then there are Meat Roasters, Joint Carvers, Bread Bakers, Kitchen Lads. They have cooks' caps in various styles, decorated with herons' feathers. And their standard—that is a cook-pot."

"A cook-pot," they all cried out, "an actual, regular cook-pot?" The children, who had refused to go to bed, shrieked with laughter as they climbed on his knee.

A couple of hours later they were in the bedchamber. The taper still burned. The window was open, the fountain splashed. Angelina slept, with her right arm softly bedded, the hand hanging open over the edge of the narrow couch. A waft of orange-water scent came from the curling red-brown hair, mingled with a faint, not unpleasant suggestion of roast meat. Cervantes saw his helmet lying at the table's edge; Angelina had tried it on in bravado a little before: and with her red-brown locks, and bare young breast, had looked like some rustic female deity in an allegorical painting. Cervantes smiled, and gently straightened her pillow.

Two weeks had passed. "When we are married," she had said today for the first time, quite simply and casually; she seemed to take it for granted.

And why not? Would it not be for the best? Here was a friendly, confiding human creature who offered him domestic satisfaction and simple well-being. An inn-keeper in Lucca, a citizen among the citizens of a little state that found modest security amid the storms of the time—certainly, his heart's dreams had been far different from this. But he had been six years a rover, and had not yet advanced so far as to relieve his own from sordid cares. "Church, or sea, or courts of Kings": he recalled the fortune-bringing trinity. But the saying seemed not to have applied to him. He had got no further as soldier. The letter to the King, promised by the good Urbina, Don John's letter, never came. It never would come. And without such patronage there was small hope of military advancement. To become Captain in the ordinary course one must have served ten years as ensign; and he was not yet even ensign. Once he had dreamed of fame as a poet—he smiled reminiscently. The strophes had streamed from his pen, and Master Hoyos had been full of praise. That was long, long ago. Every young gentleman in Spain did as much. It would have been shrewder of him to shave his pate and hope for a benefice. But they were all dead in Rome. That too was over and done with.

He put out the candle with his insensitive stump of a hand and fell asleep beside Angelina. It was seldom that he dreamed, but tonight he did so. He stood in front of his tower in the Vatican. There were low-hanging clouds, the thunder rolled and bluish lightning shot across the night. The tower, already leaning, fell with a mighty crash, the air was full of dust and ruins. But he stood erect among the falling stones. Fumagalli's saying, those words from a more than human mouth, echoed in his ears: *Si fractus illabitur orbis*—"and if the whole round earth be o'erthrown, let the ruins find one undismayed."

He sat upright in bed. It was already dawn. The helmet lay on the floor and had rolled partway towards the bed. Angelina was awake too, she grasped his arm. "I was dreaming that they had shot you," she said.

"My helmet fell down. Sleep a little still."

Two hours later he confronted her in the garden, equipped for travel. "What can you do with a cripple and a beggar-soldier?" he said. "You deserve something better and you will find it."

She clung to him, she wept aloud uncaring who should hear, she enfolded him and kissed his mouth and breast. He made the parting brief. He did not look round. He went off by the northern gate, near to the inn.

When he had got outside he paused. But there was nothing to see, no house, no church; the dense leafage of the tall trees on the inner wall hid the town from view. By the gate, even this early, German foot-soldiers were dicing round a drum.

He made stout progress in the August morning and reached the sea. By the fourth morning he would be with his regiment in Genoa.

But when on the second day he had put the harbour of Spezia behind him and was marching along a straight, treeless road, he saw afar off a troop of soldiery approaching. Nearer by he recognized Spanish uniforms and presently the pennant borne in front: it was his own regiment.

He greeted and questioned them briefly. Nothing had come of the action in Lombardy, they were on their way back to Naples. It was trying, this aimless and futile to-and-fro. He fell in and went along. The rear began a hymn as they marched, in honour of the Virgin—but at the second verse they knew no more and stopped perforce. It was midday, the wind raised little whirlwinds of irritating dust. Cervantes coughed, changed his place and fell in at the front rank, near the standard.

The standard-bearer was a big, stout fellow, a good head taller than Cervantes. They walked along in silence. All at once he felt himself seized in an iron grip and held. The whole troop had to halt.

"Verily it is he!" cried the standard-bearer, his bass voice breaking with emotion.

"Who am I then, name of a Turkish pig?" cried Cervantes wrathfully, and wrenched himself free. Then he recognized his brother Rodrigo.

CHAPTER NINE

El Sol

Nothing happened in Naples. The city was full of lounging troops. Rumours of warlike operations rose from day to day and melted away like foam. King Philip had forgotten the East. The heretical Netherlands were the thorn in his flesh. Already Holland and Zeeland were boldly threatening to secede in the face of the whole great Spanish monarchy.

Cervantes passed the summer days sadly in the teeming city of the South. His money was wasting. That would have been no misfortune, for Brother Rodrigo stood at his side with the new pay of Lombardy in his pocket. He had no cares. He pressed upon his brother what he had. From the first day he hung with childish idolatry on his elder, found all his exploits incomparable and prophesied great things. Miguel often had to smile as he looked at him. "I am a duodecimo edition of you," he said once—a bookseller's jest of which the unlearned Rodrigo most likely missed the point, apt though it was. The ensign looked like his brother, but everything about him, limbs and features, was enlarged and coarsened; the eyebrows more arched and bushy, the aquiline nose standing out like a promontory.

After a month of it Cervantes had enough. "I am going,

Rodrigo," he said abruptly. "Perhaps there will be a ship soon."

Rodrigo agreed at once. "Let us go, Miguel mine," he said. "A fine idea. But tell me whither."

"To Spain. Home. Will you come?"

It was an admission of bankruptcy. After six years' absence, and five years' service, he was returning home, a cripple, without rank, without a ducat, reduced to sitting in the antechamber of the chancellery at Madrid, to showing his mutilated arm and begging for some petty office. There was no more talk of a prince's recommendation. When Captain Urbina met him, the good man's red face grew redder still as he looked away.

But they had luck with the homeward voyage. It was now the middle of September, and on the twentieth three galleys were due for Spain. Seldom did a single ship dare the perilous crossing alone. Cervantes announced his departure to the Captain, who was more embarrassed than ever.

From early morning the brothers kept watch at the Molo, near which the ships were anchored. Their boat, the smallest of the three, was somewhat pompously named *El Sol*. Their baggage was negligible: arms and knapsacks, that was all. There was a mixed assemblage of travellers, the military predominant, but also officials of the Viceroy returning home, as well as priests and merchants, women and children. There was excited chatter and laughter. Pedlars swarmed, thrusting their wares on everybody in the strange delusion of their kind that the traveller is anxious to load himself down with useless trumpery. Two men with fife and drum deafened the ears. On the open landing-stage two others were having a parting shave.

Directly behind the Molo lay the huge old Castle of Aragon. The Viceroy lived there and with him, as his guest, lodged Don John of Austria. Lepanto lay far in the past, and the review of the fleet where Cervantes had first beheld that elegant and glorious prince.

On the right, beyond the little basin, the new war arsenal was rising to the sound of hammer and saw. Cervantes caught himself looking across with a sort of envy: those workmen were being used, they could see something rising under their hands.

A cannon fired from the Castel dell' Ovo announced midday. The flags went up on the galleys. The passengers filed on board. The heavens were radiant in bright sunshine, but a gentle mist lay over the bay. The rocky walls of distant Sorrento lay in blue shadow.

"Why do we stay, Brother?" Rodrigo asked, and got up. "Let us board with the others."

Cervantes unconsciously hesitated to take the decisive step. It seemed to him that to leave Italy was to acknowledge all hope fled. Still seated, he turned and looked back at the tiered city. So he sat, and they were almost the last. Then he saw a man, a soldier, running towards them round the corner of the palace and across the almost empty square. Hand to his eyes, he recognized the Captain, running and shouting even from afar and waving a paper in his hand. His helmet sat as crooked as at Lepanto.

The trumpeters on the galleys blew the first signal. The rowers replied. Urbina, fiery-faced, came up in triumph.

When all else had failed and the last hour was come, he had cast military etiquette aside. He went to the Castle of Aragon, in his brightest armour, with fluttering scarf and his order on his breast. At the entrance his courage almost failed: nearly two hours he walked up and down before the triumphal arch which now formed the entrance on the landward side. The bronze doors were closed, in the left-hand one a cannon-ball was stuck—it fretted Urbina's very soul not to know how it got there.

But the midday gun told him that there was no time to lose. He found the Captain-General in his room, sitting gloomily over a late breakfast. He knew the Captain and why he came: the business of that Cerveedra or whatever his name was—this was the fourth time he had been at him. As though it were so easy to ask favours of his royal brother at the Escorial!

He looked at his officer with weary eyes, underneath which pouches were beginning to show. Urbina put down his papers on the table among the dishes. To simplify matters he had written out a draft of the recommendation, in fact two, one shorter than the other. He gave Don John the choice, and renewed his plea, modestly but firmly. The brave man for whom he pleaded was sailing this very day. He would feel his honour wounded, himself injured by his superior, if his plea were again refused. He fairly shook as he spoke.

No reply. The prince continued to chew, apathetically. Urbina dared the uttermost: with trembling hands he loosened his order, the Cross of Santiago, from his neck and threw it rattling down on top of the papers, all among the sauces.

The young man sat up and stared into his officer's honest and embittered face. Then he beckoned to the servant and having got a quill signed the document nearest to him—it happened to be the shortest.

"Now let me eat in peace," said he. "Don't come back."

Urbina hastened down the steps, gay as a lark. And met coming up, together with his military suite, the master of the house, Viceroy and grandee of Spain. Success went to the Captain's head. There on the stairs he bent his knee before the astonished Governor, thrust the second document under his nose and breathlessly told his tale.

"With pleasure," said the Viceroy. "Come into my room." Perhaps it flattered him to think that his word could be of importance beside that of the Grand Admiral.

Cervantes heard little of all this. The trumpet had blown twice. He held the documents in his good hand and tears streamed down his cheeks. Rodrigo stood reverently by, delighted but by no means surprised: why should not people do their utmost for Miguel? "May the Blessed Virgin be with you!" said the Captain. And that was all.

A south wind had come up conveniently; it drove the little squadron on its way, past Cape Misenum and the roadstead at Procida. But then came a calm. The three ships stuck close together and slipped northwards along the Italian coast. It would have been madness to venture upon the open sea unless they must.

The voyage was long, but merry. Everybody was glad in the prospect of home; on board the *Sun* was no single unhappy soul. The oarsmen were not slaves but free sailors, who rowed in time to their own music.

And merriest of all was Ensign Cervantes. He never tired of conning the documents—the evidence of his brother's honours past and to come. He knew them by heart, he quoted them to merchants, monks and women, to all and sundry in his perfervid bass: "A soldier whose claims had been neglected, but who has won general regard by his valour, prudence and faultless behaviour!"

He who owned these honours sat for the most part quiet in the poop and read. When the boat skirted the Tuscan littoral he did not read, but gazed shorewards to where not many miles away the Emperor's walled town lay behind its groves.

They sighted Genoa, and had for days in view the brilliant Ligurian coast, with its jagged line of Alps rising abruptly behind it. This was the sixth night, and not a breath of air stirred; yet by the next midday they must reach Marseilles and in another twenty-four hours sight the Spanish coast.

Wrapped in their mantles the brothers lay on deck. Rodrigo slept. Cervantes, as he turned on his side to address himself to slumber, felt his letters to King Philip rustle at his breast. They meant well-being, they meant security for his own; perhaps, even, they meant fame. They opened the gates to life.

But at midday the storm came up on the south-west.

CHAPTER TEN

The Dead Kings

The funeral trains crossed Spain: from the north, from the south, from the west, they came to the centre. King Philip awaited them.

How long had he not been yearning to live united with his dead! All too slowly arose that palace and cloister for the departed of his house! The spot is remote and sinister, stark cliffs surround it, pitiless storms swoop down. And here, twelve years long, the work had gone on; twelve years had King Philip watched over it. Madrid saw him but little. He was waiting.

At first in the hamlet close by, where monks lived huddled in the little houses, in one room of which they made a chapel, with a great crucifix painted on the wall and a bedquilt stretched beneath the roof to protect the altar from the rain. The space was so small that the ministrant tripped over the feet of the kneeling King.

No better were the quarters of the King, the greatest prince on earth. The priest's house boasted no windows and no chimney-place; it had a single three-legged wooden bench.

After the eighth year the monks moved into the still unfinished palace, and King Philip with them. The damp was very hard on his gout. The grandees in his train despaired, the monks themselves groaned in secret. Monks love to be left alone.

He sat among his papers in a couple of poorly furnished rooms near the temporary church and regulated the affairs of two hemispheres. All about him the confusion and noise of the building; all about him still the desert. Close up to the mounting masonry yarrow grew—a tough and rugged weed almost impossible to root out. Stone blocks lay about, brought up from the quarries by teams of twenty, thirty, forty oxen. The creaking of the two-wheeled crane, the blows on the scaffolding, the hissing of saws, the hammering of smiths, the pounding of stone-masons, the axes of woodmen in the forests near by—none of all that disturbed the waiting King.

But it took too long. Only the eastern and southern wings were finished of the mighty foursquare plan. Of the church that should rise above the dead there was little yet to show. He gave the order to leave all else and build the vaults. His desire was overmastering; he could wait no longer.

Hour after hour he sat at his desk, studying maps and mileage tables, methodically working out the routes of the processions. The dead of his house lay widely scattered. It would take so and so many days; at this and this place halts would be made overnight; at such and such cross-roads certain trains would meet; at a certain spot they should all unite; and on a fixed day he himself—at last, at last—would greet his dead. He exercised much care in choosing the great ones of the earth who were to accompany the dead: the Duke of Alcalá, the Duke of Escalona, the Bishops of Salamanca, Jaén, Zamora. They had to pay for the honour too: each one chosen bore all the charges of his train. So strangely was mystical yearning married to thrift.

He had good ground to count the cost. The blood of Spain was ceasing to flow. In the very midst of world-domination, the mother-country was drying up. It was coming to pass in the name of God.

The King did not ask if the world understood him. Outside the Habsburgs there was no world. Never did he concede the name of Majesty to any foreign sovereign. Majesties were only those dead whom he was awaiting.

They were coming from cathedrals and cloisters where they had lain asleep: from Andalusia and Estremadura, from Old Castile, from Madrid. And among them was not one who was once happy. Theirs was an other-worldly destiny—not for them was earthly life and earthly bliss. There came Juana, mother of the Emperor, with melancholy and insanity in her blood; there came Philip's mother, the Empress; the Queens of Hungary and France, the Emperor's sisters, who from outside yet laboured at the edifice of his glory; there came the young Queens, Philip's wives, sacrifices to premature maternity; there came the children of the house, too weak to live; there came the half-bestial Don Carlos, absolved by death, now welcomed by the father who had forbidden him to live. And from Cloister Yuste came the Emperor Charles himself.

The distances were great, the roads bad. The expectant man in the Escorial knew every milestone passed by each procession every hour. He himself had arranged every detail down to the smallest: the number of nobles in each escort, of chaplains and mendicant friars. The retinue of each corpse was apportioned with the most meticulous etiquette:

to that Infante eighteen pages, to this Queen twenty-four. So many ells of crape went to each horse. Gold brocade covered the coffins, each had a coronet of special shape according to rank and precedent.

The whole plateau was parched with summer heat. The folk made holiday, lying in the dust along the roads. All the cities were draped in mourning, the poorest village or heap of stones flew the crape-shrouded red and yellow flag. The nights were spent in churches, where masses and litanies for the dead were sung, while the bearers lay sleepless on the stone flags, wrapped in their mantles.

At length the waiting time was past; a herald brought word: the trains had met, they were coming on.

It was a dark and dismal day; tattered storm-clouds flew low over the Escorial. The King issued from the unfinished portal of the vast, unfinished vault.

The great square was still unpaved, the ground uneven, the yarrow not yet burned away. A mammoth catafalque had been erected, all black velvet and gold brocade, and three steps leading up to the flat surface where the coffins were to lie. The baldachin was supported by columns wreathed in gold.

The King, in ceremonial mourning, stood alcne beside the catafalque. He wore the cap and vestments of the Golden Fleece, the open robe whose lapels were finely embroidered with a recurrent pattern of the Lamb. In his hands he held a crucifix. His gaze searched the sunburnt steppe, the tragic heart of his domain; it ranged for miles and miles, to the far-distant mountains of Toledo. In the middle distance a pale shining marked his city of Madrid.

The funeral march swelled on the breeze and the sound of prayers. Uphill wound the foremost train; the eagle standard was visible: the coffin of Charles the Fifth led the way.

King Philip knelt down. On his death-bed in Yuste the Emperor had held in his hands this jewel-encrusted cross; so in his turn he would one day hold it.

Now, in this hour, he gave his father account of his charge. Alas, the hands that hold the cross can no longer hold united God's kingdom on this earth. Gone for ever are those glorious days when Europe was one in the community of faith. God has permitted abominations to come to pass; His world grows dark. Everywhere is rebellion, heresy and delusion. England, Germany and the North are long gone to perdition, the Habsburg Netherlands are in profoundest spiritual unrest, France is ready to make peace with the heretics; while the Mediterranean east and south, the Habsburg Sea, is in the hands of infidel prophets, from the Atlantic to the Holy Sepulchre and from the Holy Sepulchre to before Vienna.

Yet he need not shirk the reckoning. He had always been ready to render all to God. For the sake of the pure dogma he reigned at enmity with other States, his creatures drew their daggers against renegade princes, his best provinces were desolate, his treasury empty; Moorish industry and Jewish wisdom were hounded and burned. Soon he would be alone with the dead of his own seed, with whom alone he felt himself at one in the citadel of faith where they now gathered.

The organ sounded from the unfinished interior. Salvos echoed from the troops brought up for the purpose. The Prior, the crucifix in his hands, issued from the entrance, which as yet boasted no doors. Chanting from within mingled with that of the oncoming trains.

The royalties had now arrived upon the broad platform, in front of their vault which stretched out unequal arms to embrace them. King Philip lingered in a trickle of rain to oversee the ceremonies, during which the cases were taken from the wagons and borne up on to the stage. The organ music and salvos, pealing of bells and chanting went on, the bishops in mitre and pallium blessed the dead. Low clouds of incense floated off in the rainy air.

It was over. The coffins, arranged in a long row by order of precedence, covered the huge slab. Each of the departed was designated by initial and special coronet. But in the very centre, isolated in proud majesty, rose the sarcophagus with the closed crown atop, the imperial standard at its head and the pall embroidered thick with the eagle, symbol of imperial power.

The heir stood there, drunken with melancholy. Ah, might he but prolong this moment for ever! It was his greatest. Not even in their vault would he ever again embrace them as now with his glance—these who were of his blood, his mission, his destiny, his certain faith. This review of the dead was fulfilment at last, fulfilment of his ecstatic faith, fulfilment at the same time of his profound and morbid, unquenchable craving for order. Only death preserves order.

But now—like some primeval ravening beast from its lair—the storm swooped down from the mountains, a howling tornado.

It was the scourge of this sinister spot. The monks feared it as the embodiment of a personal evil, as a Satan defending his kingdom and solitude against the rising might of the new fortress. But never had his violence raged as today.

In a single second all the ordered magnificence was

gone. The coronets shivered, the standard bowed, the palls were whirled away. The mighty baldachin billowed up like a sail on the high seas, then split asunder; the golden pillars crashed down. Soon there was nothing left of the whole proud catafalque but a naked scaffolding. The draperies snapped and rattled, it would have been dangerous to try to hold them. As with giant hands, the symbols of Habsburg might and power were snatched into the air, and tatters embroidered with eagle and crown whirled away across the stony fields and into the forests. "Our wood has blossomed out in brocade," the wood-choppers would say, on the morrow, as they took their midday rest under the ilex-trees.

The bishops' mitres rolled in the dirt. The robe was wrenched from King Philip's shoulders; he stood there, a fragile figure in his black under-garment, before the naked sarcophagi of his dead.

CHAPTER ELEVEN

Dali-Mami

The storm came out of Spain.

They had left Marseilles behind and shortly afterwards the mouth of the Rhône. A small village was in sight upon a headland. It had a grey church with a battlemented watch-tower which made it look like a fort. A boatman said that it was called Les Saintes Maries.

Here it was the sou'wester attacked them. It came in gusts of such violence that the little squadron was separated in a moment. *El Sol* was alone, a cold, driving rain lashing her decks. Everybody tumbled down the companion-way, save the Captain and two mates. The rowers crouched with their mantles over their heads and laid into the oars, for the helpless little ship was being driven against the coast. It got darker and darker; lightning flashed and thunder answered.

In the bowels of the vessel discomfort reigned. They were all lifted up and dashed down again, the ship lay on her side and they rolled in a heap, women groaned and children screamed pitiably. The air grew worse and worse.

A violent shock, and a rebound. They had run upon a rock; this was the end. But there followed a second shock, even more frightful and on the other side. Men dashed up the companion, Cervantes among them. They did not get far, for the companion was crowded, they looked into the mouths of pistols; shots cracked and a Spaniard fell, clutching behind him, dragging the others down into the hold, which echoed with screams and lamentations.

No opposition was possible. Almost no one was armed, and those who were stood helpless in the narrow space. Cervantes succeeded in getting on deck. It was the work of a moment to trip him, bind him and toss him to one side like a bale of goods. Close by he saw the Captain lying in his blood, and a few of the sailors hung dead over their oars. The storm had died down, a thin rain was falling. The deck was full of corsairs armed to the teeth, roaring among themselves.

Below deck he heard shots, trampling and shrieking. Then one passenger after another came tumbling out of the hatch, their arms tied behind their backs. His brother was nowhere to be seen. The commander appeared to be a certain lame, thick-set man, in splendid garments, dripping wet, and with an agraffe in his turban. He carried a curious cudgel, a sort of flexible life-preserver with which he gave free emphasis to his commands.

Cervantes pulled himself up painfully in his bonds and peered over the edge. The *Sol* had been doubly boarded, two ships lay to port and starboard, secured by grappling-irons, while a third privateer was not far off. They probably came from some lurking-place in the delta of the Rhône.

The rain had stopped; the sun came forth. The limping commander put up his hand and peered about him. There came a cannon-shot. Cervantes knew that one of the Spanish ships carried two small guns. The lame man shrieked an order. They began to drive the prisoners across the gang-planks on to the corsairs. It went too slowly; they expedited the process by picking up the fettered men by feet and shoulders, giving a heave and tossing them across. Cervantes flew through the air, crashed against a bank of oars and lay dazed.

When he came to himself, the vessel was in easy motion. He lay for'ard, and about him were many of his fellow-passengers, tied up and arranged in rows like packets. Many were blood-stained. The weather was clear and fair. The lame commander stood by the mast with his life-preserver clipped under his arm. Detached and contemptuous, he was setting down notes in a book. He had a fat, white, by no means Oriental face, evilly distorted by a drooping eyelid.

On Cervantes' right lay a Jesuit Father with a slash on his forehead; he gazed straight before him, with a fine, collected air. On his left was a lady of middle age, wife of a high Madrid official. Her coiffure was a wreck, the rain had distributed her rouge in streaks over her face. The present calamity had been recognized as possible and dreaded from the first; but now that it was here, it had something so improbable and crazy about it that Cervantes, to his own surprise, felt a laugh rising in his throat. He could not suppress it; in his fetters, as he was, he bent over and laughed. His neighbours turned incredulous eyes upon him.

Afternoon and evening passed. Nobody spoke. Nobody brought the packets food. All the sails were set, disproportionately large ones for so small a craft. They moved without light. "I described it all quite correctly in Lucca," Cervantes thought. The galliot flew southwards over the open sea. In three days they were in Algiers. . . . The Spanish coast must lie to their right. Honour and a future had awaited him there; he felt the papers at his breast. With a tremendous effort he forced himself to forget them. Then again it came to him that Rodrigo was nowhere to be seen. But he felt quiet, a feeling of security possessed him. The starry night was cool—he might sleep. Gently he drew his left arm out of his bonds and was able thus to find a more comfortable position. There are circumstances under which it is an advantage to possess only one hand. He fell asleep. He slept not at all badly.

Next morning they were all kicked awake and systematically plundered. Two of the freebooters searched each defenceless prisoner, two others held open a great bag into which everything was dropped at random: money, coins, ornaments, buckles, handkerchiefs, gloves, girdles and boxes. The lame commander stood by and saw to it that no florin and no bangle missed the mark.

A man in a green shirt and dangling black cap knelt above Cervantes, who blew in his face to avoid his stinking breath. It was quickly done: the corsair contemptuously held up a few coins and the precious papers. Cervantes bit his tongue as the princely recommendations disappeared into the all-embracing sack. He had the sense not to say a word.

They had let the woman next to him stand up. She writhed and complained as the searcher went relentlessly over her body. Her lamentations did not sound very genuine; even now she remained affected. But suddenly Cervantes felt his inaction intolerable. He forgot reason and self-control in the service of this *poseuse*, and with one of his bound legs got so in the man's way that he tripped and fell grotesquely to the floor. He got up, mad with anger; but the lame commander, grinning all over his white face, yelled furiously at him, apparently to the effect that he should get on with his work. As he passed on, he gave Cervantes a glance of unmistakable approval.

One of the crew came and gave out food: a grey-coloured biscuit made apparently of grit and barley, with a handful of black olives. The prisoners were lightened of their chains, some of them stood up and stretched—certainly the heavily armed corsairs had nothing to fear.

Cervantes almost enjoyed the sorry meal. He watched the official's lady bite affectedly into her biscuit, and perceived that the coquettishness in her raddled face was directed towards himself. Now and again she heaved a melancholy sigh. He decided to move away and seek Rodrigo.

He spied him presently at a distance, sitting, his feet still bound, but quite sound, under the barrel-shaped awning. The faithful lad stretched out his arms; but two of the deck watch drove Cervantes back to his place with threats. He avoided the neighbourhood of the female and lay down at the edge of the boat between the Jesuit father and a Sardinian arquebusier.

They were passing a rocky island under a spanking breeze. There was a bay, with a chalky landing-place, and in the background a pretty Moorish town.

"Ibiza," said the Jesuit. "From here it would be no distance to Spain." Cervantes nodded. He could see himself landing at Valencia, touching and kissing the soil of Spain. Tears rose—but he mastered them and they did not come again.

Self-observation was not his habit. But—so much he had

remarked—small vexations troubled him more than large. Any annoyance, a quite minor disappointment or injury, remained with him for days. But when destiny struck hard, and misfortune came, he proffered his brow, came to terms and was quiet. His life would not end in an Algerian prison; he swore it and he knew it.

The Jesuit was tranquil too. And with reason: for him, indeed, the affair was an incident. It was unthinkable that his Order would leave him in the lurch. His ransom would come in four weeks, there was a regular tariff for clerics. He chatted with Cervantes, and told him the names of their captors. The lame man was Dali-Mami, an Albanian. They had fallen into the hands of one of the most famous of the guild—and one of the cruellest too. He bade Cervantes cast his eye upon the rowing slaves—poor devils without commercial value, who would sit at their oars till death released them. One was earless, another lacked an eye—souvenirs of some passing displeasure on the part of Dali-Mami. It was said—but the Jesuit did not vouch for it—that Dali-Mami was in the habit of hewing off the arm of some laggard oarsman and using it for a cudgel to beat the others. It might easily be true; the man's cruelty seemed to know no bounds. Most shocking of all, it seemed that Dali-Mami and most of his colleagues were born Christians, from Greece, Dalmatia, Italy and elsewhere, and as apostates from the true faith behaved much more atrociously than Turks or Moors. There was no computing the punishment that must await these renegade ruffians in the hereafter.

A member of the crew now came up to Cervantes and with marked politeness of manner signified that the latter was to follow him to the mainmast; there standing on a wooden chest was a glass of wine and a piece of smoked meat. "The Rais sends you this," said the sailor; "flesh, and wine, which you may drink, since you are a Christian." He grinned. It seemed improbable that the pirate ship carried intoxicants for the sole purpose of giving captured Catholics to drink. "And you may go about freely, the Rais permits it."

Cervantes pondered as he drank the strong red wine and took a few bites of meat. He determined to give the rest to his brother Rodrigo.

The ensign was blithe as a lark. He ate gratefully. And seemed not the faintest surprised at the distinction with which his brother was treated. He smiled significantly and with a certain pride under his bushy brows. Cervantes' mind misgave him.

"Will you explain to me," he said, with drawn brows, "what it all means: this wine and meat and the face you are putting on?"

His suspicions were confirmed. It was a bad business. When the booty was sorted his documents had been found. The Rais had the name of Cervantes cried from the poop, where Rodrigo was sitting with bound feet. He answered the call. No, he was not Don Miguel—that was his brother, who was for'ard in the ship. Quite right, a soldier, who had lost one hand. Yes, they could see for themselves from the papers what manner of man he was: not in everybody's behalf would the Captain-General of the Christian forces address a letter to the Spanish sovereign. He advised them to bethink themselves before they touched a hair on the head of Don Miguel de Cervantes Saavedra. What was this Miguel's rank, they asked him, in whose affairs the masters of Christendom took pen in hand? Rodrigo took refuge in mystery. One gathered from what he said that this was a nobleman, very highly placed, a grandee of some very special function. All of which, Rodrigo thought, could only do good. Miguel would be pleased with him.

"Unhappy man!" Cervantes cried. Then he felt remorseful; laid his hand upon his brother's shoulder, and added: "But you meant well."

The lame man was not on deck. Cervantes sought for him and was admitted to his presence. He sat writing at a table in a tiny cabin.

"Yes, I know, you are the grandee; your case will be dealt with presently," he said, not ill-naturedly.

"I am no grandee, and you will get nothing out of me."

Dali-Mami paid no attention. "Two thousand ducats, eh? That is no money at all for a man like you."

"Of course not, I'll give it you tomorrow."

"By next month, certainly. Will you write at once? I will see that it has safe conduct."

"Listen to me, Captain," Cervantes repeated. "You are mistaken. I am no grandee, I am not rich, I have no friends to ransom me. I am a plain soldier, without means, no higher than a lance-corporal."

"Yes, and on behalf of a lance-corporal the Admiral of the fleet writes to the King! Bah!"

"Read the letters. Then you will understand."

"How so, then?" Dali-Mami picked up the sheet from the table. "This is a warm and urgent recommendation. There is nothing here about a poor soldier."

"That is one. Read the other, the one from the Viceroy."

"Ah! So the Viceroy wrote too. And all that for a lance-corporal. It seems to me you manage your affairs very well."

"But read the second one."

"There isn't another one. A poor subterfuge."

"Have them look for it."

"The first one is enough for me."

"You are an ass!" yelled Cervantes. "A silly, pig-headed, thick-skinned ass!" He thought it would be better to be slain on the spot than to sit years on end at an oar, waiting for two thousand gold-pieces which would never come.

And the Rais did indeed start up. His eyes narrowed with fury, his lips pursed and he seized his flexible cudgel. But then he sat down again and drew a long breath.

"Now you have proved your identity," he said calmly. "Only a nobleman could be so insolent." His voice was so well controlled as to be a little too sweet.

Cervantes left him. Oh, Rodrigo, Rodrigo! But he began to feel in his heart an obscure pleasure in the destiny whose sport he was. Yes, in utter freedom of spirit he could ask himself whether this fate was wholly undeserved. Did it thus repay him for his heartless rejection of love and goodness when he left the gates of Lucca as one pushes behind him with his foot the bark which has brought him safe to shore? If such were the case, then he was paying dear. Snatched away into the unknown, almost in sight of home; the instrument of his destruction those very documents which were to make his fortune; his brother's love the grave of all his hopes—he felt as though he were swimming alone upon a dark sea, with no bark in sight. Well, then, he would go through it. He who has forgotten the fear of death is strong.

By midday of the fourth day the corsair lay beneath a radiant sky opposite the city of Algiers, a pyramid of little white boxlike houses, crowned by a citadel at the top. They were welcomed by salvos and joyous cries; the arrival of a ship with booty seemed to be a signal for general rejoicing. "To the Badistan, to the Badistan!" half-naked children sang and chanted.

The Badistan lay close to the sea and the Grand Mosque: a pretty little square, equipped as a slave-market, with posts and counters. The men were divested of their clothing, amid a rain of comment; a mound of discarded garments piled up. All this was soon done, it was the legal and customary procedure. Then clothing was dealt out. Cervantes, Spanish grandee and protégé of the Crown, got what the others got: the coarse shirt, the clumsy breeches, a sort of caftan reaching down to the knees, a pair of slippers and a red cap. They tossed him a woollen cover as well, and with that he was equipped.

Then the auction began. Turks, Jews and Moors moved about among the chattels, feeling over shoulders and legs.

Cervantes was put on one side, he was not offered for sale. Some gentlemen from the police, in long green mantles and turbans of white felt, thundered up to him on slippers shod with iron, and bore him off, with three companions of his lot, to the near-by bagnio.

He was driven into a large, gloomy, vaulted space, where it smelt damp and musty. The green-clad gentry loaded him down with irons and chains. He realized that this distinction, too, he owed to his brother Rodrigo. The more uncomfortable they made him, the sooner would the two thousand ducats arrive.

CHAPTER TWELVE

Algiers

The pirate kingdom of Algiers—by no means an ephemeral organization, since it bid defiance to the great powers for more than three hundred years—has not its like in all history. It was a blend of fantastic unreality and good business. A blood-thirsty tale with a thrifty moral.

In that pyramid of white stone houses, huddled together and smelling to the burning heavens, there dwelt some fifty thousand human beings, of stocks most recklessly mixed.

Since early times the Berber ranged here, the dark Numidian, whose near relatives dwell by the Nile and in Senegal. Phœnicians sailed early to this coast, traded, settled and built. Then the Roman came to hold sway over Punic and Berber; the African province was an imperial storehouse for grain and fruit and oil and wine. Latin was the prevailing tongue. Also Greek; but that was later, when the Empire was ruled from Byzantium. But by then the name of Rome was no protection. Germans landed, conquered, and destroyed the porticoed cities; they in turn were defeated, scattered, and absorbed. The Eastern Empire, too weak to endure, could still have its victories. When Islam came, soon after the death of the Prophet, it triumphed on its first invasion. Far and wide it seized the power; in Spain it founded its greatest kingdom and highest culture. But it fell out with its own, on African soil. Rome's mission was not yet quite extinct; as yet Arabian blood was only a drop in the melting-pot. Early in the dawn of the second millennium, however, huge swarms of roving warriors from the Eastern deserts broke in—plundering, slaughtering, trampling savages. The feast of blood lasted ten years. By then all culture was uprooted, the stores were bare of grain, North Africa desolate for ever. The national triumph was consummate; Arabic became the ruling tongue, in a sea of subservient Berber, with only a vague underwash of Roman, Hellenic and Phœnician sounds.

A strangely mingled population, then, a starved and desert region, a thousand miles of the rock-bound Mediterranean south coast, within striking distance of the most flourishing countries in the world. The stage was set, the rule of the pirate States began.

It would have been Spain's affair to put an early end to the business. She had hounded out the Moors, she was mistress in her own house, and ruled over the treasures of the Indies. She tried. Some coast cities surrendered, cloisters were improvised, mosques turned into churches, garrisons set. But that was all. Africa was then forgotten. The troops were not provisioned or armed. One after another the port towns were lost again; Oran was barely held.

As for Algiers, the Spaniards had fortified a rocky reef within calling distance of the shore. And on this peñon, the "thorn in the heart of Algiers," a Spanish nobleman lay with a handful of soldiers and waited on his own destruction.

It came through Haireddin-Barbarossa. He took the

rock, slew the garrison, had the nobleman bastinadoed to death; destroyed the fort, built a causeway to the mainland and thus created the secure harbour which was the main base for all the corsairs thenceforth.

He offered Africa to the Turkish Sultan in Constantinople, as a present on the palm of his hand. He became his Kapudan Pasha and Beylierbey. He commanded a Turkish army. He himself was a renegade, of Christian blood, of the scum of Europe.

So were the "kings" who from then on reigned in Algiers. So were the Rais, the bandit aristocracy of the city. So were the Sultan's janissaries, his officers and generals, and the upper court officials in the Seraglio at Constantinople; so were most of the viceroys, viziers and admirals in the great kingdom of Turkey.

For the Grand Seigneur had selected for him every year certain Christian boys from all the subject lands. Only the finest and strongest, and of tender age. They soon forgot parents and home, and knew no fatherland save the barracks or the Seraglio. None of them sought to get away; they all clung fervidly to their wild new gospel.

Hosts of volunteers, men and boys, were always coming in. The lost, the strayed, the disillusioned or merely the adventurous took shelter under the banner of the Crescent. They "became" Turks. It was a career. There was complete lack of prejudice: no claims of nobility or tradition of inherited bravery barred the way to the advancement of the lowly born. Everyone without exception had access to every rank and fortune. These renegades were the strength of the kingdom. It was no advantage to be born a Moslem—indeed, it stood in the way of advancement to the highest posts.

The barbaric prestige of that warlike religion was a powerful cement. Charles himself, Emperor and lord of the Christian world, tried to corrupt Haireddin Pasha, son of the Greek potter. He offered him an alliance, Spanish troops, sovereignty itself, if he would forsake Turkey. Barbarossa remained steadfast. And when the Head of the Roman Empire appeared with six hundred ships off Algiers, the pirate stronghold bade him defiance. He landed and attacked. Charles' foremost lieutenant, the standard-bearer of the Order of Malta, thrust his dagger into the Eastern Gate, which closed in his face. It remained closed for centuries. Algiers was impregnable.

The Sultan's plenipotentiaries bore various titles: Aga, Bey, Pasha—the people called them "king." In reality, these kings were tenants. They rented the whole pirate business, which was based upon the power of the janissaries. Chests and bags of gold went regularly to the Bosphorus. Opposed to the King was the Guild of the Rais, ship-owners and pirate captains, the economic backbone of Algiers.

For this whole city was an enterprise, the stock-in-trade of which was stolen goods and the lives of men. If the buccaneers did not make raids, everybody would have died of hunger. There was nothing grown. The countryside was a desert. Trade was confined to "imports."

Claim and counterclaim were very strictly regulated between the crown and the guild. Booty was divided according to a fixed tariff. There was no better bookkeeping in Antwerp or Augsburg. With hands from which the blood was not yet wiped they stood and gesticulated over rates and charges. They plundered cities, pillaged ships, stole regardless and herded men together like cattle; but twelve per cent precisely, not eleven or thirteen, belonged to the King. Twelve per cent of the ransom too, of course.

Prisoners from every country in Christendom were the "goods" that crammed these strange warehouses. There were thousands of prisoners, speculated in from the moment of their arrival. A vigorous man was sold at auction on the Badistan for fifty ducats, in expectation of a ransom of three hundred; but meanwhile the invested capital must yield interest. So the man was hired out, as labourer or beast of burden, and the purchaser drew three ducats a month. Some he might keep in his own house—these were regarded as the lucky ones. For in daily intercourse a man could not continue to be thought of as a bale of goods. Hard to whip him if your children sit upon his knee. Most fortunate of all were those who were taken into a Jewish household, for there mishandling was out of the question, and so, almost, was severity. There were slaves who after a few weeks in a Jewish household held the reins in their hands.

The slaves who lived in the bagnios were the property of the King or of the municipality. Theirs was the harshest lot. They were badly fed and did hard labour in heavy chains—on buildings and fortifications, in mills, or in the harbour. When the ransom was long in coming their case became desperate: such worthless chattels were sent to the galleys. But companioned with them in the bagnios were prisoners of rank and means—or imagined wealth and imagined means—from whom it was hoped to extract, by cruelty, extortionate sums.

Trinitarian monks were the link between officials and slaves. From time immemorial it had been the function of their Order to collect the "alms" and arrange the ransoms.

They worked hand in hand with the prisoners, enabling them to correspond with their families. The religious fanaticism of the renegades paused before the practical utility of these men. King and captains dealt with the monks as the heads of a large firm deal with trade representatives.

The pirate State was also a religious centre. Within its narrow limits were more than a hundred mosques. But religion left off where business began. For a slave to be converted was an unwelcome occurrence, prevented where possible. The owner would not be cheated of the blood price.

But for a slave to try to escape was worst of all. Could a piece of property be permitted to set itself up as owner? Greed and cruelty avenged every such attempt with frightful punishment. Above all, fear must reign; and they could not be careful of the means. The hooks outside the gate were always plentifully adorned with Christian heads; the vultures of Algiers had feasted centuries long.

And all this was State policy. For upon these unhappy men, for ever hungry, weak with lashings, almost never free of chains, drudging to pay their monthly interest or else mouldering in the bagnio, the whole State lived: the city, the religion and every several inhabitant of Algiers.

The King, or Bey, or Aga, or Pasha lived in his palace with the crescent flag and the great gold ship's lantern on the roof. The captains lived in the houses of the lower town, or outside the gate in villas whose bald, forbidding walls concealed cool courts with fountains and charming interiors gay with coloured marbles, faience and inlaid woods. Upon these prisoners lived King and Captains, Cadis and Muftis, the Mudirs and Muekkits, the Imams and Khetibs in the mosques, six large and a hundred small; administered justice, decided matters of faith, held prayer and song and made the calendar. Upon them also lived the janissaries in their cloistered barracks, picked militia, in their chefs' caps and women's petticoats, looking both reverent and foolish at once. Upon them lived the tradesfolk—that cut and sewed and dyed and hammered, and soled shoes, and roasted and baked, in the open booths which lined the long Market Street by the port. So too the whole scabby, bastard, lounging population of the crooked and slippery maze of lanes that mounted in steep terraces to the Kasbah shooting up at the top. Likewise the floating population of a thousand prostitutes, in brilliant rags and tinny jewellery, who squatted in every passage and gateway to rob the robber citizens; and the hordes of slim and perfumed lads who were their more prosperous rivals. And finally, the numerous Jews lived on them too, hunted from Spain and tolerated here, moving in black garments among the brightly costumed throngs.

And like the costumes, so the speech to be heard in these alleys was variegated too. A gratuitously harsh patois, in which Spanish, Italian and Portuguese made a wild marriage with Arabic and Turkish. There were even Greek, Gothic and Phœnician elements in this *lingua franca;* more plentifully than all, the Berber still—the accents of Jugurtha's wild Numidian horsemen.

Life was easy and amusing in the pirate State. There was always something to look at. A parade of the King and his halberdiers, or a review of the janissaries to the sound of trumpets, fifes and clarinets. Daily public whippings in front of the palace, when the white flag was mounted on the Grand Mosque at midday; executions in diverting variety before the East and West gates. Boisterous festivals, commemoration of the Hegira, or of the Prophet's birthday, the great feast of mutton and the joyous feast of lights with which the month of fasting closed. The Badistan was never empty, there was always business at the port; ships came in loaded with plunder and gold convoys sailed off to the Bosphorus. With blithe good consciences the populace laced their beef and mutton stews with oil and strong spices, drank down the fiery, forbidden fig brandy and watched the weal-marked slaves rooting in the filth for scraps.

Such was the nature of that cruel and calculating and altogether crack-brained world into which Miguel Cervantes, a devout, courageous, soft-hearted and imaginatively gifted man, found himself cast, a victim.

CHAPTER THIRTEEN

The Slave Don Miguel

With the genius of man it is as with the beauty of women: it can be asserted but not made perceptible in words.

A man may have had naught but misfortune; may have taken part in great enterprises and remained obscure. He may be mutilated and beggared. A gate seems to open for him into a brighter future, but the iron wings shut in his face. The man is inglorious, unknown, a mere cipher, apparently foredoomed to rot in chains. But meanwhile something great and mysterious has happened within himself. From him issues a fire that gives warmth and light; that touches all who come near, that arouses confidence and affection as the April sun summons blossoms out of the bare brown soil—a power which even his chaffering slave-drivers cannot withstand. And so, thanks to that mysterious splendour of our humanity, he is preserved throughout the long season of peril, that one day his life may bring forth its meet fruit.

Cervantes' good fortune—if good fortune it was—began when after a few days they took him out of the damp vault where he had been put. He found himself in an upper story of the bagnio, where there was air to breathe. One long side of the space was entirely open, without rails or beams.

The place was a three-storied shed, arranged as a square about a court, in the centre of which a fountain plashed. The sun stood high and the court was empty, so that its white sand blinded the eye. No one was to be seen in the open chambers. Cervantes turned himself about in his with a clank of chains. The background was divided off in little compartments, with rings in the wall, and straw bedding. It was like a stable. Here a few figures squatted, shifting with a noise as of horses stirring in their harness.

The hall only filled up at sunset, when the labourers were driven in. Grey bread and a thin soup were given out. It took an hour to fix on chains for the night; the watchmen seemed to have been ordered to make sleep impossible to some of the prisoners by means of the heavy and complicated fetters.

Cervantes sat in his corner, his arms and legs already stretched out and his doubled night-fetters ready to put on. But the green-clad men passed him by. Sweet was that sleep of his with legs stretched out.

He started up when something cold touched his temples, and saw beside him Dali-Mami, dressed in a highly elegant and urban burnous, with his flexible rod in his hand, as usual. It was bright daylight in the hall.

"Glad to see you sleeping well, Don Miguel. Though not so well as in your four-poster in Madrid. Yes, yes, I know, you have no four-poster, and you are no grandee. But if you call me ass another time I must strike you dead, whatever the loss. I could only stand it once."

And he gave his halberdiers an order over his shoulder.

One of them disappeared and came back almost at once with a short, light fetter, soldered to a ring.

"Have that put on, Don Miguel, and wear it on your foot. Only a suggestion, as you see. Everything else is removed. Your days down below have shown you how things *can* be, here. Why should a gentleman like you starve with two hundredweight of iron on him, when at Madrid honours and fair ladies wait? But write five letters rather than two: if one friend should not have the two thousand liquid, another will! And now enjoy yourself in Algiers."

It was almost possible. He was assured a rude shelter and some sort of food, and by day might go about as he would, even though with a rather clumsy attachment on his leg. It was not alone his supposed rank which had won him freedom. There were enough gentlemen of station in the three bagnios whose lot was never eased nor fetters lightened all day long. A curious sort of grim partiality on Dali-Mami's side was playing a part. Cervantes shrugged his shoulders over the idea and went off to seek his brother in the teeming city.

He found him the very next day, in a house in the lower town, near the Bab-Azoun. There in a long dark entry leading from the street to the inner court, Rodrigo's massive silhouette showed at a distance, black against the light. He was sawing wood and whistling.

Cervantes stood still a moment. Then he passed under the carved roof that overhung the entrance and called to his brother.

The ensign told his news, in good spirits. He had been purchased on the Badistan by a Jewish physician, old man and old inhabitant, a widower whose slave had lately died.

"Very good victuals, Miguel mine. And the Jewish dog is extremely friendly—really hardly a dog at all, it is only a way of talking. He speaks Spanish with me, I have already told him about you."

"I should not always tell everybody about me, Rodrigo! It is not always a good thing."

Just then Doctor Salomón Pérez came from the inner court, in a little cap showing the silver side locks beneath, and a long black silk caftan.

"I am summoned," he said, in the purest Castilian. "Rodrigo, you must carry the medicine-chest." And he directed upon Cervantes the gaze of his dim, brown, deep-set eyes.

"You are the brother of my house-mate," said he; "it is plain from the facial structure. How has Your Grace found things in Algiers?"

At this subservient address a mingling of emotions, pity, amusement and shame, filled Cervantes' breast. As though illuminated by a lightning-flash in the night of time, he saw the whole unregarded destiny of these exiles. What must have happened to the forefathers of this learned man, that he could speak so to a slave!

He had his mouth open to make the usual protest. But an unaccustomed stirring of practical good sense made him close it again.

Was it sensible to destroy the legend? It had its advantages. It had given him freedom of movement. It gave him time to concert the plans which were already darkly stirring in him. Why should he seek to bury himself in the cheapest category of human chattels?

He answered: "Thank you, Señor Doctor. Things are tolerably good with me. And I rejoice to see my brother in the house of the learned, for knowledge softens the heart."

"If it does not make it arrogant and unfeeling," said Salomón Pérez, wagging his head severely.

The ensign had brought the bulky medicine-chest out of the house. Cervantes looked after them as they went off, the slender figure in silk in front, the brother in his red slave's cap following with the black strapped chest on his shoulder. They disappeared to the left, upwards along the city wall, in the direction of the Kasbah.

A week later every nook and corner of the place was known to Cervantes. He sat on many a stair of the climbing city, talking and looking on. And presently, all unsought, a piece of luck befell him.

How many slaves lived in Algiers? Fifteen thousand? Certainly ten. They all had need to communicate with their homes, but not many could write. There were public scribes, of course, but they did not know the languages, were too dear, and their letters too empty and stiff.

Cervantes sat under the horseshoe arch or in the shadow of the wall and wrote for such as these. His swift pen made eloquent every appeal, suited it to the character of sender and recipient. Always he began by having the recipient described to him, let his own fancy dwell upon the figure and visualized the varied destinies with which he dealt.

Everybody confided in him; they followed at his heels through the streets. After a month he chose a stand for himself and was often besieged. He took small coins in payment, but only from those who pressed them upon him.

His stand was outside the wall, before Bab-el-Oued. Leaving the city by this gate, one had on one's left a height with a kind of little cloister and the tomb of a saint, Zaouia Sidi-Abd-el-Rahman. And here, beneath a tall, old, solitary cypress sat Miguel Cervantes and wrote his letters to Andalusian peasants, Mallorca fishermen, the subjects of Italian states, to patrons, chancelleries and cloisters.

Sometimes, too, he sat there alone. Then he rested, gazed and mused. Bab-el-Oued and the city walls were hid from him by bushes, and on certain grounds this was good. He looked across rolling green countryside and saw the sea. This sea, with which his life was bound up, on which he had been blindly battered. The Mediterranean Sea, cradle of the two great ideas which nourish the souls of men: Greek freedom and Jewish compassion. That sea, now beleaguered by sinister powers raging more furiously than any storm.

At the beginning of the year it grew suddenly cold. He spent some weeks "at home" in the bagnio, in his own corner, or in front of another man's niche. Monotonous wailings filled his ears. He remembered the precious pastime of his youth and began to write verse. It was not as it had been: no breathless ambition, no prize beckoned him from the judges' bench, no Master Hoyos hailed his pupil as a future Mendoza or Boscán, with loud acclaim. He was aware that a great new literature was flourishing in Spain; there was of late an incredible concourse to the theatres. But he was cut off from all that. All that he wished was to sing a little to himself in his captivity, to remember and recall. The thought took shape in him that he would make a cycle of his latter years, these years which seemed to have the fullness of a century. He began—since one place was as good as another—with a trochaic elegy upon the death of the gentle Acquaviva; the lines flowed sweet and effortless from him; then he read it over and tore it up. It was all rhetorical and empty, nobody reading it would be moved by the gentle charm of that youth in the purple. But perhaps the heroic would go better? He drafted an ode on the battle of Lepanto, in stormy iambics that rang and glittered. It pleased him for a day. But in the night he woke with the lines in his mouth:

> The Lord in strength puts forth His arm
> And guards His faithful sons from harm.
>
> All glory and honour to His name
> That grants the victory to Philip's Spain.—

and knew that they had come almost word for word from a poem by Herrera. In the early dawn he revised his work —but without much confidence. It all seemed to him bombastic and swollen, and left a flat taste on his tongue. "What are you at, Don Miguel?" asked a Valencian priest who was among the prisoners, as he stood before Cervantes' alcove. "Even at dawn you are already writing." "I am writing verses, reverend Father. It is better, at least, than hunting for lice." But he had his doubts none the less.

In February a mild and springlike sun began to shine. He betook himself to his place by Sidi-Abd-el-Rahman. He hardly ate even his soup in the bagnio. He ate nothing. He went unshaven.

He no longer denied the legend of his origin and station. He even did something to feed it and keep it alive: leaving about forged letters from Madrid merchant friends in which methods of payment were discussed. Sometimes the letters disappeared. Dali-Mami on his evening round would lick his chops at the fat sums mentioned. That two thousand ducats, an enormous sum, was not at once forthcoming seemed only natural.

Actually, of course, Cervantes had done nothing. To whom should he write? To his parents and relations, whose wretched plight was one of his gnawing cares?

But they had been bestirring themselves none the less. Rodrigo, despite Cervantes' stern interdiction, was in correspondence about the ransom. No Trinitarian Father crossed the sea to Spain without several of Rodrigo's letters. Their orthography was questionable, but their matter was urgent. He himself, he said, was well placed; but Miguel's fate was wretched. Nobody in Spain could know how dreadful the bagnios were. His brother must be released with all possible speed, for everybody's sake. And then he let gleams escape him of Miguel's brilliant future prospects. He developed imagination. He even told lies, though they went against his simple nature. Miguel's clumsy foot-ring became iron bars and heavy chains.

The deaf attorney Cervantes and his silent wife, the daughter in the cloister and the other who went about with men, imagined the lot of their sons and brothers, sweating and labouring in chain-gangs. Miguel's own letters sounded more cheerful, but that they ascribed that to his pride and his forbearance. They sold whatever they could in any way spare, they tried to borrow; Sister Luisa importuned her superiors, and Sister Andrea bought neither gowns nor adornments from the gifts of her lovers, but set aside *real* after *real*. They petitioned, they sat whole days in the antechambers of the officers of the Crown, they lived on nothing but bread and onions.

But the sums which they could accumulate were pathetic. They did not dare mention them to Miguel. Rodrigo had forbidden it.

Cervantes knew nothing of all this. He was well enough, he might have been content.

But he was not. He had been, until lately, but now his painful unrest increased with every day. He suffered. As the spring advanced he was torn with anger, misery and rage.

Once—before Lepanto—the bare report of the atrocities in Cyprus had plunged him into fever. Now daily, with his own eyes, he saw the like. The times were harsh, he was a child of the times and was harsh against himself. But imagination, his lively senses, forced upon him the feeling of another's torture. And what he saw was too much.

The penal system everywhere was of frightful severity. The stake, the wheel, dragging to death, pulling apart by horses, breaking the limbs one by one. . . . Men lost a hand for stealing a few copper coins. In all the states of Christendom the cripples of justice swarmed in the streets.

So it was here, in the sink of the old world, where the sorry riff-raff of humanity seethed, and avarice, fanaticism and cruelty reigned as nowhere else. Executions, mutilations, torture, were daily spectacles, the shrieks of the agonized as common as the braying of asses and the bells of the water-sellers; beatings, which nearly always led to death, were as regular as the daily market. When you passed the Djenina, where the King lived, you saw the unhappy delinquents stretched out naked in the square, a green-clad official squatting at head and foot, two others applying the lash in time, shouting to each other the number of the blows: a hundred and fifty, two hundred and fifty, four hundred. Then the crushed and bleeding mass was shoved on one side. At half-past two the white flag was lowered on the Grand Mosque: finished for the day.

There was a new king in Algiers. Ramdan Pasha had been recalled, and an Italian renegade took his place. His name was Andreta but he now assumed the name of Hassan-Veneziano: certainly one of the most frightful men of his age. He had got his position by paying large sums to the dignitaries of Stamboul and to the Sultan's wives; and had now set to work to recoup himself from the proceeds of the business which he had bought. Woe to the prisoner who dreamed of flight! He introduced new, ingenious and protracted forms of martyrdom. This new despot leaned towards frightfulness: he was cold, methodical, sensual cruelty impersonified. He was even too much for the Moors and the Turks, who were openly horrified. The traditional hanging, beheading, strangling and burning did not satisfy him. He preferred choicer methods. For instance, impaling: a pole was driven through the victim's body lengthwise, the King laying bets with his train as to the spot—eyes, mouth, cheeks, etc.—where the iron-shod tip would appear. There was no lack of material on which to gratify such tastes. He might see a slave column working somewhere, declare himself dissatisfied and summarily order that the batch should lose their ears. If in lighter mood, he would then have the troop trot round the square before the Djenina to the shrilling of the janissaries' pipes, the bleeding appendages tacked to their foreheads.

But not only the Christian slaves suffered thus. He terrorized his soldiery; even the guild of Rais revolted against him, by reason of his petty and malicious schemings. He was hated throughout Africa—and at the same time admired for his savage intrepidity, which was as boundless as his bestialities.

He looked like a picture-book pirate: upstanding, pallid, lean, with a scanty sprouting of red beard and glittering, inflamed eyes. Those who got close to him asserted that he smelt of blood.

Such was the man to whom the one-handed slave, Miguel Cervantes, offered defiance—whom he, in a certain sense, subdued.

For the moment, indeed, Hassan had driven him from his stance by the Zaouia. Folk who wanted letters written found him no more. The execution square before Bab-el-Oued was too frightfully occupied. True, the green shrubbery hid gate and walls; but the shrieks of the victims were always to be heard, there was the smell of burning flesh, the stench of decay from the corpses to whom burial was denied. Those who had been bold and desperate enough to think of escaping from hell were left here to rot, to encourage the others!

But even so escape remained Cervantes' goal. No more did horror cast him upon a bed of fever—that time was past. He wanted to escape, to take as many comrades as possible with him into freedom and to rouse up the Christian world outside to take arms against the infamy.

CHAPTER FOURTEEN

Three Traitors

Oran was occupied by Spain. It was twelve days' voyage distant—if this short route along the coast had been anyway possible for an escaping man. But it was too well watched. No, the most audacious must make a wide detour, far to the south, then aiming back at the coast and reaching Oran, with luck, in three weeks. No one had ever succeeded in this as yet.

There were no roads: only rocky heights, desert and bands of marauders. A guide was indispensable.

By early spring Cervantes had found one. A dare-devil of mixed Portuguese and Moorish blood, twenty years in these parts, as much at home in Fez and Tlemcen as in the Algerian oases; nimble and lean, but with nothing else to recommend him in looks: a dirty complexion shading off to green, and a nose too short and wried as though by some brutal and mocking thumb, not even very young. This dangerous piloting of eleven prisoners was to be his last profit-bringing undertaking; then he would give up "the whole thing"—whatever that meant. He carried his notes of hand sewed up in his haik: ten of them, for Cervantes, conscious that he was a beggar, would promise nothing—though Rodrigo had very likely done so secretly for both. And now Rodrigo, towering above the little troop of fugitives, was trudging beside his beloved brother across slopes of rubble and through dry river-beds.

The strain on the ill-nourished bodies grew considerable after the fourth day. Up rocky cliffs and down them again, under a sun that scorched like summer: no shade, no human habitation where they might shelter or refresh themselves. Now and again a cave in the clay, in front of which fat-bellied, sore-eyed children goggled after the twelve. And now and again a sudden silhouette emerging from behind a rock, a rider in a flutter of rags, but armed and forbidding.

On the sixth day their rations failed. In a hollow they saw sheep grazing before a few huts, and shepherdesses. They tried to buy one of the sheep but could come to no agreement, as money was unknown or not coveted. So they quite simply took the mutton, frantic with joy at the prospect of a meal.

They ate towards evening, at the edge of the great Metidja. Giant cedars, of regular growth and each proudly distinct, clothed the slopes of the mountain ranges far and wide. Their branches extended parallel at an even height, forming a solid roof like a dome.

"Where are we?" Cervantes asked their lean guide. "What sort of place was that which you so mysteriously led us round about today?"

Their leader squinted down his crooked nose. "Teniet-el-Had is the name of the place, Don Miguel, and its inhabitants are an insolent and malicious lot." And he moved away.

The mutton was roasting on a cedar-wood fire, the resin giving out a pungent odour as it burned. They all crowded round the flames, for the spring night was cold in the uplands. Before the joint was even done they tore the flesh from the bones. The Europeans smacked their lips and licked their fingers. Soon they all fell asleep under the trees, wrapped up in what they had. The upper Metidja was full of a pale milky brightness from the full-moon which swam in a clear sky above their tree-roof.

When they awoke by morning light to rub their stiff limbs, no guide was to be seen. They called, they hunted, then stood helplessly about, not daring to look the situation in the face. Until suddenly one of them, a merchant from Murcia, cried out and felt over his clothes, then desperately searched the spot where he had slept, and finally groaned out that he had been robbed. A small leather bag of doubloons which he had worn bound to his naked breast, a treasure guarded with infinite care, was lost; the grim-faced man had taken it and gone hence. That smaller but tangible sum had been more real to him than all his ten notes of hand. So he had left them in the trackless wild, six days from Algiers, fifteen from Oran, ignorant of the country, without weapons or food.

They all began to wrangle and lament. Each wished to be the first to have perceived the character of the man, each wished to prove that he had held out longest against the foolhardy enterprise. These brothers in misery all but came to blows. But at length they united to blame Cervantes, who had concocted the plan, arranged the means and even produced that fine fellow of a guide.

All perfectly true, he said at once, and it was only natural that such being the case they should now take him as their leader and follow him westwards. The cedar forests, he had seen them on the map, lay above their goal. They had only to follow them westwards as the sun travelled, to arrive without fail under the walls of Oran.

But for them all there was but one single cry: they must go back. Six days' travel on a route they knew seemed better to them than any journey into the unknown; and as they should be returning voluntarily they might hope for pardon.

A quarter of an hour later they set off. The brothers stood at the edge of the wood and looked after them.

"Two of us will get on much faster than eleven," said the ensign, enchanted with the thought of marching with his beloved brother towards liberty. "Come, then, let us be off; what are we waiting for?"

But Cervantes stood silent and irresolute. The returning fugitives had long since disappeared behind a spur of rock.

"It won't do, Rodrigo," he said at last. "We must go after them."

The ensign was not usually one to grasp obscure allusions. But this time he did. "They will not thank us for it, Miguel mine."

"Of course not."

And that was all.

Their reception in the slave state was not unfriendly. Their owners had been furious at the loss of property, but when it returned itself they saw no need of great severity. Harder labour, worse quarters and a few beatings would suffice, considering they had been led astray. Cervantes declared himself the moving spirit and none of the nine contradicted him. He was sentenced to the bastinado, three hundred blows—as good as death.

But Dali-Mami prevented the sentence from being carried out. He had his one-handed slave close-fettered in the bagnio. Cervantes sat in his corner draped and hung with irons as a bride with roses. The Rais would now and then appear, test the chains and manacles with the air of a connoisseur and address the rebel with sinister threats. But on the fifth day all the irons were removed. His clothing had gone to rags on the flight. A new, clean, unpatched outfit was given him: shirt, breeches, caftan, slippers and cap. The symbolic foot-iron was forgotten; otherwise all was as before.

But Rodrigo's lot had worsened, alas! For Doctor Salomón Pérez had taken another servant and the ensign was put with a gang for municipal service. Miguel found him, naked among the naked, toiling under the burning sun upon a new bastion at the edge of the Kasbah.

"Not for long, Rodrigo, not for long," he whispered. The ensign smiled, in happy confidence.

Rodrigo had to drudge for a year. Every morning he rose from his straw with a rattle of chains, full of expectation that Miguel would that very day perform the miracle of liberation. But as it was, when freedom beckoned, he refused.

Two Trinitarians arrived with ransoms. Among them three hundred ducats from the Cervantes family. Miguel was amazed. His lively imagination had no difficulty in picturing the deprivations, the self-immolation represented by that sum. Well, at least it spelled release for his brother.

But Rodrigo had been completely obstinate. These three hundred ducats were a first instalment on Miguel's ransom —and nothing else. "How so, instalment?" asked Miguel, almost with violence. Two thousand ducats, as he had perhaps forgotten, was the sum demanded by Dali-Mami. And from where else in all the world a single goldpiece could come, nobody knew. He would not leave his brother, the ensign said, and the money was not for him.

Miguel looked at the gentle, obstinate face and then down into the blue shadows beneath them. It was a hot noon in May, and they sat together under a high wall belonging to the fortifications of the Kasbah. Rodrigo had leg-irons on both legs. He and his fellows might rest at this hour, because their overseer could not stand the sun. The sea was so bright that one could not look at it. The white flag had just gone up on the Grand Mosque by the port. The daily executions were about to begin.

Miguel raised his head. Scarcely a minute had passed. A keener observer than Rodrigo would have noticed that in this minute something decisive had happened.

"You will take this money, Rodrigo," he said very firmly. "You will go back to Spain. I need you there. If you are clever I shall be free in a few months."

"May be," said the ensign, grudgingly.

In August he went. The formalities took that much time. At the last moment his ship was searched down to the smallest cranny. Nothing suspicious was found.

But things were happening. Slaves were disappearing. Never many at a time, one or two each week. It was incomprehensible what became of them. Suspicion fell upon Miguel Cervantes, but he was going innocently about, writing his letters, and everywhere expressing his joy at his brother's freedom.

The missing slaves were not far off.

An hour's walk westwards from the town, between the

sea and the hills, there was a strip of land called El Hamma, where frequent floods produced a luxuriant vegetation. Here, along the shore, one of the upper officials had hewn himself a garden out of the wilderness, a sort of tropical park, full of palms and bamboos, myrtle and broom. The master seldom visited his distant property, and it was guarded and cultivated by a certain Juan from Navarra—a pleasant soul, who liked mostly to sleep in his wooden hut and let the plants of God's garden mingle and marry as they would.

Cervantes had won over this gallant good-for-nothing. He was told that if he wished to see his native land again he might join the Spanish ship sent by Rodrigo, which would touch at the gardens some night soon.

The spot was well chosen. In the most retired spot in the park there was a natural cave, which at some time had been further hollowed out by human hands. The fugitives trickled into this cave, by ones and twos, leaving no trace. They were sternly forbidden to leave their damp refuge by day. Juan de Navarra kept watch for them.

There was the problem of provisions. Nothing edible grew in the garden but a few roots and berries. They were all afraid to undertake the perilous trip to the city and back. Everybody felt relieved when on the third day the youngest among them came forward. He was a Florentine nicknamed "the Gilder" (though nobody knew whether he had ever practised the art). It was said of him in Tunis that he had changed his religion several times; but nothing really definite was known.

There were now fifteen of them in the cave. Cervantes, as already suspect, was to join them last. He had concerted with Rodrigo that the attempt should be made on the twentieth of September. The night before he left the town. As he approached the gardens from the hilly land in the rear, he recalled that on a twentieth of September *El Sol* had set out from Naples. And he had to banish a vague misgiving.

The day passed and the night and seven days and nights after that. No ship was to be seen. Had his brother failed? Had a mishap befallen the vessel? Almost without hope they kept watch the last night, a moonlit twenty-eighth of September. And at the eleventh hour the ship came in sight.

When they saw it they fell on their knees. It came gliding on, upon a perfectly quiet sea, a small, one-masted cutter, obviously drawing so little water that it could come directly to land. Cervantes praised his brother for this in his heart; also for the choice he had made of sailors familiar with this part of the coast.

They all stood there with uplifted arms, waving but making no sound. They almost thought to hear the splash of oars in the moonlit water.

Then there came shrieks from many voices—wild, menacing, guttural voices. One could not tell whence they came, whether from people on the shore, abroad at this late hour, or from the water.

The vessel retreated. They did not dare call. Their hearts almost stopped beating when they saw the rescuer disappear.

"Friends, they will come back," Cervantes said. "They must await the right moment."

But three agonizing days went by before they returned. They had had to send the Gilder for more food; he was away when the cutter appeared, at early dawn, before sun-up. The vessel cruised cautiously about outside, awaiting a signal. On the beak they could vaguely see a tall man, apparently bareheaded.

They all urged that the signal be given and the vessel boarded at once. Every minute was precious.

"And the Gilder?" Cervantes asked.

"Why is he not here?"

"Because for the twentieth time he is risking his life for us."

But were they not right? Better one should perish than all. He longed, he anguished, to give the signal. But he could not. His fancy pictured the Gilder hurrying into the garden, their bread in his hands. Finding no one. Cave, garden and harbour empty, fifteen traitors on the way to freedom!

They pressed round him, rebellious. "How long will you wait?"

"Till the sun is up. He never comes later."

"But give the signal. That is not running off."

"It is running off. Once we are on board they will sail."

"Then they will be cleverer than you," one of the men said roughly.

The man spoke the truth. What was this urge in him to tempt fate to the uttermost? He had no right to do so —and now no longer the power.

For they were giving the signal themselves. Despite him, they waved. Cervantes drew a deep breath—within himself. He looked aside. Juan de Navarra was just bringing his bundle out of his hut; he was going with them.

Then from behind them in the garden came noises of crackling wood and many footsteps. It was Dali-Mami, the

Rais, with a troop of armed men. At their head came the Gilder, wearing a turban.

Who knew how long he had plotted treachery? Perhaps he had despaired of success, perhaps a sudden burst of malice guided his act. He stood impudently at Dali-Mami's side, who had paused to enjoy the prospect. This was indeed a dainty morsel.

The wrath of the betrayed burst out against Cervantes. So great was their rage against him whose loyalty to the traitor had delivered them all up to death, that they almost forgot the treachery—or even to be afraid. Wild-eyed and with lifted fists they crowded round him cursing. He shoved them off. "I'd take pleasure in killing you," said he to the Gilder; and the expression on the face of this sensitive and death-devoted man was such that the traitor crawled backwards and took refuge with the armed men among the trees.

"You will not be killing anyone," said Dali-Mami. "They will hack off your right hand too, before they hang you. And your friends' left hands, so that they can be like their leader in future."

"To mutilate the others will only be a loss to you. And it is not necessary either. Nobody will dare to escape when I am dead."

He said it with a convinced and convincing seriousness. He knew his mind. Whatever he touched went wrong. He believed no more in his star. His obstinacy had endangered all these people. And he would do the same again. Here, in this incident, the pattern of his whole life sketched itself in vague and shrouded contour. And to such a life he clung no more.

The Rais gave a sign. The fugitives were surrounded and driven to the gate. At the end of the train the traitor, Dorador, in his new turban, slunk towards the expected reward of his treachery.

The Rais and two of his train remained behind. He strolled up to the mutely waiting Cervantes, daintily nipping his life-preserver.

"Of course, Miguel," he said, "I have long known that there is nothing in your rank or your ransom. It has amused me to pretend up to now. But what you are not, you can become."

"Elevation by the rope, you mean? I know."

"One of the greatest corsairs, Horuk-Barbarossa, Haireddin's brother, was a one-handed man like you."

Cervantes said nothing.

"What do you expect from your own? What do you want in Spain? Take the turban! I will set you free. I will give you a ship. You will make good use of your one hand. Is it a bargain?" And he offered Cervantes his right.

Cervantes did not move.

"What prevents you? Your God? He has not markedly prospered you. Your King? He does not know you. Your companions? You saw how they cursed you. Believe me, the whole breed deserves nothing better than to have its head crushed."

"What will be done with my companions, Rais? Will you spare them?"

"Why speak of these vermin? Think it over. I will not ask you again."

He looked Cervantes in the face, turned round, whistled to his men as one does to a dog and went off with no more words.

Cervantes stopped alone in the garden. The sea was vacant. The cutter had sought open water.

Two days later Cervantes learned that one example had been made, and that the most innocent of all, Juan de Navarra, had been hanged by one foot. Dali-Mami and the official who owned the garden walked up and down under the gallows and watched the man being choked with his own blood.

Cervantes' life, in the following years, was strange, yes, marvellous indeed. He, who in the code of the rulers of Algiers had many times deserved death, went about in complete freedom and no one touched a hair of his head. No one drove him to work. He lived in the bagnio. If it occurred to him to spend the night elsewhere, sleeping under the stars, the watch greeted him when he came back like a returned acquaintance.

He had a wide circle of acquaintances: the slaves of all Christendom, the sailors of the Rais, the jewel-bedecked women under the gates; soldiers, clerics, monks, tradespeople, officials, Jews that were scholarly and Jews that were commercial. Children knew him. He was talked about. That a monster like Dali-Mami spared him, had obviously in some way taken him to his sinister heart, was itself so astounding that many whispered of witchcraft. They were not so far from the truth.

He was provided for; particularly after the privilege of settlement and trade had been granted to a number of Christian merchants. The houses of Baltasar Torres and Onofre Exarque were the most important. When anything difficult had to be drafted, Cervantes was called upon.

He might have been satisfied. But he could not come to

terms with what he hated. He had not even been able to get accustomed to the abuse of the beasts of burden. If he saw a little ass in the crooked streets, a pot-bellied rider on its back bigger than the animal itself, and goring the festering back with his spur, the blood mounted to Cervantes' head and he could scarcely keep his hands off the man. How could he endure with calmness the sight of King Hassan's daily mounting atrocities? The gallows were never empty, the ground before Bab-el-Oued was slimy with blood; the number of executioners was not equal to their tasks. "Hardly a Christian here has his two ears on his head, and lucky he who still looks out of two eyes": it is written in a letter sent home by a certain Neapolitan.

It is likely that Cervantes might have escaped by himself, for no one guarded him. But he still set before himself the task of liberating many. Failure had not daunted him. He sought a justification for that existence which seemed to him so lamentably ineffective and small.

Two years after the second attempt he again got to the point. And again it was the fateful month of September.

The Christian merchants settled in Algiers had pledged themselves to show no smallest favour to Christian slaves. Should they break that clause, their licence to trade, their property, even their lives were jeopardized. But Onofre Exarque, the richest among them, could not say no to his one-handed secretary. He fitted out a ship for him.

Not a paltry little cutter, but a stately armed frigate, large enough to hold sixty escaping Spaniards. It came from Cartagena and anchored off Cape Matifou, five hours from Algiers—where the Emperor Charles had once embarked his shattered army, and himself last.

The fast of Ramadan, that year, almost coincided with the month of September. Aid-es-Seghir, the feast of lights which closes the fast, fell on the twenty-ninth; they chose that night to act. Feasting began at nightfall; then would come the time. When the sated feasters rose glowing from the banquet and thronged into the mosques from whose wide-open doors streamed golden light; when from lips still glistening with fat and honey they all exultantly shrieked out the sacred name to the accompaniment of blaring, snarling music—then would be the chance to break from the swarming pirate city singly or in groups, to climb walls, to swim from the port, perhaps just simply to walk out at the city gate! The meeting-place was on the left bank of the Harrach, an hour away.

Perfect secrecy seemed to have been preserved. On the morning of the feast of lights, each of the conspirators was to receive the countersign, as assurance that all was well and no danger to be feared. Miguel Cervantes was to spread the glad tidings; they had awaited them since early dawn at their several working-places.

They waited in vain. Word did not come. No one saw Cervantes. No one left the city that night.

Once more there was treachery. This time the traitor was a learned Spaniard, Doctor Juan Blanco de Paz, one-time Dominican monk in Salamanca. His motives were probably envy and jealousy. Yellow-faced and physically ugly, he could never awaken aught but discomfort and mistrust among his fellow-men. All his words were evil and equivocal, and most evil and unequivocal the breath that accompanied every one. For this trait he was famous in this city of unwashed slaves: his nickname was the "Stinker." Yet this disadvantaged man had an unquenchable urge to please and make friends. And he felt a corresponding hatred of Cervantes, a lively, engaging soul whose popularity was a byword. He had entered the conspiracy only to betray; on the night before the end of Ramadan he told all that he knew to King Hassan.

Miguel was warned by friends in the Djenina—for friends he had everywhere—and hastened through back streets to the house of Onofre Exarque, who then almost died of fright. All his deportment, all the dignity of this wealthy man, left him on the moment. "Who knows my name?" was his first word. "Who besides you? You swore to me no one should know it."

"And no one does, Don Onofre."

"You swear it by the Virgin and your own salvation?"

"Be assured."

"Assured! You will shriek out my name, when they break your limbs one by one, or slowly skin them out of their joints."

He hid his face in his hands and leaned against the wall. Cervantes waited.

"It is more than one can stand," he heard at length the faint voice saying. "You could not be silent. Go! Vanish!"

"Vanish? How so, Don Onofre?"

"It needs must be. I will hasten to the Rais, I will pay what he asks. If I beg you off, the danger is past. You can give me a receipt for the money."

"It would be a lying receipt, Don Onofre. I could never redeem it. And it would be madness too—for it would only direct suspicion upon yourself."

"You won't?" asked Exarque, his face blank with astonishment and fear. "What do you want? To be tortured to death?"

"We have not got that far yet, Onofre."

Nor had they. He hid. In the noisiest heart of the city, in the Market street, he sought his hiding-place. Three days he sat in a sort of hole in the house of a Jewish cobbler to whom he had once done a favour—and called himself to account.

Had not Exarque's astonishment been justified? What possessed him, always to drive everything to extremes? Why had he to tempt fate to the uttermost? Whence this mysterious sense that this was not the end, that nothing could touch him? For what destiny did he feel himself reserved? He peered into himself as into water, and saw nothing in the depths.

He was cramped in his hole. Above him he could hear customers cheapening the wares and the swarming family of his host indulging in a gush of conversation. Twice in the day they brought him highly seasoned food: his retreat stank powerfully of onions.

They had just brought down the midday meal, he had a bite in his mouth, when he heard his name called loudly in the street, to the sound of the crier's rattle. The slave Miguel Cervantes was being hunted; he was a criminal; all who sheltered him were criminals too, their lives were forfeit. Then the rattle again, and silence.

The trap-door was lifted. The round head and beard of his Jewish host showed against the light. "I heard it, Elias," Cervantes said. "I am coming."

Upstairs he blessed in departing the two eldest sons of the family, laying on their heads his glorious, mutilated left hand—and the next minute stood at broad midday before the Djenina.

King Hassan's armed guards were posted about the

square. He was seized. They bound his arms against his back, and put a rope round his neck, ready for the gallows. He was led inside and presently found himself before Hassan-Veneziano.

King Hassan's state couch, of green and yellow cushions, was spread between the centre columns on the narrow side of a vast inner court, where three fountains played. Erect beside it stood Dali-Mami, this time without his life-preserver, and a court official whom Cervantes recognized by his costume as the Aga of the Two Moons. He whom they called the Stinker lurked behind in the shadow of the arcades.

King Hassan was dressed with ostentatious simplicity: a simple white burnous, not very fine, yellow slippers, and above the fez a white turban, without agraffe. Apparently he had no wish to distract upon externals the impression to be created by his personality. Very quietly he measured with his brilliant, red-rimmed eyes the rather weakly man before him. Then he turned his gaze upon Dali-Mami, lifted his eyebrows, shrugged his shoulders as though to say: "Is that all?" and began the examination.

It came out quite soon that the Dominican had magnified the extent of the plot. He had told the King that the frigate would hold two hundred people and that this number had been ready to flee.

"So, you audacious villain," said Hassan, "you were going to steal from us the enormous sum of forty thousand ducats. Do you admit it?"

"The dog who betrayed me," Cervantes replied, "has exaggerated in order to increase his reward. The frigate has room for sixty prisoners."

"So you admit your guilt?"

Cervantes bent his head. The rope slipped off his neck and lay looped at his feet. A servant sprang to replace it, but Hassan motioned him away.

"These sixty you will name to us. Begin!"

The Aga of the Two Moons advanced, writing tablets in hand.

"Further, you will name to us the man or men who financed this enterprise. It means a good deal of money."

Miguel's manner was pleasant, almost deprecating. But everybody realized at once that this silence was not to be broken down.

The King beckoned. Beneath the horseshoe arches on the long side of the court appeared four men, two in green on the left and two in violet with black turbans on the right. They had long, oddly shaped instruments in their hands.

"Look," Hassan said. "When the flail will have asked you twenty times, your answer will be ready."

They were really flails, their flexible part set thick with sharp nails; the bare sight was enough to make one feel them biting deep into the flesh.

Cervantes was seized from behind. With practised swiftness they tore the clothing from his body and threw him naked on the stone slab, face downwards. The assistants knelt at his head and feet.

He shut his eyes. He felt not fear or dread, but astonishment. He had not believed it would come to this. Well, now it was happening, and he tried to call upon the saints to help him. To his horror he found that he could not fix his mind upon them. Was he no longer a Christian, then? he asked himself, shuddering. And if not, why was he lying here? He breathed deep—as deep as he could under the pressure of the hangmen's legs—and awaited the first blow.

Nothing came. He felt the weight lifted. He opened his eyes and raised himself on his elbows.

"You are too weak," he heard the King say. "It would be the same as killing you. Get up."

Cervantes stood up. Perfectly naked, blinking in the strong light, he stood there, five paces from the King's couch.

"Hearken! I will spare your life if you will name the guilty. Each of them would have betrayed you a hundred times over, be sure of that. Who are they?"

"Four Spanish noblemen, all four long since free and returned home."

"Name them."

Cervantes rattled off a number of names, just as they came into his head, high-sounding, improbable, fantastic—a jumble of *omez's* and *anto's* and *igo's.*

And now the incredible happened. Hassan-Veneziano, that savage bloodhound, was overcome with laughter. He did not mean to laugh, he was probably ashamed of it; he held his hand covered with red hairs over his great crooked slit of a mouth, his bloodshot eyes narrowed with enjoyment, and sounds burst from him which sounded more like something rusty creaking than like human laughter. His long, lean form rocked to and fro. Dali-Mami and the rest looked on incredulous.

"I will buy him of you, my friends," he said at last. "It is not too much, what you have said. Four hundred ducats—is that right?" Dali-Mami nodded his puffy head.

Hassan nodded over his left shoulder and the traitor came from under the colonnades.

"Well, Stinker, you have done us good service, you shall be magnificently rewarded."

He felt in his girdle and drew out a single gold-piece, held it between thumb and fore-finger so that it glittered in the sun, and then flung it at the other's feet.

"But that is not all. Go to my head chef. He will give you a tub of butter. A whole tub; you can lick it all up," he said with gusto—and God knows what withering contempt there lay in just this kind of payment! "Stoop down," bellowed Hassan. "Pick up the ducat with your stinking mouth and crawl back into your hole!"

But the revenge he had prepared for the traitor he visited also to some extent upon Cervantes too. He kept him in close arrest, of a singular kind. At the entrance of the great court, between the first and second horseshoe arch, he had him chained to the masonry. His comfort was consulted with cushions and covers, and he was protected from sun and rain. A long, thin chain gave him freedom sufficient to move about the court—a chain made expressly out of pure silver.

Hassan kept the one-handed slave as though he were some valuable, untamable animal. "My famous leopard," he would say to guests, leading them past the alcove where Cervantes sat writing. For he gave him liberty to do what he would, and all needful materials for the same. His chain was loosened every day, that he might wash at one of the fountains. And every second week the barber came and trimmed the leopard's beard.

Did this man who "smelt of blood" consider Cervantes

a kind of talisman? A waiter at table repeated words he had heard Hassan say, that "the city of Algiers, ships, slaves and property, would be safe so long as he kept his one-handed slave under his eye."

So there he sat, and hour after hour had before his eyes the inward life of that notorious Djenina. He learned to know the motley host of officials of the corsair court, and its ceremonial, a grotesque mingling of East and West; had his ears assaulted three times a day by the trumpets, drums and clarinets of the royal band; saw court held and torture carried out in front of the yellow-green cushions—mutilating, impaling, beheading; saw the flags washed off afterwards and the "blood-scented one" stroll upon them in the cool of the eve; came even to hear something of the sinister state business there transacted—a privilege vouchsafed to few.

He came to know, earlier than the city knew it, that Hassan was to be recalled. And felt some curiosity as to his own fate when that happened.

They were in the third year of Veneziano's tenure of kingship and lease. Palace intrigues had begun earlier than usual in Stamboul. The name of Hassan's successor was already mentioned: Djafer. By means of enormous bribes and by accusations against Hassan, he made headway at court. But as yet the affair hung fire; for many months the Leopard still wore his silver chain.

And many a sharpened quill was worn out, the pile of written sheets rose high. The result was a play, or something like a play, the title being *Life in Algiers*. He wrote down his torments: the sufferings of the prisoners in the city of Algiers. Would not others be appalled by that which had appalled him these five years? He dreamed of smuggling his manuscript across the sea. One of Spain's famous theatres should play it, opening the eyes of King and nobles; perhaps his play would be the signal for a crusade which should eradicate this African plague-spot.

But no. It was impossible. He soon saw it himself. What he wrote was too confused, too arbitrary, too literal, the plot too badly knit, the whole too much a mixture of the amazing and the amateur. Ah, no: not with the sword, not with the pen either, was he to achieve greatness. He was still the scholar of Master Hoyos' Academy. Still, and for ever, a beggar and a cripple.

But his legend rose ever higher and surged like a wave about the walls of the Djenina. Letters went to Spain, Italy and France, telling his tale. He was famous and beloved.

CHAPTER FIFTEEN

Home-Coming

The four royal ships lay ready to weigh anchor, in the harbour of Algiers.

All day long boxes and bags had been lowered into their bowels, the incredible profits of Hassan-Veneziano's three-year lease. His own galley, largest of the three, lying high out of water, her sides be-written with gilded script, the crescent waving at her purple poop, lay already manned at the quayside. Only one of the gangways was in use. The other, laid with a red carpet, was for the sole use of Hassan. The red carpet ran from it across the square and past the Grand Mosque to the door of the Djenina, like a street of blood.

Cervantes was chained to one of the rowing benches nearest the mainmast; the inside seat, since he was no good to pull the strap. He bethought him of the date: the nineteenth of September. Night was falling. They would sail at dawn on the twentieth. The recurrence of the pattern faintly amused him.

The rowers slept, squatting and crouching among the benches. Their irons clanked. He was fastened only by his own silver chain. He did not sleep, but contemplated his lot: how, like a boy, he had been defiant, had scorned his own salvation more than once, had set himself up as a saviour for the many. Now it was too late. Once carried off to Stamboul, there would be no return. To perish somewhere in the broad Turkish realms it seemed would be his lot.

He knew just what had happened. Since the day when Hassan's recall became known, the Trinitarian Brothers had redoubled their efforts. Fray Juan Gil, Procurator-General of the Order, had come himself to Algiers and ransomed many of Hassan's slaves. His means had been scanty and the bargaining keen. But in the end more than a hundred Christians were freed. They were already off across the seas, to their own villages and towns.

Hassan had refused to surrender Miguel de Cervantes. He played with the Procurator-General. He could not say enough in praise of the one-handed man, his courage, his fortitude, his learning, his dignity. The old worn-out legend of Miguel's noble origins was trotted out. A thousand ducats down might make Hassan consider a sale—even that would be dirt-cheap.

The new day came, in radiant beauty. Guns went off and from all four ships the trumpets gave insistent, crashing signal of departure. Cervantes looked back at the shore, alive with people. For the last time he looked at the blinding white walls of the Grand Mosque, the squat and gloomy Djenina, from whose roof the golden lantern had disappeared; the white pyramid of the Kasbah topping the whole. And it was almost as though in this place of manifold sorrows he was leaving his home behind.

Two sailors stopped before him; one stooped and loosened his silver chain and told him to follow.

Under the purple hangings of the poop sat the departing King, clad in unaccustomed splendour. On his knees he held a scimitar with a jewelled hilt.

Hassan did not look at Cervantes, seemed not to notice him, gazing away from his "leopard" across the sea which should bear him from his kingdom.

A janissar-Aga, standing beside the King in skirt and chef's cap, opened his mouth and spoke:

"Cervantes, you owe the officer on board nine doubloons."

This was the traditional tax when a rower was freed; everyone knew the practice, Cervantes too. And so he knew that he was free.

He said: "I have no money." And this was his first free word.

"Give your silver chain," the Aga said. "We can break it into nine pieces." His words sounded prearranged.

Cervantes took off the chain. He waited. As nothing else was said, he turned away and mounted the gang-plank. It was the nearest one, with the regal carpet. Scarcely had he reached the shore when the carpet was drawn away, the end of it splashed in the water. Shouting arose on the quay, drowning the silver trumpets; and he saw King Hassan's ship glide away.

When the free man, an hour later, came before the Procurator-General, who was lodged in the house of Torres the merchant, he was received with little cordiality. It seemed that Hassan had finally agreed for the sum of five hundred ducats: this now Miguel owed to the Brotherhood of the Trinity. He gave his bond—and that was his first free written word.

"I had some doubts," said Fray Juan Gil, "about taking up the order for your release; reports questioning your worthiness had reached me. You will have to justify yourself."

Justify? Against whom? The Stinker.

The Dominican had been ransomed, and to compensate him for all he had gone through he had been made a member of the Holy Office. But spite was still burning his belly. The tub of butter stuck in his crop. And most of all he feared that his treachery would be found out when Cervantes came home. He tried to forestall him: while Cervantes still sat chained with his silver chain, the Stinker was poisoning his reputation. He accused him of scoffing at religion, of leanings toward Islam; but also of betrayal, debauchery, all sorts of dissolute conduct. The Holy Office sent word to the Procurator-General to investigate the charges before negotiating the release.

The public voice of Algiers spoke out stoutly for the accused. The departure of the galleys impended; Juan Gil laid out the purchase price. But there must be exculpation at the hands of the Inquisition. The monk would be forced to demand this to exonerate himself.

And so began the years of his freedom for Miguel Cervantes. Instead of returning home rejoicing to his native land, he had for weeks to tread these all too familiar pavements, begging testimony after testimony, to prove, in smoothly servile language, that he was no heretic, not a Moslem in secret, no whorer nor falsifier nor sodomite, but rather a true son of the Church and a man of goodly life. Thus was constructed a long, involved, obsequious document, in which witness after witness recorded his views. If one who did not know Cervantes were to read it, he would have envisaged not a brave, good-natured, free-hearted man, but a conventional, careful conformer. But this was necessary. With that kind of weapon the Stinker must be fought.

By the middle of October the Procurator-General, Juan Gil, declared himself satisfied. On the twenty-fourth Miguel Cervantes set sail for Spain. Five years and a month he had been in Algiers. His heart felt joyless; only slowly and painfully did hope lift her wings.

The little ship captained by Antón Francés carried besides himself five other ransomed men, and Fray Juan Gil travelled with them.

The voyage went off briskly. After all, what a narrow channel it was that divided the slave colony from the Spanish coast! With a favouring wind one sighted Spain by the second evening. A domelike mountain was the first thing to appear above the waves.

"The Mongo," Messer Francés said to Cervantes, who stood beside him. "Does it make your heart beat?"

No, Cervantes' heart knocked not a throb the faster. The weeks of waiting, begging, recording had worn him down more than all the danger and deprivation.

"Mongo?" was all he said. Then: "Where do we go in?"

"Into Denia, where I live," said the Captain.

Miguel did not remember the name. It must be some tiny port.

Would any of his own be waiting for him? His sister Andrea perhaps? The deaf father? He would rejoice at the reunion. And would constrain himself to believe in the future and future honours. He was not old.

"Do you know, perchance, Messer Francés: is the King in Madrid?"

"Not in Madrid. The King is on the Portuguese border.

The Queen is lying ill there. She may have died in the meantime."

The Queen? Which Queen? Did time stand still? Was it yesterday he had composed his poem for her death?

"What Queen?" he asked then, aloud.

"What Queen?" The little pot-bellied man in the light-blue scarf looked at him shrewdly from one side. "The Austrian, to whom he has been married ten years. You did not know?"

Cervantes did not answer. "Is Don John of Austria with him?" he asked once more.

"Don John—why?"

"He did me a kindness once."

"Don John of Austria is dead."

It was like a knife-thrust. But why? Not because the news was a death-knell to any vague hope of his. Or because they had been of about the same age and now the other's stormy life was ended. And what else was he to Cervantes, that vain and glamorous prince, that last shallow mirror of the chivalry of Spain?

The Captain, being a well-informed man, told him how it had happened.

A pity, truly. Such great and manifold hopes—and such an end! Africa, Greece, Genoa—he aspired after them all; nothing seemed too high. Not the crown of France, nor the crown of England. At last they had sent him to the Netherlands. There too glittered a vague hope. He failed—he was bound to fail. Perhaps—but Messer Francés only hinted this—perhaps that was why they sent him. At thirty-three he was a worn-out old man. And his last request was only for a grave near the bones of his father, the Emperor. That would be a reward for all his services.

"And they granted that?"

"They granted that."

"Did he die in Spain?"

"In Flanders, Don Miguel. Among his soldiers, in a hut on the open field."

"That was good."

"Yes . . ." Antón Francés drawled reflectively, "that was good. It seems his skin was black when he died, as though he had been burnt. And when they opened him, his heart was shrivelled."

"But now he lies in the Escorial?"

"They had to divide the body. And send it home secretly, in four packets. He was so much hated by then. Yes, now he lies in the Escorial."

It was growing dark. The dim lights of Denia showed close at hand. It seemed to Cervantes that after twelve years, entering his native land once more, he came in by the back door.

Part Two

CHAPTER SIXTEEN

First Evening

The house made him sick at heart. He had expected, of course, to find his parents in modest circumstances—but nothing like these three dark holes, with glassless windows, on a desolate court behind the Calle de Atocha.

A feast was held in honour of Miguel's return—a hot supper. He remembered what an extraordinary occasion that meant. A thick stew of meat and vegetables, eaten with bone spoons and smelling strongly of cabbage and garlic. They even had wine. The drinking-vessels did not match—and the trifling fact saddened Miguel quite unreasonably.

And how sad it was to see his father fall upon the food and seem to forget the occasion in the feast! He was quite white, a bony little old man, with jerky motions and almost entirely deaf. Miguel winced when he had to shout to make himself understood. Then it occurred to him that perhaps shouting was a mistake; he lowered his voice and articulated with much movement of the lips—and that was still worse. He fell silent in sheer embarrassment. His mother, who had grown much smaller too and, though not past the middle fifties, was like a little old woman, kept nodding to him, while the tears stood in her beautiful, great, dark eyes, shining in the flickering light of two candles.

He had looked forward to seeing his brother Rodrigo —but Rodrigo was away. He and his old regiment were with the King in Portugal, or "on the islands"; one did not know which one. They answered his questions about Rodrigo in monosyllables, as though he had left home on bad terms with his parents. His mother began to talk of Luisa, to Miguel's surprise, who had almost forgotten the existence of this sister who had taken the veil; he could hardly recall her convent name: Sor Luisa de Belén. But he showed the greatest interest, to please his mother, who sat more erect and seemed to grow younger as she talked.

Luisa's cloister, named La Imagen, was the one with the strictest rules in Spain. The nuns, barefooted Carmelites, lived by the precepts of the great Teresa of Avila. Their clothing was the coarsest cloth, their bed a straw mattress, their food salt fish and bread; their day was made up of work and prayer. They might receive no presents, cherish no friendships; they might not even shake hands in the cloister. Luisa had lived under this rule for years. She was particularly god-fearing and much respected for her fine character. The year before, in her old age, Teresa had visited Toledo, travelling by way of Alcalá expressly to see the pious Luisa of Bethlehem. And, her relative youth notwithstanding, they had now elected her Subprioress.

Miguel Cervantes looked at his mother. How her glorious eyes sparkled as she told him of the serviceable sacrifices of this child of hers! He had been long absent from Spain; but how well he understood even now that not himself and not Rodrigo but only Luisa, far away in her cell, fed the maternal cravings! The Absolute! The almost impossible! Such were his nation. Religious faith, even the austerest, was not enough for this Teresa and her followers. They thought with insane fervour to enforce miracles like those of the early Church. All the barriers set up by reason and a temperate attitude toward life must be done away with. Solitude, flagellation—these alone would open the gates of Heaven. Endless unity with God was the goal.

Miguel understood his mother's feelings. The career of this barefoot nun was her joy and consolation; it made up for the worldly courses of her other children: the two sons, who as soldiers recked too little of their salvation; and her eldest daughter, of whom the same was only too true.

Andrea was sitting with them at the table. She was a well-developed woman of thirty-six or thirty-seven, perhaps a little heavy already; with regular features, and a complexion rather spoilt by rouge. Her clothes were in the fashion: tight stiff stays, narrow sleeves, a ruff; a great hooped skirt with ribbons and galloons and bead embroideries. But a closer view of all this elegance showed that the materials were cheap and shoddy and worn out.

Of her, too, Miguel knew but little. A letter received in Naples long ago had mentioned a little daughter, who might be now eight or ten years old. The father, a Señor Figueroa, had been mentioned too, and for a while Miguel had supposed that his sister was married. But a few years later the little niece was suddenly referred to as Costanza de Ovando. Miguel had concluded that his sister lived in a sort of free wedlock with one man after another. But the truth was otherwise. Miguel knew too much of life to mistake: love, for this weary woman, was a trade—he saw it, and it pierced his heart. For was not his the guilt, or anyhow a part of it? Some of the ransom money, he knew, had come from Andrea.

He looked her full and cordially in the face. She cast down her eyes and went a flaming red. So she had done when Rodrigo's name was mentioned. Had his simple feelings been outraged and had there been scenes between them? Did she fear the same now from her other brother? Yes, that was it, she was afraid. It went to his heart; he seized her hand and held it fast in his. Whereat Andrea quite simply began to wail aloud, leaning upon his breast. The father looked on mistrustfully and shouted across to know what it was all about. Nobody answered. The mother's lips moved, she murmured something.

After supper Miguel looked at the house. There was not much to see. The flickering candlelight displayed the few poor casual effects of those who change their dwelling often. At the end his father beckoned him aside and opened a little chamber: Miguel stared in surprise at some primitive apparatus and a store of little bottles. "My laboratory," said the old man proudly. "You did not know that even in my old age I could change my profession."

The truth was, his law practice had entirely dried up. From Seville, from Burgos and Valladolid he had been driven by hosts of learned rivals, and in uncertain Madrid had come to his bold resolve. Purging and blood-letting and the names of fifteen drugs or so he could still learn. Business was good, he told his son; the trick lay in the enormous cheapness of his charges: two *reales* for blood-letting—hardly a barber in Madrid would work for such a sum. Riches, of course, could not be had that way. Not the riches made by high-class swindlers whose treatments only began with inhalations of gold vapour. Of course, profound secrecy was highly important.

Miguel would have liked to throw himself on the bed to hide his eyes, and see no more. These pathetic souls had scraped together enormous sums for him—so had the sister who just now had flung herself on his breast in gratitude at being pardoned. Pardoned? He to pardon them! Had he not prided himself all the time on his constancy and daring outside in the diverting world—and meanwhile things had gone here so that the family had not four wine-glasses alike to set on the table!

Only these glasses and the wine were left on the table, the supper had been cleared away. They were waiting for his tale. He felt like a criminal. His mother's eyes, as she sat beside him, fastened upon his left hand; he saw it, drew the famous stump out of sight and hid it behind his back.

CHAPTER SEVENTEEN

Unica Corte

In the years of his slavery he had often pictured to himself with what joy he would walk down the well-known street the first morning after his return. This scene had become for him symbolic of his home-coming.

But it is seldom that men's dreams find literal fulfilment. On that first morning a cold wind lashed the rain in torrents through the dirty streets. He stopped at home in his parents' house—though it looked still sadder, if that were possible, in the cold November daylight than it had done by candle-light the night before—and held forth to the neighbours who came in to feast on the sight of the much-travelled man.

Early on the next day he went over to the near-by Puerta del Sol, and found the gateway missing. They had torn it down. He looked uncomfortably at the place where it had been and at the wide, marshy suburban street in building beyond. Often he had entered by this way from Alcalá, through a fine forest of well-grown trees that extended to the Puerta itself. Of the forest naught was to be seen, the surrounding tract had been ruthlessly cleared. To get building material they had hewn down without reason or compunction.

What the returned wanderer saw was the beginning of

the process by which Madrid was to be turned into a capital. It had been that in name for twenty years; but actually it was only a poor little hole with a maze of dirty streets. King Philip's whim to make it a capital rested only on the fact that Toledo seemed heathenish to him—glorious old Toledo, in whose streets Arabic was still spoken.

He indeed showed himself but seldom here in his "Unica Corte." He spent more time in his cloistered stronghold with each year that passed. But he kept his court here.

And that was numerous and costly. Thousands of men fed from the royal butteries. Roast, fowl and game, fish, bread, chocolate, ice and oil—all came to them from the King. The candles alone cost him sixty thousand *thaler* a year.

One might have thought that the requirements of so many magnificent mortals would have stimulated industry and trade. But there were few signs of that. What was required was imported: in all Madrid there were only two small factories, one manufacturing porcelains, the other carpets. Nobody worked at all in this Unica Corte, and not much in the other cities of Spain. The treasures of the Indian Islands, of Mexico and Peru, flowed through the land, without fructifying it, and were poured into overweening enterprises of the Crown. The peasant still hacked at the stony soil and perished in unthinkable misery.

And Madrid, the product of the royal whim, devoured all; it remained the official centre for place- and preferment- and privilege-hunters, for elegant idlers and splendid swindlers. And also it remained and became their centre, the place for humanistic studies and academies, of painters, poets and actors.

And first and foremost for the theatre. The time was past when wandering actors set up their stage here or there outside the gates. For a year and a half now the city had possessed a regular public theatre, where there were performances almost daily, summer and winter. Cervantes knew that—had heard of it where he lay in the Djenina, chained with his silver chain.

He would gladly have gone. A regular theatre! Three hundred days in the year! But he had not the money, had not even the few *reales* for his board and lodging, and had still to lie with his father and mother in their dismal quarters.

It was unfortunate that the King, from whom all favours flowed, was now in Portugal. But his father consoled him. He had not been idle. He had made Miguel and his claims known to the city fathers, the War Ministry, the Chamber of Commerce, the President of Castile, the King's official secretaries, the gentlemen of the Privy Council. He could not go wrong. Miguel was certain of high preferment—military or civil, one or the other.

But when the invalid and his deaf father began their visits, mounting the stairs of the several chancelleries, things wore a different face. Certainly everybody knew the elder Cervantes. He must have been in these antechambers dozens of times. The clerks lifted their brows and looked meaningly at each other when he appeared. They gave brief and ironic attention to his inoffensive and somewhat weakly companion. But if they actually got as far as one of the authorities—a subordinate councillor, perhaps—they encountered nothing but mechanical phrases, and were advised to appeal in writing. King Philip's "say it in writing" was the sovereign prescript of the entire government.

Miguel was surprised at the blitheness with which his father accepted this treatment. He obviously preferred his illusions—and his deafness served him well, sparing him most of the subterfuges and lukewarm explanations. Quite tranquilly he would mention other places to try. Quite tranquilly, albeit in a loud shriek which made Miguel cringe with embarrassment, he would recount his son's deeds and his merits. If you could believe the old man, Lepanto, without his son's assistance, would have been a crushing defeat. Though certainly nobody in all Spain cared a fig for Lepanto now! It was even a drawback to have had to do with it, now that the princely Admiral of the enterprise had departed this life more than a little under a cloud. And there was a glut of heroes. They owed money in every public-house in Spain, where they molested the paying guests with their boastings. Tunisian and Algerian adventurers were as cheap as herrings. In all the chancelleries mountains of addresses piled themselves up: *Que Vuestra Majestad me haga merced* . . .

By the end of three weeks Miguel Cervantes understood. After three hours' wait they were leaving the offices of the Council of Castile, in the basement of the palace. "We are making no progress, Father," he said in his ear. "You have done all you could and I am truly grateful. But these clerks are no use. I will go to the King. I will throw myself at his feet. I am going to Portugal."

The father was dismayed. He made a long face. These visits had become a part of his life—he did not want to give them up.

"I am going to Portugal." Easily said. Even his clothes were too bad—he had bought a suit second-hand when he arrived in Denia. And where could he borrow money? One thinks, after long absence, to return to a city full of acquaintances and friends—and finds oneself alone.

He sought his old master, Don Juan López de Hoyos. Master Hoyos was dead. Miguel heard the particulars from his successor, a talkative gentleman. Three years ago it had happened. He was hearing a class. He had just read out the *Conquest of Alcocer* from the *Cid* and had reached the final lines:

> "To God who rules above us
> Be praise and homage brought,
> Because in such a battle
> Victorious we have fought."—

when he collapsed across his desk, and it had sounded, almost, as though a knight had fallen down in his armour.

Miguel had had little in common with his fellow-students of those days. In any case, they were scattered all over the kingdom of Spain. When he met one, full of office and dignities, the man's manner was just that of the secretary whom Miguel had encountered in the War Ministry: quite particularly formal and inaccessible, so soon as he recognized the retired soldier. Even his former fellow-prisoners were scattered, not to be found. His family's connexion was exclusively among the poor. Without a sou in his pocket he walked the streets of this Unica Corte.

Then he bethought himself of his play, and set out to realize upon it. But the firm of Pablo de Leon, which once had printed his pastoral poem, *Filena,* had gone out of business. When he neared the house in the Calle Francos, there met him an old woman who sang the praises of her establishment; she had six extremely pretty girls all at his service, and further could summon material for his enjoyment, all sizes and ages, from the neighbourhood, did he so desire. She had been about to enter into more detail, but stopped on a study of Miguel's clothing. He smiled to think that a house of joy had sprung up in what had been the cradle of his first-born child—and continued, with his manuscript under his arm, on his search after a publisher.

The name of Blas de Robles was known to him from seeing it on title-pages. Señor de Robles received him at once. A drama? Very good. Where were the others? The others? Cervantes asked. Was he so unfamiliar with the custom in literary matters as not to know that usually twelve comedies were bound together, making a handsome book that would sell well?

If that were the case, Cervantes answered, then he would have to come back in another eleven years, for his Algerian play had taken him nearly a year to write. To be sure, there had been certain disadvantages. . . . And he told Señor Robles a few things about his silver chain, about Hassan and so on.

"Try to get a performance," said Robles. "That is the quickest way to earn some money. Have you seen Gerónimo Velásquez?"

Cervantes looked at him inquiringly.

"You are a great dramatist! All Madrid runs to his performances every day in the Corral, and you know nothing of him. You must learn the productions of your contemporaries. Before all, Lope!"

"I don't know, Don Blas, how much it costs to get in. Too much for me, anyhow."

The bookseller reached in his drawer and took out two crown-pieces, very thick, heavy, solid currency.

"You can go a good many times for the sixteen *reales*, Don Miguel—you do not precisely need a loge, do you? It is not a present. We shall reckon it in the first piece of business we do together. And take your piece to Velásquez at once, into the theatre. He always needs plays."

CHAPTER EIGHTEEN

Theatre

When Cervantes entered the Court of the Cross, about the second hour in the afternoon, he was amazed, and captivated. This was entirely different from the booths where, as a boy, he had listened to Rueda's now obsolete comedies.

The place was what the name indicated, a great paved court, formed by a background of unusually high houses. The stage, elevated some four feet, took up one of the narrow sides. It was open and empty in front; the three sides were hung with coarse painted cloths, the background a landscape with a Moorish castle, left an elegant salon, right a garden. A depression in the floor, with a trap-door, represented the technical apparatus.

Cervantes stood wedged in a thick mass of men that filled the square enclosure, laughing, chattering, already somewhat impatient. Round the three walls were tiers of seats. All the back windows of the houses were boxes. The first story of the house opposite the stage made a sort of latticed and projecting ladies' box, to which jests of not the finest sort were shouted up: one could see a fluttering and glittering of ruffs and rouged red lips and moving fans.

What a host of idle men in broad daylight! They all

seemed to know each other. Cervantes stood rather isolated, holding his fat manuscript under one arm. Here and there came a pushing and shoving in the crowd, as a pedlar of fruits or pastry made his way through to a client, without intermitting his clear loud crying of his wares.

The play was a comedy, called *Lovers Ever Find a Way*. The hand-written posters at the entrance gave the author's name: Señor Lope Félix de Vega Carpio. It was not only from the bookseller that Miguel had heard this name in the past several days. He was still quite a young man, this Lope, miraculously gifted; he had simply appeared one day, out of nowhere, a dramatic star of the first magnitude.

The impatient scuffling of the pit had increased. The cry arose, in tones treble and bass, of "Begin, begin!" A hundred voices bleated and bawled. A sturdy fellow stood next to Cervantes, with a somewhat abandoned and reckless air, who at brief intervals put his fingers to his mouth and whistled so shrilly that his neighbour feared it would break his ear-drums. Then all at once this same man turned to his neighbour and in the floweriest Castilian offered to hold his manuscript, since, as he expressed it, "the gentleman must under the circumstances find the holding of a packet embarrassing." Miguel thanked him profusely but did not dare to accept. After all it was his last hope that he was carrying under his arm. . . . Then they both turned their attention to the stage.

First came an introductory concert of guitar and harp, and then a fulsome eulogium delivered by a costumed page, to bespeak the favour of the audience; and then the comedy began.

The plot of this three-act play was a wild and whirling

game of hide and seek played by the whole cast; in which everybody turned into everybody else all the time: the nobleman into the doctor, the bull-fighter or the miller, the soubrette into the gipsy lad or the gardener's daughter, the gardener's daughter to the Moor or the student, the student to the ghost, the ghost to a hump-backed mute; until at last, after an inexhaustible flood of verse and rhyme, of terzettos and quintettos, romanzas and redondillas, through the intervention of fairies and gods and dragons and prime ministers, four newly betrothed pairs stood before the footlights of the uncurtained stage radiating bliss and singing their lively final song.

To Miguel Cervantes it all seemed a clever and lively but after all empty and somewhat silly pastime for the big children in the parterre, who greeted each joke and each unexpected turn with noisy shouts. On the other hand there would be whistling and abuse when one of the masks embarked upon a long verse speech. That they did not care for, the "gente de bronce," the "mosqueteros," the "infanteria" who had been referred to with such flattering wit in the prologue. What they wanted was furious action and a lot of metamorphoses; the trap-door must be constantly in requisition. But the noisy ones were most likely mistaken: for Cervantes the virtue of the whole resided precisely in those literary speeches—so full of exquisite charm and harmony, wise and moving, pensive and merry at once. It was clear to Cervantes that this Señor Lope was far more than an ingenious and inventive buffoon.

The audience here got their money's worth! There were no pauses. An act was scarcely over when an interlude began, designed to give the audience no time to draw breath. They were quite primitive scenes, played like lightning off the reel: in the one after the first act there was an astrologer, a policeman and two vagabonds, and at the end of it the astrologer had lost his telescope, the policeman his bandolier and sword. The one after the second act had no meaning at all, it was quite frankly slapstick, full of coarse oaths and witticisms, and ending in a free-for-all scuffle to top off.

Cervantes had stood a good three hours, when *Lovers Ever Find a Way* had ended with the chorus at the footlights. The sun was down; it was growing cool. He withdrew to one of the back benches and watched the twilit court empty of its audience. He had been told that Director Velásquez lived in one of the tall houses at the back.

But he was saved the trouble of hunting. For scarcely was the last of the audience gone when three men appeared upon the stage, from behind the hangings. Two of them were in ordinary clothes, the third was an actor still in his costume. He put down a candle upon the round table left there from the last act. The two others took place right and left.

The whole length of the court lay between Cervantes and them. He was almost invisible in the fast-gathering darkness, sitting very still not to call attention to himself. And he was at once entirely taken up by what he saw and heard.

It was neither the actor, in his burgomaster's dress and regalia, nor the man on the left, obviously the Director himself, who interested him. It was Señor Lope Félix de Vega from whom he could not take his eyes. He had heard of him that he had read Latin at five years old and written plays at twelve, but not really credited it until now, when he saw in the flesh this successful man, upon whose chin the hairs had scarcely sprouted. He bounced about upon his chair, cackling with a high metallic laugh which did not seem even yet quite mature. A woman had joined the three, a tall, handsome, full-bosomed wench, not virtuous, from her appearance; she listened to the conversation in silence.

The rehearsal for the evening did not take long. The serious business was the arrangement of the programme for the next weeks. Little Don Lope—as the watcher in the darkness learned with amazement—seemed to take it for granted that almost the entire repertory would be by him.

If they wanted a pastoral piece, like the Italian comedies, very good, he could supply them. Personally he did not care for the genre, it gave no scope for wit and invention, and it was artificial; but never mind, he was willing. And he held a scrap of paper to the candlelight and read off some titles which he had put down: "The Love of Albanio and Ismenia," "Bilardo," "The Shepherd Hyacinth."

Very pretty titles, Velásquez broke in, but could he not see some of the pieces?

"You have only to command, as you know, Don Gerónimo. Tell me the number of roles and the general tone of the piece; if you want mostly emotion or mostly burlesque, in three days, two if necessary, you shall have it. Of course the pay goes up from sixty to eighty *thaler* if the thing is urgent; I do not like to give up my nights. I have a better use for them," and he leered at the full-bosomed lady.

For his own part, he went on, plainly under sensual inspiration, he would much rather just now write a few Amazon pieces, plays in which Doña Elena Velásquez would find brilliant roles—it was a thousand pities how little joy she had shown of late in acting.

There the Director could wholly agree with Señor Lope. He did not see, himself, why his daughter should be behaving so coyly. Probably she was waiting for the years when she could take the part of a toothless procuress.

And with due gallantry Lope replied: four or five decades would have to pass before that happened. Anyhow, she had but to command, and on the instant he would offer her on his knees a play about the renowned Doña Lucinda, who avenged her honour, wounded by the King of Arcadia; or about the beautiful bandit of Estremadura, who dwelt in her castle among the hills, and first beguiled and then murdered all the men who found their way thither, until she too was overtaken by her fate.

The father remarked that certain pieces had lately found favour in Seville and Valencia, in which an infidel, a Turk or a Moor, had the chief role. The author had let fall something about such a plot, had he not?

The lively young gentleman did not wait to be asked twice. He was glad to be reminded, he said. There could be nothing more effective than the criminal drama about Hamet, the Moor, which he was at the moment carrying about full-fledged in his brain. The nameless man in the dark, with his manuscript, felt his courage oozing away, as the other sketched a plot dealing with a proud and noble pirate named Hamet, taken prisoner by the Christians, who perpetrates frightful cruelties out of longing for his beautiful dusky sweetheart, then escapes, is retaken and finally makes an edifying end on the gallows, after conversion to Christianity. There was a particularly effective bit, the author remarked, when the Spaniard who stood as godfather proved to be he whose wife the Moor had slain in a jealous rage.

Capital, Velásquez said: amorous, sanguinary and orthodox—a most happy combination. A piece which must certainly be written without fail, and soon. And they should need a realistic piece to go with the fanciful, and then they should be provided for four weeks: something in recent history, something national, which was always exciting, a victorious battle.

"You do not need to tickle me long before I laugh! What do you say to the Siege of Maastricht?"

"Capital," cried all his hearers at once. The Siege of Maastricht had taken place the year before.

"I will bring the whole army on the stage," Lope declared. "Don't be afraid, Velásquez, you only need to hire fifteen ragamuffins for a few *maravedis* and let them lay about them behind the scenes. It will come cheap enough—I will give you the whole magnificent action of the Duke of Parma, with soldiers cursing and yelling in French and Spanish and Flemish and Italian; the Duke himself taking the trench shovel in hand and laying hold of the spokes of the wheels to bring the cannon up; clouds of powder-smoke, ringing of iron on iron, dust from horses' hoofs; and right in the middle—yes, that is the plot—two women running, a Fleming and a Spaniard, in men's clothes, dragging up munition, both of them in love and fighting a lively battle of words among the cannons; and the Spaniard"—he looked up once more at the bosom of the voluptuous Elena—"wins the battle at length with her tongue, just as the Duke does with his cannon."

At this point for the first time the actor became vocal. He was a big, pot-bellied man, with uncommonly good-natured features and a bass voice rather spoilt by drink. He liked the idea of this siege of Maastricht. It would be a play after his heart, and in the role of this valiant and gifted Duke he found at last something which exactly suited him.

They all laughed. He was annoyed. "That's all right, Gutiérrez," declared the Director. "Actors are crazy people, who knows that better than I? But not so crazy as that. You want to play the lean, keen, elegant Duke, and everybody in Madrid knows how he looks from his pictures. The infantry in the parterre would tear up the stage! What do you say, Lope?"

"I would not say that by any means! Señor Gutiérrez is so emotionally gifted that he can make people forget physical discrepancies. But it would be a pity for him to play the Prince!"

"A pity?" asked Gutiérrez, wrinkling up his forehead. "Why a pity?"

"Because anybody can do that. A conquering young hero —anybody can play that. For you I should conceive another part," and he sketched with lively eloquence a figure which he had obviously thought of that very moment: a gruff old Spanish colonel, full of coarse wit, flesh of the soldier's flesh, their burly idol, whom at the close they carry across the battle-field, with his gouty legs sticking up . . .

It had grown cold. The conference was nearly at an end.

People came and took down the hangings and betrayed the bare, unmortised walls, behind which, presumably, Director Velásquez lived. Then table and chairs and candlestick were borne away.

Cervantes remained sitting in the dark court, with his manuscript upon his knees. He still sat. He had entirely given up the idea of showing the Director his piece. He sat in front of a bare, high, unmortised wall. There remained only the King. The King was in Portugal.

They seemed to be asleep, in the parents' house. He had his bed in his father's medicine-closet. As he lay down, he felt something hard under the pillow: it was eight gold-pieces, rolled in a scrap of red cloth. That could come only from Andrea. It was the journey to Portugal.

He coloured violently, alone as he was, kissed the scrap of cloth and put out his light.

CHAPTER NINETEEN

A Little Relief

The journey in winter through Castile and the desolate, uninhabited Estremadura was very hard. But in Portugal the oranges were in blossom in February. A softer, kinder air enveloped the sore-tried traveller. Here it was good to breathe. His heart seemed to divine the possibility of rest, of joy, of freedom from care.

He found the King in Tomar.

Philip had gone to Portugal in mourning. But if he felt sorrow, it could not endure for long. He had been blest in his courses—even though their full extent was yet unknown. He must have been happy—and he almost was. Here and now, for the first and only time, he might pause, and hold his hand.

The soft, expressive landscape of Lusitania, lacking the violent contrasts of Spain, appealed even to that parchment-preoccupied monk. He looked at Portugal like a man who has eyes to see the beautiful, a heart to perceive the aromas given off by the creative processes. His letters to his children at home at this time are full of excursions, of flowers and nightingales. Sometimes indeed there comes in an account of a heretic burnt; and he sends them the list of heretics, that they "may know who they are."

He had scarcely needed to conquer his new kingdom. The Portuguese campaign was an armed picnic.

A young and rashly enterprising king had fallen in battle against the Moors, and his dynasty was extinguished. Philip was among the heirs, his rights were not less than those of the others, his power vastly more. His army easily dissipated every hostile effort sent against him by the nobles, and Portugal became a province of Spain.

As in a dream, as in a game, a great thing had been accomplished. The peninsula was now a closed kingdom, with one man master between the Pyrenees and the sea. But there was more than that: Portugal's colonies fell to Philip.

A vast empire was thus formed. New, broad and precious possessions came into being in the West Indies, Mexico and Peru. Brazil became Spanish. Over large tracts of Africa waved Philip's red and yellow flag; in Muscat in Arabia, and Persian Ormuz; in Goa, too, in Eastern Asia, in Calcutta, Malacca, Java and Macao. Lisbon became his second capital, after Paris the largest city of the Christian world, a centre of trade second to none. And not only the gold and silver countries belonged to him now; he drew in tribute wood from Brazil, sugar from Madeira, carpets from Persia, Chinese silk, Indian spices. Elizabeth in Westminster looked on affrighted, so did the Medicis in the Louvre and the Doge in Venice, at this concatenation of power and riches in a single hand.

For it all seemed unconquerable and indestructible. Who could rise against a Greater Spain protected by mountains and waves and an invincible army; against a great king who literally commanded the resources of the entire earth? And yet—what could make this king a beggar, begging money among his subjects, mortgaging mines and harvests; so that between Lyons and Milan, in Genoa, Augsburg and Antwerp there was no bank in whose books his name did not stand; and in twenty years he twice declared bankruptcy and dragged the whole financial system of Europe with him into the abyss; how came it that he, the over-exact, pedantic book-keeper, left his people in unexampled poverty, bled it dry, finished it, bequeathed it as a beggared state? What happened to bring all that about? What must have been the spirit of the man?

Well, then, it was of the spirit alone and not of life. Of the spirit that counts as naught our earthly pilgrimage and our earthly joy, anything earthly at all, that scorns the plough and the hammer, that grasps only the cross and the sword, that in fantastically distorted ambition knows but one goal: the purity and unity of the Faith throughout the peoples, the universal triumph of the holy Letter of the Law.

A world kingdom had fallen, as it were, into King Philip's lap. But how little that is, how nothing at all, when what one wants is the Absolute, the Impossible; when all one's life one tilts against the overwhelming, to the point of sublimity, to the point of madness!

Cervantes found the King in Tomar.

The little town was full of military and court folk; above it towered the citadel of the Knights of Christ, where Philip had his quarters. The ear of the King seemed as inaccessible as ever. But the first persons whom he met in the city were two people of high birth and station whom he had known in Algiers. And he had been scarcely two hours in the place when he met that elegant Madrid dame, the wife of an official in the palace, who had fallen into

Dali-Mami's hands at the same time as himself. She recognized him at once; to his horror, for her coquetries had not become more fascinating with the years. She presented him to her husband, and took occasion to mention, evidently not for the first time, his chivalrous bearing on the deck of the *Sol*. Cervantes smiled, remembering how he had put out a leg and made the corsair sprawl on the floor. Her husband bowed low before Cervantes and offered his services with every appearance of sincerity. In Madrid nobody had cared to acknowledge his acquaintance; here in Portugal he found himself on the very first evening the centre of a friendly circle. Everyone took thought for him. They showed him the way.

As early as the third day he received a gratuity from the King, to the amount of fifty ducats. It might be due to his recommendations, to an impulse of generosity on the part of the King, or to sheer luck. But a week later there followed a royal command, an honourable commission.

The Governor of Oran was to be made a knight of the Order of Santiago. Cervantes was to convey the patent. He was paid a hundred ducats journey money.

It was an ambassador's mission—or a letter-carrier's, as you chose to interpret it. Cervantes had no doubts. This could only be a beginning, the first step towards an important position in the service of the Crown. He was a man of roving and extravagant fancy. His belief in life, for ever belied, and at last beaten down, had come back in full force. He was on the way to riches. The hundred and fifty gold-pieces were but a small advance payment, they were a retainer. He saw himself rewarded with a post on the Council, as a diplomat, as commander of a regiment. All these were such highly paid posts that they would secure a bounteous living for his family. Andrea too. . . . He was so secure in his position that he did not think of sending money at once to Madrid. What he had he needed for the moment. It was even too little.

Purveyors of luxuries had quickly gathered round the court in Tomar, mostly Genoese merchants. He bought a Flemish ruff trimmed with lace and a particularly elegant hat, a silvered dagger and a silvered sword. He was travelling for his King, acting as agent between him and the African viceroy; it would have been very tactless to neglect his appearance. The burden of many years had fallen from his shoulders. Glowing, like an impatient boy, he drank the first draughts of good fortune.

His ship sailed from Cartagena; he travelled with hired horses through Andalusia, seeing as though by roseate lightnings the cities of Cordoba and Seville. His galley lay ready in a deep inlet of the sea, it seemed to be waiting for him. When he went on board he was greeted by the crew with the thrice-repeated hail which was reserved for persons of high station. For one day and one night they glided through the mild and flattering flood; then in the morning light they lay before Oran.

This was the city which once in vain he had thought to reach as the goal of long wandering through the rocky wastes. Now he was borne hither by a puff of wind or the breath of a princely protector. All trials were at an end, at last. Never had his step been so light as when he trod the steep lane up from the port and crossed the swaying bridge over the gorge, to Red Fortress, the Governor's seat.

The fragile old officer welcomed Cervantes like a messenger from Heaven. This patent was more to him than a mere honour. He was in continual want of money: a numerous and worthless family in Spain consumed his substance; but his new rank as knight of Santiago carried with it the enjoyment of a yearly rent, in his case four thousand *thaler*. It meant a carefree old age, a satiated family. The tears ran down into the General's dyed beard.

In the evening there was a banquet. The wine was a fiery Valdepeñas, treasured for long years. Don Miguel de Cervantes Saavedra sat as of course and at ease among the gentlemen, served and listened to most attentively.

After the banquet the General took him aside and opened his heart. The opportunity had come at last. He did not doubt that this was the most direct route to His Majesty's ear. He would be perfectly frank. One lived in Oran as in a besieged fortress. Its governors still bore the title "Captain-General of the Kingdom of Tlemcen." But he had only once dared to show himself in Tlemcen. He did not trust himself with his soldiers ten miles away from Oran—not three. He was thankful that he could still hold the city. All too true it was that they were neglected from Madrid. The soldiers' pay was in arrears; for months they had been almost without munitions, most of the cannon were seventy years old; you could scarcely move them for fear of their dropping to pieces. How was it to be explained that precisely in Oran such careful husbandry was practised? Would the Señor Ambassador take care to present the picture as it really was?

Cervantes hearkened, agreed, promised. He knew better than anyone what neglect was doing in Africa. He had learned it on his own body. It cried out for redress, he knew. As earnestly as did the Governor, he believed in his mission.

He was borne far on the wings of his imagination. At night in his vaulted stone chamber he dreamed that the King had given him a fleet to conquer Africa. Algiers, Jijella, Tabarca, Tunis—he would tear the crescent from them all. He saw himself like a figurehead on his own flagship, following the rocky coast, the red and yellow banner in his hand.

The King was in Lisbon when Cervantes returned. He betook himself to the sprawling, badly built palace. A secretary received the thanks of the Governor, looked absently at Cervantes and catalogued the document in its proper place.

He withdrew. He waited. Nothing more happened. He announced himself and applied for audience; he got no answer. He sought out the upper officials. They knew him not. He went down to the lower ones. They left him sitting in the antechamber. He sat for hours, just like his father.

He remembered his highly placed friends. They were cool. He sought the court official and his wife, but they had returned to Madrid. He had to change his quarters for cheaper ones, finally for a hovel. In populous Lisbon he went about without a sou in his pocket. His lace ruff went to rags. He sold his silvered dagger and sword for money to get back to Madrid. It did not suffice; at great pains he borrowed the rest.

He had been no ambassador, only a letter-carrier. He had been paid with one hundred and fifty ducats. Probably the whole mission to Oran had been only in order to book the expense under a proper heading.

CHAPTER TWENTY

"Paradise of Liars"

When he went back to the dwelling on the court in the Calle de Atocha, strange people lived there, a shoemaker and his family. They said that the family had moved from Madrid. God knew what sort of new hopes his father had conjured up! A bundle had been left, with Miguel's small effects. He took it, thanked them and left.

He found a room on the Plaza Matute, just behind the Colegio de Loreto. This he rented, without knowing how he should pay. When he opened his bundle, his slave cap from Algiers lay there on the top.

He put it on and looked at himself in the cracked mirror. His face was sunken and faded, temples and beard were already grizzled. Truly the cap fitted him—it was more than just a souvenir. He had only exchanged one slavery for another. He had no prospect of getting out of debt: debt to his parents, to Andrea, to people in Portugal, to the superiors at the convent where his other sister was a nun. He was in debt to the Trinitarian Brethren who had bought him out of slavery, in debt for the ship chartered by Rodrigo, in debt to Exarque the merchant for his frigate. He revelled in his misery, conjuring up the whole series of his creditors as he regarded in the glass the grey face under the red cap. He knew definitely that there was no shadow of a hope of paying them. He had no bread for the morrow.

It was a strange neighbourhood, this where he had taken rooms. The little square near by had been lately christened the "Paradise of Liars." That was its official name. A Bohemian quarter had sprung up, the Court of the Cross was not far distant, and another stage, the Prince's Theatre, had lately been opened. It played to audiences as large as the other. The quarter was populated by swarms of actors, poverty-stricken, picturesque, noisily gregarious; there were musicians, jugglers and dancers and a luxuriant female attendance. Authors were like flies. Everybody lived on chance windfalls and loans, and sat about in the cafés dramatizing themselves.

A sense of honour exclusively and nationally Spanish reigned in this Bohemia. Everywhere chivalry had become a matter of exterior forms. If you looked askance at a man, out flew his dagger. It was not exceptional to find gentry lying in the mud of the street after having satisfied some punctilio upon each other's persons. But here round the "Paradise" honour was even more ticklish. Hysteria and vanity will quickly generate ideas of revenge. If one actor had stolen another's part; if a poet found himself savagely criticized—a dagger-thrust was held to be the most convincing retort. You defended like that of a virgin queen the honour of any light young female with whom you might happen to live for a couple of weeks. The snobbery was ferocious. Card-sharpers who filched each other's little tricks would none the less call each other "Your Grace" and carry on conversation in the third person. Egregious boasting was the order of the day. All of these poetasters had Iliads and Æneids on their stocks. They lied shamelessly; each knew that everybody else was doing the same, and yet each expected to be believed. But for everybody the chief thing in life was the theatre, the great magnet, the certain hope. For there one could actually earn money: fifty to seventy *thaler* for a single piece.

Only, of course, the public was too exacting. And the Directors too. Even authors of reputation, like Artieda or Armendaris, did not often succeed in being produced. Lope was the only sure card.

He was a monstrous exception. The whole theatre of the period began to depend upon this single youth. There were six travelling companies who played him almost exclusively. He dominated the repertoire, in Seville, Burgos, Valencia. King of the theatre, marvel of nature, the Phœnix of Spain—so people called him. Distant managers sent messengers to his house, with orders, entreaties, cash, laying siege to it, camping in the garden, till a piece should be finished. Though at the very beginning of his career, he was passing into a proverb. "Made by Lope"—it was the phrase for anything which looked, sounded or smelled exceptionally good, and people used it who only vaguely knew who Lope, or even what a theatre, was.

Cervantes saw him almost daily. And it was the incredible truth that the man could finish a piece of some three thousand lines between one sunrise and another—less time than a professional copyist would take to write it down—and he had time to live as well! His love-affairs were the talk of the "Liars' Paradise." They were numerous, despite his relations with the voluptuous Elena Velásquez, who, moreover, had married and was now called Ossorio. The two sat daily in the "Leon Arms" and for Lope never it seemed as though time pressed. On the contrary, he enjoyed himself; the thick incense of flattery and sycophancy seemed the breath of his nostrils. He never noticed Miguel Cervantes, other than as an elderly, rather silent man with one hand and no signs of any profession. Although they continually met and even spoke to each other, Lope was not sympathetic. Something about Cervantes made him uncomfortable.

Miguel regretted it. He highly admired the famous man. Upon that earliest impression of him, other and stronger ones had followed, and every few weeks a new volume came from Lope's pen, each containing twelve plays. Truly here was genius. It was quite possible that none of these arrived at actual perfection; but all of them at least had scenes of such genuine and lofty poesy as to make the heart stop beating. Here was all that could be desired, to stir or to exhilarate the heart of man: a continuous, full and sparkling flow of tragedy, humour, folly, wisdom, fantasy and homely shrewdness. Its variety was incomparable. The man took his material wherever he found it. All occasions were alike to him: a royal murder, a novelty or yesterday's state scandal, Tasso or Ariosto, an illustrated flysheet, the legend of a saint, the latest coarse jest told in an alehouse. Any country served his turn: Spain, Greece, Germany, Persia, Poland, America, any place in the world.

The young man did not stand upon his dignity. His mood changed abruptly, he knew no moderation. There was an endless stream of scandal about the fair Ossorio; and Lope was ridiculously vain, had an endless appetite for gross flattery, would appear good-natured and generous one moment and poisonously foul-tempered the next. If you took him to task, he had no hesitation in denying his own word: he knew nothing about it, it must have been somebody else. In truth it was, he changed from hour to hour, a Proteus of a hundred shapes.

And Cervantes found that his creative activity was of the same nature. It seemed to him that this vast flow of productivity had not anything to do with a single writer or single works. It was more like ceaseless eruption of nature herself; nature, not intent upon limits or consequences, inexhaustibly, irresponsibly producing issue after issue from her teeming womb.

But, nature or no, it was certain that this phenomenon barred the way to the stage for all contemporaries, including Cervantes. Some time since, of course, the latter had made the acquaintance of the producer, Velásquez, and also of his rival, Gaspar de Porres. But when he modestly mentioned to them his half-finished transformation-piece, *A Comedy of Confusion*, or *The Death of Selim*, a tragedy the scene of which lay in Constantinople, they looked benevolently at him and thought of the five or six Turkish and transformation-pieces which they already had in prospect from Lope. Cervantes' position worsened daily. His landlord at the "Leon Arms" filled his glass only half-full these days. He considered turning scribe again—but who that could not write had letters to write in Madrid? Now and then he earned a few *reales* writing dedications for authors to put in the front of their books. He wrote one for a poetry-writing Carmelite father, one for a man named Juan Rufo who had composed a tedious metrical life of Don John of Austria. Five lingering strophes were devoted to the Battle of Lepanto alone. It was rather mortifying for Cervantes when the whole epos, which he had praised redundantly, turned out to be a shameless plagiary. It closed that avenue.

He took his courage in his hands and sought out Señor Robles anew. The good-natured business man reflected a little. Had he ever thought of writing a pastoral novel? No, not in verse: a novel, like the famous *Diana*. The public never tired of that sort of thing. Three new impressions of *Diana* had lately come out, and its continuations and imitations were almost equally successful. Those by Gil Polo had already been translated into five or six foreign tongues. Even a Latin version was being made—probably for the monasteries. Could Cervantes do anything like that? It was advisable to use some classic female name for the title, so that the book was at once placed in the line of the inimitable *Diana*.

A sort of contract was arrived at. Cervantes received a small advance payment.

He went to work at once. He sat out the days in his half-dark room and polished his prose and verse, for this *Galatea* of his was to comply with the prevailing mode and be a mixture of both. He did not enjoy the work. In this unreal, perfumed world, this false Arcadia, not a breath of air stirred. These discreetly lustful nymphs with bow and scarf, these cooing shepherds—it was a cheerless routine. While he was confecting their cloying charms, and making his couples utter exquisite dialogue, he had no feeling in his blood for what he wrote. This precious chirping and trilling, this pedantic rhetoric, had nothing at all to do with passion as felt by the heart of man. He was writing for the fashion. And would rather have made shoes, had he known how.

He was getting on for forty. His life had been empty of

love. The disillusionments of youth lay far in the past. He had embraced women in all the cities whither his adventurous life had swept him. Mostly they were such as a man forgets, even while they lie in his arms. If he felt that one whom he liked was clinging to him, he wrenched himself loose. How could he—soldier, cripple and beggar—have anyone depending on him?

Now, however, precisely now, while he cut and hacked at these empty love jingles, love pounced down upon him like a bird of prey out of a dark cloud, and thrust its talons into his heart.

CHAPTER TWENTY-ONE

Ana Franca

She gave herself out to be the daughter of a gentleman of the court, and called herself de Rojas: Ana Franca de Rojas. But her father had probably been a German soldier (people said so, and her blond hair seemed to bear them out). Her mother sold false jewellery and cheap cosmetics in a gallery in the Calle Toledo. That was whispered on the first evening into Cervantes' ear.

Otherwise he had kept aloof from the women in the "Leon Arms," for fear of having to invite them. Today he pushed regardless past two men who sat beside her on the bench, shoved them out of the way and began to talk. Flattered by her obvious conquest, the blonde smiled. He did not even let her speak (there was time for that), but talked himself in an experienced vein, between homage and irony. He ordered fruit and cake and a sweet Tarragona, with such an air that the landlord was convinced he had come into money, and brought the order without a word. Silence fell all round the table as they listened to this once taciturn old soldier relating one jovial or thrilling anecdote after another. He breathed in her nearness with rapture, the fragrance of her clear skin and of a cheap, pungent perfume, which he found rare and priceless. She was flattered by the expense into which this strange *señor* plunged for her sake; before an hour had passed he felt under the table her leg close to his own—its touch went through him so that he lost his breath and had to lean back.

At the first moment, when she was still at the door, he had thought to see again the Venetian girl, Gina, of whom these ten years past he had certainly not thought. But Gina would be already old. This girl was young, gloriously young, not yet twenty. And the resemblance was merely superficial. This fair-skinned face was not so broad, the nose and mouth were more self-willed, the blond hair was a different shade, paler and drier. The grey-green eyes had some likeness to those others—perhaps it was only their expression. This gaze had a strangely provocative power, a measuring coldness—there was no kindness in it.

It was growing late. The *posada* was nearly empty. They got up together. When they were by the door the landlord came up with an inquiring, even threatening look. Miguel felt in his pocket, took out all that he had and thrust it into the man's sticky hand, not caring whether it were too little or too much.

It was a moonlit September night. As she walked beside him, he saw that she was smaller than he had thought. She seemed slender; yet one could divine, beneath the shawl wound round her bosom, and the narrow skirt, a sturdy, well-developed woman. She walked with that swaying lightness of step that indicates sensuality. When they reached the door of her house he stopped and embraced her. She made no resistance. For the first time in years he felt regret for the loss of his hand—it was bitter, to embrace her and caress her only with one.

Connexions were easily made and broken in those days, round the "Liars' Paradise." By the third day she was living with him on the Plaza Matute, and he took a still smaller room, next his own and communicating with it. The landlord wanted rent in advance. Cervantes copied out the first two songs of his *Galatea*, rushed to Robles with them and received ten *thalers* in exchange.

Ana Franca had, it was quite clear, no connexions to break when he took her to him. It was all very sudden and irresponsible. She was one of those unattached creatures whom men toss to each other like coloured balls. Such women become old suddenly; at thirty-five they are finished; they become receivers or go-betweens or sell trumpery at street corners. It took Ana Franca some while to realize that this was different, serious; that somebody loved her.

He sat in the little room and hacked away on his novel. It was desperately slow work. Some sentences he re-wrote seven times—with the verse it was even harder. And it halted, it had no melody. But what was a poet if he could not write verse? So obviously he was no poet. He felt no inward relation to his subject. Nor did he need to. He wanted success, he wanted pay. He dreamed of the embroidered hoop-skirt he would buy for Ana Franca, of the rouge-pots which she coveted.

She lay in bed next door, munching cheap sweets. That was the life she loved; she knew no better, and felt it a hardship that she must rise toward midday, fling on some clothing and buy vegetables, herbs and a little mutton fat to make a stew in their landlady's kitchen.

To him it was enough that she was there. He felt an unquenchable craving for this sound, fresh body, which even indolence could not make flabby. He had never enough of the sweet-sharp odour of her. And the ever-aloof and measuring gaze of the grey-green eyes spurred him on to such mad extravagances of passion as scarcely belonged to his age.

He did not ask himself if it could last, what would be left some day when desire ebbed. It would not ebb, it was for eternity. He had found the one woman in his life. He possessed that joy.

Her few and limited ideas seemed to him wise and witty. It never occurred to him to talk to her of his work. It was weeks before he even knew whether she could read—she had learned, it seemed, but as good as forgotten how.

She gave no thought as to what he would be doing there in the other room. Men have various ways of scraping together the money women need. This one wrote, with the hand he had left.

But about the theatre she was not indifferent. It meant something to her. Six months before, she had had a part with Velásquez, as an English slave—presumably on account of her blond hair. It had not really been a part; she had only knelt, half-naked, to receive the blows from a lash which a jealous favourite had decreed. But these ten minutes on the stage, two evenings in succession, had sufficed to give her an enduring appetite for that world. To act, that meant to move about on the stage in exotic garments, or better yet with none, while a packed audience of men stared with wide-open eyes that unmistakably communicated their unmistakable desires.

Miguel thought to please her by procuring her a place

in the women's gallery, now and then. But she always came back in a bad temper, complaining about the wenches who had pushed themselves into the front row so that she saw nothing. She had less to say about the plays themselves. And when one evening Cervantes so far conquered the pangs of jealousy as to seat her opposite to the great Lope himself at the "Leon Arms," that hero made no impression at all upon Ana Franca. Probably she thought that the dialogue—sad or merry—on the stage was made up by the actors themselves. For she gazed with humble admiration at those who came to the tavern, found their echoing periods beautiful, their bombastic gestures most refined. She often referred to a certain Alonso Rodríguez, who had acted for a time at the Court of the Cross but was now in Valencia. It was he who had got her the walking-on part which she regarded as the climax of her existence.

There came an afternoon, and an evening, when Ana Franca did not come home. Miguel waited. He waited the next day, helpless, inconsolable, prostrate. He could think of no reason, there had been no quarrel. . . . On the third afternoon she was there, her face badly made up, strange odours in her clothing. She forestalled any scene, by straightway announcing that he had not the least right to make one. He gave her nothing—look how she was forced to go about! What good was it for him to be sticking there in that room and coming to bed all inky, when after four months there was not a frock, a shawl, even the thinnest gold ring, to show for it. No, he might kindly just keep his hands off her.

Plainly, she was parrotting somebody else—her mother, or a friend, or the lover whom she had managed to find.

Cervantes fell prey to utter misery. He shook with jealousy, with mortification that he had nothing to give. He realized upon what it was he had bestowed his heart. But it was too late, he was bound; could neither cut nor tear himself free. He began to speak. Never had he thought that he should one day so speak. He insisted, he shook her, he sought by any means at all to strike a spark out of this so seductive body. She looked at him, offended, with her strangely measuring gaze. She understood not at all what he meant. At last, with contemptuous acquiescence, she drew him to her firm, white bosom. What else was it he wanted? What else was he talking about? And he, conquered and shame-faced, took with avidity what she offered.

He sat next day over the third book of the *Galatea.* And suddenly noticed that he had been writing for some time almost mechanically. He had intended to compose a customary and affected lover's lament. But when he read over what he had written, it was a mixture of over-emphatic prose and halting, unskilful verse. A lover's lament, indeed, but overwrought and bizarre, bursting in gouts from an overladen heart. Not an academic shepherd cooing to an orthodox nymph; but a man enslaved, shaking and rattling his heavy chains, and madly thinking to extract music from them.

Not a word of it could be used. The whole exiguous web of his novel would have been rent asunder. He tore up the three pages.

Once more there was not a sou in the house. He skulked about the "Paradise" and waylaid his fellow-writers (any who had ambition and a little cash) and offered them eulogies in verse which he would put into his work. He would take them with him to his immortality of fame. Actually, he spoke of immortality, quite cynically and sceptically, in order to earn five *reales*. But he never got enough. And Robles the bookseller refused, albeit sympathetically, to advance him any more—in the author's own interest, he said; who would otherwise have nothing more to expect when the book at last appeared.

Then Miguel went to his sister Andrea. She lived with her small daughter in rather better circumstances than before, in two cleanly rooms, paid for by a friend. She was very proud of her housekeeping, looked older and more like a little bourgeois. But there was not much money in the house; her friend gave her only enough for necessities and kept weekly accounts.

Andrea knelt down before her chest of drawers and took from the bottom of the lowest drawer several rolls of stuff. Kneeling, with a kindly smile, she reached out one of them in her arms to her brother. It was a fine and especially durable taffeta, the costly gift of a former lover, which she had kept by her as a kind of last resort. The Genoese, Napoleone Lomelin, who kept a pawnshop, would certainly give twenty ducats for it, perhaps thirty. He knew the rolls—they had been once in his possession.

Cervantes borrowed a little cart near by, for the five bales were too heavy to carry, and went to the pawnshop. "Are you taking it to the flag-makers?" the children asked him in the street; for the taffeta was striped red and yellow. There was enough of it for fifty Castilian banners.

So there was fresh linen for Ana Franca, the debts were paid, even in the "Leon Arms," where they had lost faith in him. Ana Franca was in a good mood. There was no repetition of that earlier excursion; the weeks passed for Cervantes in a kind of happiness—petty, restricted, wretched, yet happiness of a sort.

He began, as the custom was, to advertise his book before it appeared: giving readings, circulating pages, and seeking some highly placed patron who would accept and pay for the dedication. He found the man, after some search: one Ascanio Colonna, Abbot of Saint Sophia, a member of the princely Roman house. He was a somewhat finical man, and principally won to the undertaking because he was told that Cervantes had years before been a member of the household of the sainted Acquaviva. It must be expressly so stated, in the dedication, he stipulated. Cervantes promised.

When he got home, joyful at his success, he found Ana Franca in a frozen fury. She was with child. And rather far advanced. She had noticed nothing, had not suffered, and had only became convinced that very day. Her feelings were quite unequivocal: she saw in the prospect merely misshapenness, suffering and trouble.

And they grew daily stronger. She looked out of her grey-green eyes with scarcely concealed hatred at the man who was the author of this mischance—the cripple, the pauper, the paper-waster. One day she came home half-dead: she had tried to throw off her pregnancy when already so far advanced, and had of course not succeeded. The doctor and the drugs ate up their remaining cash, but she got well. Nature insisted on making this unmaternal being a mother.

Cervantes cared for her with untiring gentleness. In secret he rejoiced. Since it was so, he would marry her. Perhaps the child would be a son. A little son—his, much more than the mother's. He would teach him, form him. He would tell him the tale of his adventures, that now no one wanted to hear: of Don John, Dali-Mami, the King of Algiers. A little son—that was a little immortality, and of the greater he dreamed no more.

But in the weeks before the child was born, their need was worse than ever. A lone man might be poor, might owe; but a poverty-stricken parent was the wretchedest creature under heaven. What if the book-dealer would pay no more? What if Colonna yet refused? And the hostile criticism which can kill an author, above all the poisoned tongues of his own colleagues! He must silence them. An idea came to him. . . .

He would tickle them all at once. Not mention one and another with praise in his novel, but all of them together. He would set up a huge steaming chalice of incense for the whole of Spanish literature. And when even the poorest rhymester drew the thick incense into his nostrils, his face would expand in a grin—and the *Galatea* would be saved.

He threw himself into the work. He took great pains with the list he made; cast back in his memory, kept adding fresh names. Then he began the composition. In the last, the sixth, book of *Galatea* the muse Calliope appeared in full moonlight and sang to her harp before the assembled shepherds and shepherdesses an eulogium upon Spanish poetry.

There were one hundred and eleven octets, exactly eight hundred and eighty-eight rhymed lines. A strophe was devoted to each author: to Baca, Bivar, Garay and Vergas, to Pariente, Romero, Maldonado and the rest. The great Lope himself got no more space than the others.

He had place in the one hundred and fortieth strophe, and he was not called Orpheus or the new Euripides; in fact his praise was relatively sparing. Perhaps the poor eulogist tried to indicate by this sober sincerity his conviction of the man's genius.

The whole was a triumph of disingenuousness. He had taken in his hand a most discreditable weapon, with which to tilt against overpowering odds, against the envy, malice and stupidity which for ever throw their protean shadows across the path of every true man.

Ana Franca's hour had come on apace. And what nature gives to so many maternal souls only at the price of blood and torture, she granted to this woman with lavish hand. The pains were slight and short; soon there lay beside the scarcely wearied woman a green-eyed little creature, with a tiny aquiline nose, who made next to no outcry. It was a girl.

Four days later she was christened, with the name of Isabella. The mother was strong enough to go to the church. Even the priest noticed how stiff she was. At home Cervantes had to remind her to nurse the infant.

But yet he was glad. His book was about to appear, and the two births together appealed to him as a lucky omen. Perhaps his *Galatea* was better than he had dared to hope and would carry his name a little forward into the future.

Robles the bookseller proved himself a skilled man of business. The book was to appear on a Wednesday in May; on Monday he paid down the remainder of the honorarium, a hundred and sixty-seven *thaler*. Cervantes received the sum in silver in a leather bag.

His first visit was to Andrea. She accepted less than her due, and embraced him with joyful tears.

With all the remainder of that splendid sum he went back to Ana Franca. She was sitting in her chair fully dressed, gazing with tranquil eyes straight before her. Beside her, on a table, the little Isabella rested on her cushion and gazed outwards with the same tranquillity.

Ana Franca only nodded when she saw the money. His joy was quenched. He tossed the money with a rattle into a drawer of the table whereon the child was lying.

On Wednesday he was early at the shop. The copies of the *Galatea* were not there yet, but might come at any moment. Señor Robles expected them with the post from Alcalá, where they had been printed. At last the cart stopped before the shop, piled high with books. They all set to work to unload, the driver, two clerks, Señor Robles and Miguel too, making himself as useful as he could with his one hand. The whole salesroom was full of the fat, heavy quartos.

Then Cervantes sat down with one of them in a boarded-off back room of the shop, and enjoyed that pleasure which every author knows. He enjoyed it with a throbbing heart, for this was truly his first book, the other earlier ones being nothing but cheap paper pamphlets.

Blas de Robles and his printer had done their work well. Good paper, clear, fine type, not too much text on the page, prose and verse set off with practised taste. Engrossed on the title-page the arms of the patron, Colonna, the prince's crown above the column, with the proud device in bad Latin: *frangi facilius quam flecti.* Cervantes turned over the pages of his book, read a few sentences here, a strophe there. He had been too fearful: it was all good! Only when at the end of the volume the pages containing the *Canto de Calliope* came open of themselves, he did not read but hastily turned to another page.

He went home, his book in his hand. Ana Franca was not there. The rooms seemed blatantly empty. He looked round. He opened the cupboard. Ana Franca's clothing and small effects were gone. He opened the table drawer. Half the money, counted out with precision, had disappeared. In a corner on the floor small Isabella lay in her cushions and looked up at him seriously with her grey-green eyes.

CHAPTER TWENTY-TWO

Cross-Roads

He had been seven hours on the way, now riding his mule, now walking beside it. If what they had told him at the stable was right, he must soon come to where the road branched off towards Toledo.

He had gone out of his way in order to follow the Aranjuez road for a while. But it had been a mistake. True, it was the route used by the court; but even so it was full of holes, and so deep in dust that he could have written on the back of his beast

It was a pretty little animal he had hired, and strong; with extraordinarily long ears that moved expressively as it went; with head, mane and tail be-tasselled and be-braided in ribbons which had been gay when they set out, but which now were a uniform, whitish grey.

Perhaps after all it would have been wiser to stop at the inn and await the cool of the day before setting out. But it had been a hateful barn of a place built of bare bricks, boasting a table and three stools and nothing more; and the people seemed so dirty and disreputable that he had paid his six *maravedis* to sit and rest a while, and then moved on. He needed better lodgment than that, for he was not alone.

Something stirred in the left-hand pannier; he thrust back the linen cover. Little Isabella lay there, neat and cleanly; she lifted her head and blinked up into the staring light.

It was for her sake he had undertaken the toilsome journey; he was taking her to Toledo.

No more than three months had passed since the evening in May when he had found himself suddenly alone with the infant. Ana Franca had vanished, for good. Some vague and dubious information had reached him that she had been seen with Rodríguez in Andalusia, in various places. That was all he knew, or ever was to know. Spain was an easy place to be lost in. All the larger cities had their bad quarters, acknowledged and avoided by the police. Wherever was Cervantes to look for her? In Valencia near the olive market, in the Percheles at Malaga, the horse fair at Cordoba, the Rotonde at Granada? It would be vain. And even more vain to try to win her back when he found her; vainest of all to try to live with her.

He had to learn to accept the inevitable. And the situation was not without its humorous side—being left like this with a new-born girl-child on his hands. He found a wet-nurse. Isabella throve. But the peasant woman saw that Cervantes clung to the child, and her demands became exorbitant.

Andrea offered her services. She would bring up the infant on the bottle. And she had her own child's clothing left over.

He refused. He loved poor Andrea, and was unprejudiced too, and her taffeta he had accepted. But this he could not do. Andrea understood, though she wept her easy tears as she acquiesced.

Then, most opportunely, word came from Toledo. His mother wrote: "Bring me the baby, Miguel; it will take me back to the days when you were a baby. And there are other reasons too: there might be something here to your advantage."

It sounded promising. He could certainly do with something to his advantage. His *Galatea* had had only a minor success; people were buying fewer pastorals this year and more romances of chivalry. And his patron Colonna had been very shabby. Miguel was coming to the end of his money. With the last that he had, he hired his animal and two panniers, disposed Isabella in the one and wine, milk, bread and cheese in the other, and sallied out of Madrid at four in the morning.

They came to the road that turned off on the right hand to Toledo; you could follow it with your eyes, a bad road, without any shade, going up and down across the rolling flatland. He had still seven or eight hours of travel before him; and his courage was nigh to fail.

At the cross-roads stood a solitary pine-tree, combed all one way by prevailing winds, casting a thinnish shade. He stopped, and gently took down the panniers; the mule, being freed, began to crop the scorched herbage, with its dusty ornamental fringe falling into its dark and rolling eyes.

Cervantes took Isabella on his lap, supported her head with his bad hand and fed her with the other. She drank in long, slow draughts. She had an oddly mature little face, which could not be called pretty; the conflict between the paternal and maternal elements was too harsh. The round green eyes, sitting close to the little hooked nose, gave a birdlike, almost uncanny look to the face.

Isabella smacked her lips in satisfaction when she had done. Cervantes laid her back among her pillows and found a cool spot for her. Then he gave the mule its nose-bag. He needed nourishment himself no less but felt too tired to trouble, sat himself down and leant his head against the rugged tree-trunk.

This was a stern, harsh landscape that affronted his gaze. It was bald and monotonous, the earth was parched and traversed by wide cracks. Here the sun burned down as on the tablelands of Africa; here too ice-storms raged five months in the year. This countryside knew only extremes, it had no mean of kindly warmth. Now and then a squat house of sun-dried bricks, rarely a field with any crop, and that already harvested, in June. There were clumps of pine-trees, with small, windswept trunks. Half-dried-up patches of cabbages on the ground looked like some kind of skin-disease.

This was the burnt-out heart of Castile, the innermost core of Spain. Perhaps this cross-roads between Toledo, Aranjuez and Madrid was the precise middle of the country. And round Spain circled the world. Here he sat, with his child, at the universe's inexorable heart.

The heat of midday drowsed his eyelids together.

Through his half-slumber droned a leaden humming, a vague, monotonous sound, which seemed to be coming nearer, on the Aranjuez road, where it rose into a dusty hillock. Yes, a spot of colour was coming over the crest.

It was a herald on a tall white horse, bearing a red and yellow banner. Under the drooping velvet cap the sweat ran down his handsome face in glistening streams. He wore a stiff, square tabard before and behind, upon which the lion of Leon and the tower of Castile diagonally repeated themselves. His steed moved at the slowest possible gait, for the rest of the train was on foot. First six monks, barefoot and bareheaded, each holding a crucifix, chanting as they walked their scorching way. Then came the litter.

It was a simple leather-covered sedan, with a linen awning, borne by four servants. Other monks walked alongside, praying, their figures somewhat screening from the dust the person within. Behind followed a relay of other bearers; a picket of soldiery brought up the rear.

Cervantes had knelt on one knee to await the procession. He saw how carefully the bearers walked, how they kept their eyes on the uneven road, compressed their lips and set their feet with the utmost care.

They halted at the cross-roads, directly in front of him. He heard no order, but perhaps at a sign from the herald, they put down the chair and stepped aside that the relay might take their places. The barefooted monks continued to chant. The man in the chair slept on.

Cervantes had not thought of him as an old man. The rather long beard was entirely white, the complexion sickly, the closed lids reddened as though with weeping. His left leg hung down, in black stocking and shoe; the right, which was probably gouty, was wrapped in bandages and stretched out before him. And upon this burning day he was otherwise dressed as though for a Council of State; in the black silk mantle over the black velvet doublet, and the very tall, brimless, ribbed felt hat atop his waxen features. Thus was he, whose countenance Miguel Cervantes had so often sought in vain to behold, borne past him sleeping.

It all lasted but a minute. The four new bearers lifted

the chair, with a slow, gentle, steady movement. The herald's horse paced slowly forwards. There was a gentle rattling and ringing as the soldiers filed by. No one had marked the kneeling wayfarer under the tree.

Isabella began to scream. She lifted up her little head from the pillows and uttered piercing squalls. She almost never cried; it was like an attack. Her face was red, her mouth so wide open that one saw deep into the rosy little throat.

He tried to take her up, to quiet her. But her whole little body stiffened, with almost alarming strength. And so she roared, as though beside herself, in a burst of desperation, behind the royal retinue that with chanting and clanking wound away into the dusty distance.

CHAPTER TWENTY-THREE

The Village in La Mancha

He must get married. This was the "something to his advantage" of which his mother had spoken.

The father, who still practised his pathetic art of healing, had twice been called to bleed a certain priest who had come to Toledo from the near-by district of La Mancha. The apoplectic gentleman had actually been relieved and was loud in his praises. The third time he came as a friend, bringing two fowls and some wine, and also his young niece, a country girl who answered to the name of Catalina de Salazar y Palacios. She was tall and rather heavy, with a thick crop of shining black hair above her regular and rather empty features. Her father was dead; her mother never left her village of Esquivias.

This was her own first visit to the city, and she looked with an expression of dull amaze at the Moorish tangle of streets, the palaces, towers, churches and bridges of the ancient capital. In the evening she sat with her uncle in the clean little inner court where the Cervantes family dwelt. Things were much better with them here than in Madrid, they lived in a little house in the "vegetable market," just behind the cathedral. Rents were cheap in this thousand-year-old city where Goths and Arabs and

Castilian kings had reigned, and which now was slowly decreasing in size. The father had had some luck too with his cures. He thought himself a great physician now. But he seemed unaware of his own illness, a dropsical affliction which was rapidly growing worse; and discoursed much in a shrill voice of his grandiose plans for the future.

And he it was who talked to the priest of Esquivias and his niece about his two sons: of Rodrigo, who was fighting under the Duke of Parma against the Flemish heretics; but, above all of his elder son. His former appeals for preferment on behalf of Miguel had taught him by heart the tale of the latter's exploits and sufferings; and his liveliest pleasure was to see the credulous admiration on the faces of his listeners. Particularly la Señorita Catalina listened open-mouthed. Her favourite books seemed to have come to life. For she had swallowed whole the literature of chivalry, from the renowned Amadis of Gaul, to his son Esplandian, Emperor of Constantinople, down to his children, great-grandchildren and great-nephews; erecting in her unhappy head a dream structure of incredible marvels, superhuman courage, and invincible chastity—which corresponded to nothing at all in life as she knew it in her little village.

Old Cervantes, actually, had been entirely without motive in thus romancing. But his quiet wife did some romancing of her own as she saw astonishment and interest flicker up in the eyes of this *señorita* from the country.

She took the cleric aside. It was true—a marriage was not impossible. Perhaps it had even been vaguely thought of on the occasion of Doña Catalina's first visit to the city. Certainly she was of the right age, and had, as anyone could see, all the charms that could rejoice the heart of man. The family was good, it was more than good. On neither the Salazar nor the Palacios side had there been for generations a drop of Moorish or Jewish blood. That was an inestimable good, Miguel's pious mother would be the last not to recognize it. But as for material treasures: heroes do not as a rule get rich in this world. Miguel was not rich. The services and advantages which he would contribute—not least of which was his glorious mutilation in his country's service—must be compensated. In this matter too the uncle made satisfactory replies. Doña Catalina was an only child, heiress to a nice little property with a decent house, olive and fruit gardens, three yoke of land, house furnishings in decent array, eighteen goats, forty-five hens and a cock. All appliances for happiness were present. At a moderate estimate, one might say a thousand gold ducats.

Miguel Cervantes was weary. He had feared to be cross-questioned when he came; and sat now, grateful and relaxed, beside his mother in the little court, and his mother rocked his child. Not a question about Ana Franca had she put, she had not even praised her grandchild. But she had taken it at once to herself, borrowed a cradle of a neighbour and now rocked it with her foot as she worked.

She began to talk. Miguel listened. He was weary. If this girl were not a scarecrow and not a shrew, he would submit to the yoke. What did it matter? The mother went on, about house and furnishings, and he thought about his *Song of Calliope,* that desperate sycophantic homage he had paid to the literary genius of Spain —and all in vain. He was rejected of men. He was at the end. The village in La Mancha, fields and olive-orchards and laconic peasants who knew nothing of a Madrid failure or success—almost it tempted him. Perhaps she would make him forget Ana Franca, whom he felt still in his blood. He did not say no.

He rode over to present himself. He arrived towards evening; the bare Esquivias looked not too badly in the evening light. He found everything rather more modest than it had been represented, but Catalina did not displease him. Her almost silly innocence and infatuation had an unaccustomed charm.

For her part she hardly saw him at all. He might have been much punier and more unassuming than he was, for her he was the noble and intrepid traveller, come to life from one of her romances. But not such rosy mist clouded the vision of her mother, the Señora Palacios. Between her and Miguel there was dislike at first sight. She was a large, imposing woman of his own age, with very stiff manners. Her striking characteristics were churchly piety and an avarice which was betrayed by the narrow, sucked-in lips.

The Salazars and the Palacios were landed nobility of the pettiest sort, scarcely distinguishable from peasantry save by their pride and conceit. Three men-servants and a maid sat at a side-table. Only after the grace did the good-natured old cleric appear and greet the wooer, puffing.

Conversation did not flow. Miguel felt that he might tell some of his adventures, but the inspiration died beneath his hostess's contemptuous gaze. Only once, to his great astonishment, he delved deep down into the past and talked of the gentle Cardinal Acquaviva and Fumagalli the Canon. He was glad when the meal—mutton broth, and cheese, with a concluding grace—was over.

They left him alone for a short time with Catalina. And she, with a proud and significant motion of the head indicated to him the corner of the room where her treasures stood in rows, thirty or forty dog-eared volumes, all the Amadis, Felixmartes and Clarians, to whose tourneyings and dragon-slayings he owed Catalina's tender leanings towards himself.

Two weeks later the visit was returned. Señora de Palacios and daughter came, with the cleric, to the little house in the vegetable market. This was, since her own marriage, her first visit to the city.

Old Cervantes lay sick abed. Painfully he got up, with his distended body and gaunt face and greeted the guests in his shrieking voice. But discord soon arose—yes, even scandal. For Miguel Cervantes appeared, with little Isabella in his arms (though his mother had wisely counselled keeping her concealed) and declared plainly that this little daughter of his went where he did.

Señora Palacios seemed about to break up the party. Probably she was not sorry to have this excuse. They quieted her with difficulty. Her brother, despite his cloth, took the matter in more human spirit. Catalina blushed, bending over the green-eyed little creature. Who could say what her feelings were? It may be that she took the uncanny little maid for the child of some fairy or sorceress.

There was an uncomfortable parting, no conclusion being come to. The mother shook her head. She did not understand her son. Why could not she herself bring up her grandchild—the time being near, alas, when she would have no one else to care for?

But Miguel stuck to his guns. No marriage without Isabella, and no more said. He had loved the woman who had so basely deserted him. What was left to him of her, this speechless, unbeautiful little creature, he wanted under his own eyes.

He went back to Madrid. They could communicate with him through Andrea. He had affairs.

He had no affairs at all. Also he had nothing to live on. He avoided the "Liars' Paradise." After the unsuccess of his book he shunned intercourse with his colleagues. It is intolerable to feel that one has humiliated oneself for nothing. He did not go once to the "Leon Arms." But in taverns even more modest he sat sometimes with a violinist named Guzman or a scene-painter called Covarrubias. He had no settled living-place, and slept wherever he happened to be. And by copying work, by carrying messages between lovers, as agent, the hero of Lepanto and Algiers earned a few *reales* now and again.

At the end of November there came a letter from his mother. All was in order. Catalina had remained constant. The wedding would take place on the second Sunday in Advent.

He hired a little donkey and once more covered the road—now coated with ice—between Madrid and Toledo. This time he took the shortest route. But he felt after a while so sorry for the little beast he rode that he dismounted and led it by the halter.

In the bald little church of Esquivias the uncle-priest joined their hands together. The December wind whistled through the defective door; it was so dark that nothing could be seen of the Ascension over the altar but the illumined clouds above the Virgin's head.

No one else was present. Miguel's mother was not there, because she feared to leave her husband alone. The bride's mother absented herself in protest. By refraining from taking the hundred paces to the church she made clear to everybody her opposition. But nobody cared; they were not curious in the land of La Mancha.

Three solemn-faced peasants acted as witnesses—Cervantes knew only one of them. A few old women knelt at the back benches—this was the congregation.

As they left the church the bride put her uppermost petticoat over her head. For quite half the way they walked backwards against the storm. There was no bridal feast. The bride's mother had shut herself up. Miguel and Catalina looked after the infant, had a bite to eat, and might go to bed together.

And now arose a deadly foe—more frightful to Miguel Cervantes than fanatic Turk or bloodthirsty renegade. A foe without form or language, against whom no weapon availed: boredom.

He found it in Catalina's arms. At their first embrace he was prey to terror. For if this bond could not be knit between them, seeing they had only each other in the world, what was to be done? Lying beside her, he realized fully for the first time that this overgrown child, of whom he knew nothing save that she read childish books, was from now on his entire world. With anxious tenderness, with all the art he knew, he sought the way to her emotions. But therein lay his mistake. The much-travelled man, of so many adventures, and with senses somewhat jaded, could not understand the simple open nature of a peasant girl only half his age. He began by questioning, hesitating, trying, blaming himself. She was, as always, pleasant and friendly. She could not answer. And when all the struggles and efforts were over, of which, probably, he alone had been conscious, only boredom was left, boredom of body and of soul.

It was in everything, a brooding atmosphere, formless, all-pervading, it became his very existence. When he was dressed in the morning, he had finished his work for the day. He looked at the village street, where scarce ever a human figure showed. If you walked two hundred paces, there was the end of the village, the plain of La Mancha began, flat, unbroken, endless, swept by icy winds. The eye might rest on eight or ten windmills encircling the horizon—round windmills with revolving pointed roofs, their motionless sails creaking in their frames.

Having seen all that once, one knew it for ever. So with the village street, which as it was now would be in all future winters, with its little white windowless huts and gutters full of dirty, hardened snow.

Only the abode of the Salazar y Palacios, where he lived, had one window, in the front. It had likewise a sort of gable, and a tall wooden gate in openwork, with frozen ears of maize hanging on either side. By this one knew they were hidalgos. And he too was an hidalgo, and husband of Doña Catalina. He could do no work in the house. There were servants for that. But if he had given orders they would not have been followed. Señora de Palacios was the head of the house. If he had thought he should own anything he was mistaken. He might perhaps have insisted on having matters regulated before a notary. But he had not done so. He had been weary unto death and consented to take refuge. So now he sat at his hidalgo window, and knew that at ten o'clock the old woman would come out of the left-hand house opposite, to fetch her loaf of barley bread; but that the right-hand house would remain closed until the bell rang for vespers.

The women of his own house went twice daily to church. A few times he went too, then left off, bored and embarrassed. The Reverendo Palacios, more forbearing than his sister, did not take the backsliding amiss. "A man like you, nephew, need not make manners before God," he said complaisantly. And in Cervantes' state these words of an ignorant village priest fell like balm into his heart.

"A man like you." Useless, tolerated, he sat about in the common living-room, the only one that was warm. Señora de Palacios moved about, keeping a watchful eye on kitchen and barnyard, railing in her dry voice at the servants. Then she would come and sit down again by the stove, spinning or knitting, as Catalina did. Both of them tended the child.

For this was Cervantes' consolation, all unexpected: both mother and daughter loved the ugly little Isabella. She had, as it were, two mothers, and was the chief topic of all their talk. He had brought this green-eyed dowry into the house, and it had shoved him out—his fatherhood was a fact forgotten. Seldom and timidly he approached the cradle and addressed the infant with a man's clumsy tenderness. It seemed to him that his child shrank from him. Most likely it was only from his bearded face; but what he read in Ana Franca's grey-green eyes was Ana Franca's contempt and scorn. No, he had failed, he knew, to win the woman's being for his own, just as now he failed with the open and simple Catalina.

Of the latter's partiality indeed, not much remained—obstinately as she had stuck to the idea of the marriage. She no longer thought of Miguel as a second Florimon or Olivante; and had actually only a surface consciousness of her state as a married woman. Everything was so much the same. She was, in her mother's hands, the same as ever. The little man with one hand sitting yonder by the window—though there was nothing to look at—interfered very little with the tenor of her ways.

No one obliged him to stop in the house. But whither should he have gone? Conversation with the priest was easily exhausted: such visits as Miguel paid him grew briefer and briefer. It got dark at five. Then a single oil lamp was lighted, in addition to the one that burned always before the Madonna.

He went to the tavern. It was of the most modest kind, the only wine was a single sour sort from the district of Quero. But the host was a quiet, understanding man, refreshingly different from the cutpurses in the large cities, who affright the traveller with their greed. The peasants of Esquivias, sitting round the tavern table, were of the same stamp. Cervantes realized suddenly that he had known many ranks in Spain: soldiers, officials, priests, scholars, something of court and nobility—but nothing of the Spanish people. It had no voice. One trod upon it as upon the earth over which it stooped.

The peasants of other countries he had known. They had not been like these whom he saw, slipping in at the low tavern door in their dark smocks girdled with a thong, and their untanned leather shoes. They had not had such seamed and rugged faces, nor this proud bearing as of free men, nor such clumsy-tongued accents of utter sincerity.

He only made them uncomfortable. It had never happened that a "son of a somebody" had seated himself among them. Some behaved with suspicion, they were all rather remote, displaying a solemn, reserved politeness. Cervantes came again, sat among them and drank his glass. Nobody asked, even if he divined, what brought him among them. Misgivings disappeared. They talked again of their affairs, with long silences between. Of bad business; of how an egg fetched three *maravedis* in the city whereas they got only half a *maravedi* for it. No, they got nothing. A golden stream flowed the length and breadth of Spain, and they were watered by not one single drop. No one thought of them, they were laughed at and despised. Once it had been otherwise, in the time of their grandfathers. Then the peasant had been free, he had had the right to choose his burgomaster, the land belonged to him, the law protected him. Today three-quarters of La Mancha belonged to two proud dukes who lived in the entourage of the King. Their officers and overseers oppressed the peasantry. Whoever had a scrap of property paid heavy taxes, interest and duties.

All this Cervantes heard. Before long they talked with him as with their own. He looked at their chiselled brows and thought that a genuinely noble nobility, a prince of free, unwarped spirit, might have made this the most glorious folk in the world.

They knew all about him now, had heard the story of his stump, and more besides. They liked him because he did not boast. It did him good to sit among them. He never drank a second glass; he could not beg for pocket-money at home. At this unpainted table he won back a little of his joy and security. Had not people always liked him wherever he came in the world and sat among true men? That was where he belonged.

And in the company were, after all, a few who stood out from the staid and serious majority: comfortable, good-natured souls, though of the poorest, who joked and told stories. Not of the finest quality, yet dearer to Cervantes than the stage and literary clap-trap of the "Leon Arms."

Dearer too, he confessed to himself, than the entertainment that awaited him at home.

For years Señora de Palacios had been in the habit of reading aloud to her daughter twice weekly, always out of the same book, the household treasure, by which she swore: *The Complete Housewife* of the Augustinian Luis de Leon. This practice, which had suffered an interruption with the wedding, had now been resumed; it seemed as though the mother wanted to show that she regarded the marriage as invalid and Catalina as a young girl still under tutelage. The book itself was a capital work, full of knowledge of the human heart and of every housewifely skill. But it turned out that Señora de Palacios always read the same chapters. The gist of the matter to her was certain important precepts of the Augustinian Father; she ended her reading with them each time: warnings against love of finery, excess of rouge; against love-letters, sonnets cherished privily in the bosom, and canzonets; but above all against the highly dubious practice of reading the romances of chivalry.

Perhaps she found this last particularly pertinent, since such folly had been the means of introducing her questionable son-in-law into the house.

But her reading had little effect. Catalina continued to live in her magic world. The row of volumes grew longer and longer. Every travelling pedlar pushing his handcart through La Mancha was asked for a romance, and was generally able to produce the latest volumes from beneath his masses of shawls and stuffs.

One day, a Sunday when spring had come round, he found her sitting over her last acquisition. It was, she told him with glowing cheeks, the most beautiful and brilliant she had read in a long time. Its hero was the favourite grandchild of the great Palmerin of Oliva; and she confessed that in face of his deeds even the prowess of his ancestor paled.

Miguel silently took the book from her hand. He had long known how seriously she took it all. It was not a diversion but sober earnest; this whole world of fantasy to her was as real as that which she could touch with her hands. These godlike knights in golden harness, these ineffably beautiful princesses, chaste as ice—for Catalina, as for a hundred thousand other Catalinas in Spain, they really lived. This clap-trap about giants and dragons, guardian angels, sorcerers, good fairies; about flying horses and winged lions, crystal palaces, floating islands and burning lakes, was her daily nourishment. A whole people clutched in fancy after the impossible.

Cervantes glanced through the book. It reeked of nonsense.

"Do you really care for that, Catalina?" he asked her. "You do not see that each one of these bunglers copies from the last one and only tries to outdo him in sheer absurdity?"

"You are merely jealous."

"Why? Do you think I could not make up as much as I liked of that sort of trash?" The *Galatea* crossed his mind, that comparatively harmless product of another fashion.

But he had misunderstood his wife. She did not mean jealousy of literary fame. Of that she knew nothing. She meant jealousy of the heroic deeds depicted in her books. For books and deeds were one to her.

"Yes, jealous! What is your battle with the Turks beside Palmeranth's fight with the fifteen three-eyed giants? That is what I call heroic."

"That is heroic, is it?" Cervantes cried, between laughter and rage. "I will show you some time what it means to be heroic!"

He knew whereof he spoke. Until that moment the idea had been only vaguely sketched in his mind. Now it suddenly crystallized.

Some weeks before he had found in Uncle Salazar's little library an anthology of classic authors, and brought it home. It contained among other things a selection from Appian, translated from the Greek into bad Latin, which even so could not detract from the brilliance of the matter.

It was a description of the memorable siege of Numantia. For ten long years three thousand Spaniards defended the fortress with the courage of desperation against Roman forces thirty times as great. At last, when all was lost, they devoted themselves and their city to destruction.

Cervantes needed not to prepare. One single day, spent in a long walk through La Mancha, now faintly spring-like, wove the complete fabric of his tragedy.

The next morning, and all the next mornings, he sat in the back garden at a rickety table, and amazed the servants, who stared at the *señorita's* husband filling page after page, as in a kind of silent frenzy, without lifting his eyes. Chickens picked and cackled about his feet. A goat planted itself before him and fixed him with uncanny yellow eyes. Señora de Palacios entered the garden with a rattle of keys, stopped, shrugged her shoulders and turned back.

The text of Appian lay open beside him. He had no other books, nor needed any. He knew what his Numantian heroes looked like: they had the faces of the peasants of Esquivias. Seventeen centuries had passed, Latin, Gothic and Moorish blood had flowed in their veins; but they were as they had been. This harsh and austere land ever brought forth, beneath its inexorably burning sun, the same proud, stalwart breed. He was now its mouthpiece; from subterranean sources the stream gushed forth, in such abundance that his hand could scarcely keep pace with the flow. What issued was poetry. He was a poet. For the first time utterly a poet.

"Today," he said, smiling, to Catalina, "you shall hear what heroism is"—and prepared to read aloud. The three sat round him in the garden, Catalina, her mother, and the priest. It was toward evening of a warm afternoon.

He began—and straightway forgot where he was and to whom reading. He read wonderfully well. His voice was not deep, yet warm and ringing; it brought out the meaning clearly and with force.

He read of the frightful last days of the siege; depicted the camp and the city. The long-beleaguered folk invoke their gods. Their priests would sacrifice, but the leaders reject the omens. The earth opens, a demon appears, scatters the sacred utensils and carries away the ram with him into the depths. These are sinister portents. But the city demands to know its fate, it will face destruction open-eyed. Marquino the sorcerer, a black lance in his right hand, in his left the book, opens the kingdom of the dead. He summons back to life a boy deceased that day. Reluctantly, with groanings, the soul now clarified by wisdom returns to its abandoned tenement, and announces the destruction of the city through the hands of its own inhabitants. With the quenching of the last hope, Numantia will be ashes. No booty will fall to the victors, not one woman slave, not one single trinket. The pyre is already rising in the market-place, where all the treasure will be consumed:

> The pearl of beauty from the rosy East,
> The gold into a thousand vessels made,
> The diamond and ruby bright, increased
> With stores of purple fine and rich brocade.

Meantime, want is everywhere. The starving lie in heaps. Infants suck blood instead of milk from their mothers' gaunt breasts. Two Numantian youths with naked swords rush out of the city and force themselves into the Roman camp, to steal bread from the tents. One falls; the other, wounded to death, gains the city gate, bearing the blood-stained bread. . . .

Cervantes got so far. He drew a deep breath. These

bloody loaves of bread were a new and a powerful image. No one before him had imagined it.

He lifted his eyes. He looked at his audience.

The priest was sleeping peacefully, his heavy head drooped. But the women were exchanging a meaning look, which Cervantes caught. Catalina was inanely smiling at the same time; but an expression of ineffable meanness sat on her mother's greedy face. The corners of the thin mouth were drawn down in utter contempt—she seemed just to have shaped with contemptuous lips the words "blood-stained bread." All the baseness of gratified malice and overweening pride seemed concentrated in this woman's face.

The sheets fell from his hands. His chin dropped, he sat there as though paralysed. He saw with frightful clarity whither he had drifted. He got up and went into the house.

He left Esquivias in the night. He had spoken to no one. Words were meaningless. He would demand his child. . . . He went on, over by-roads, as the day slowly brightened, towards Toledo.

When he unlatched his mother's door, he was met by a priest in full canonicals. The house smelt of incense. His father had just died.

CHAPTER TWENTY-FOUR

The Commissary

Philip, overlord and king of the Catholic world, master of all shipping of the East, ruler over the islands and seas of the West, was an old man and ill. He was tormented by gout, his exhausted blood began to break out in sores that would not heal. The end of his earthly course was in sight. But he had not yet accomplished that to which God had called him. The time was now at hand.

He had not been idle. All his life he had laboured for the purity and unity of the Faith throughout the world. Wherever hands had been lifted against the new spirit—hands holding the sword, the assassin's dagger, the golden bribe—those hands were lifted at the instance of the quiet, the sickly master of the Escorial. He alone had sown civil war and misery in France; dismembered the Netherlands and killed their great Orangeman; again and again had conspired against the life of the apostate queen on the throne of England.

But she still lived. Mary Stuart had paid on the scaffold for the failure of the last plot. She too had died for Philip's sake. Now, in the evening of his heavy days, he was summoning all the powers and possessions of the peoples under his sway, against this England.

There more than anywhere heresy flourished unchallenged. And gained ground everywhere. Had not God given it to Castile to rule over the seas of the world? But England challenged that right. Already her captains ravaged the Spanish coast, appeared in Africa and the West Indies; they came near by their audacious forays to severing the bonds that held together the Catholic monarchy. War against England! Philip, King of England! If only that island might become his footstool, then indeed he would stand in his last days as high as he should stand, and among the clouds present to God upon his two hands a saved and pure and Catholic world.

For years the King had hesitated. But now he could wait no longer. He was warned by ministers and generals: the Netherlands must first be completely subdued. For in a storm or other sudden harm the fleet would need the haven of the Dutch ports. But the King would not listen. Was it not upon God's matter he moved, and would God permit defeat or tempest? He was urgent. He, once so deliberate, so courteous, lost his patience and railed at his servants. Their caution, he said, was lukewarmness; they were lacking in zeal for God's service.

Among those who hesitated and warned was the Marquis de Bazán, his Admiral. The King goaded this man beyond endurance: the warrior fell ill of a fever and died. The Armada was without a leader.

But since God Himself would lead, what need was there of an experienced leader? And Philip appointed as Grand Admiral of the fleet Don Alonzo Pérez de Guzman, Duke of Medina-Sidonia.

The Duke was terrified. He was an elegant grandee, of

quite peculiarly incontestable purity of lineage and blood, fabulously rich, one of the two men who owned La Mancha. But he was no sailor. In a long, pathetic letter he implored his sovereign to release him. He knew little of wars and nothing at all of seamanship—he always got seasick at once. It was no use. The Armada received for its head "instead of the iron admiral, a golden one."

In the shipyards on the Atlantic building went feverishly on. A multitude of ships, large heavy ships, impressive, unwieldy. That they were impractical was granted. And the low-lying, manageable English boats were well known. But one could not pay so much honour to these infidel freebooters as to adapt oneself to them. Powerful, much-decorated galleys, carrying troops heavily armed as for a land battle, were the only fitting retinue for God Himself.

It all cost money. State galleons and cast-iron cannon are expensive. Ten thousand sailors and twenty thousand soldiers have to be fed; and the best eaters of all are the volunteer nobility, who trooped in hordes to the lofty enterprise and were already lounging about the port towns, loud-mouthed, boasting, and dazzling of attire; whiling away the time with duelling and women-hunts.

But the treasuries were empty. The gouty man in the Escorial sat day and night over letters and papers, trying to fill them. He increased the import and export taxes: on wares to and from India, on wares from one province to another twenty and twenty-five per cent were levied. But that was not all. He quite simply confiscated the money of merchants coming from the colonies, giving them instead drafts on his own empty treasury. He sold offices to the highest bidder and created new ones to be sold, he sold titles and prebends and posts, such as *regidor* and *corregidor*, *alcalde* and secretary: King Philip had seventy thousand of these to dispose of. He took money where he could get it, and repawned the already pawned: the bankers of France, Germany and Lombardy looked askance at the royal bills of exchange. They were careful not to lose any money: a draft from Madrid, through Genoa to Flanders, cost Philip thirty per cent. Money, money—but never money enough! This King, who controlled the world's gold and silver supply, had more than once to interrupt his nightly labours over his documents, because no money was left to buy fresh candles.

His country, owning the hegemony of the world, was starving. Upon the seven million men who worked in Spain there lay like a gigantic polypus the one million noble and clerical idlers. Tax-gatherers gathered in without pity the subsistence of the poor. They took the provisions: corn, barley, maize, oil, wine, biscuits, cheese. "You will be paid," they told the unfortunates, "when the holy enterprise succeeds; here, meanwhile, is a coupon." Andalusia had to deliver twelve thousand hundredweight of rusks, Seville six thousand casks of wine; this little town four thousand *arrobas* of oil, that one eight thousand *fanegas* of grain.

The food commissioners rode on muleback through the prostrate land, squeezing the last drop out of the already dry. Where they came they aroused a dull sense of rage and despair. They broke into store-houses, granaries, cellars. They left the peasant no corn for the sowing. It was God's will.

One of these commissaries was Miguel Cervantes.

They had flung him the office like a bone to a homeless dog. He was at his wit's end. Everything had failed. In the whole kingdom of Spain there was for him, it seemed, no portion of daily bread. No more literary windfalls—nobody would even look at his *Numantia.* He had no degree, no rank, no patron. Gladly would he have become a day-labourer—mason, painter, porter: he had only one hand.

He canvassed the cities of the peninsula, crawling along in wagons where he was given a lift for charity's sake. The cities' disreputable quarters were his. Thousands of pickpockets, pimps and card-sharpers swarmed in these depths, go-betweens to the police, spies to the Inquisition. He was tempted to let himself sink into it, to the sound of copper pieces clinking in a bag. To get hold of an official position was wellnigh impossible.

Reaching Madrid he took to sitting about in antechambers as of yore, more to kill time than with any genuine hope. The clerks learned to recognize his voice without lifting their heads. Like his father before him, he would sit half the day on a bench; actually, when they one day beckoned for him to step into the War Office about a post, it came so unexpectedly that he did not understand what they said.

The authorities had little choice. Buying supplies for the Armada was truly not a very popular office. Everyone knew what it meant. Hardy ruffians were required. Some clerk must have mentioned Cervantes, an old soldier from the days of Don John, once an Algerian slave. He would be tough enough to skin the peasants properly.

He presented himself to Señor de Guevara, the head of the commissariat and Chief Commissioner. Cervantes had dreaded the necessity, for his clothing was not respectable by now, he looked like a tramp. But the elegant official did not even look at him. Breathing as little as possible, to avoid the odour of poverty, he spoke to Cervantes from his unapproachable height. He should report at once at Seville. That district was to be his field. Further instructions would come through Señor de Valdivia, Provincial Administrator of Andalusia. Pay, twelve *reales* a day.

Twelve *reales*. It was double what a carpenter earned, or a handy man in a port town. It was enough to live on, enough to send something to his mother, who had moved back to Alcalá and now lived in the neighbourhood of her saintly daughter Luisa, ailing, and cared for by the charity of the nuns.

Enough, too, to send money to Esquivias for little Isabella. For the two hidalgas had not surrendered the child. He had arrived unannounced and unkempt at the village, and there had been a row. But his conscience was not quite easy: could he really drag Isabella about with him through the underworld of Spain? She seemed to be happy with her foster-mothers, and she was thriving. She looked suspiciously at the strange, dusty man who wanted to kiss her, stiffened her body and wriggled out of his arms. But money he could send. Isabella should be dependent upon him. It was his last poor ambition.

And now for months he had been travelling the dusty roads of southern Spain. He had his animal from the government. He no longer resembled a strolling vagabond, being dressed in a dark velvet doublet closed to the throat, with a ruff and a cloth mantle, as befitted an official of the King. He had spent the greater part of his advance upon this suit. On the mule's left haunch the insignia of his authority dangled from two leather loops: the long staff with the gilded top. Sometimes he carried it thrust under his arm, so that it looked like a lance.

He had reached the depths: extortioner and oppressor of the poor. He made no bones about the realities of his task. Excuses perhaps he had. He was almost starving. He was acting for the King, certainly; he had no responsibility. If he did not do this, someone else would—and probably be harsher than he. Yes, yes. But it was all one. He could hear the voices of the men of Esquivias, talking round the inn-table about tax officials and extortioners who squeezed out their last drop of blood. Such a bloodsucker he was now become.

He travelled about the country east of Seville, from Marchena to Estepona, from Aguilar to La Rambla, from Castro to Espejo, and everywhere it was the same. The peasants barred the granaries, rolled away the barrels, took the wheels off the carts which might serve for transport. Some of them whetted their scythes. Women screamed when they saw him coming. He spent his nights only half-asleep, only half-undressed, pistol within reach, in some office of the municipality.

He lived in hell and got twelve *reales* a day for it. He was no longer a human being. He was a cog in the clumsy, creaking machinery of the state: a rake, scratching and scraping for the Armada. Only not to think! To think was to commit suicide. If he once began to think, he would have to stop. And so he succeeded in not thinking. He dropped down an iron curtain in his own mind. Behind it lay all that he had ever been. Sometimes, alone at night, he would grip into his animal's shaggy forelock with rough affection, pat its neck, and look into the mild bright depths of its beautiful eyes—and this was his sole remaining emotional outlet.

One day on the Cordoba road he was drawing near to the town of Ecija, a place of some five or six thousand souls, where he should be occupied for several days. It was the middle of a July day. He had hung his mantle and doublet at his saddle-bow and was swaying along half-conscious, in a torpor of heat. Ecija was called the "frying-pan of Andalusia"; he had been told that people died there from the heat.

Through the scorching haze he saw the little wall-encircled town lying on the other side of the river, on the slope of rounded, cultivated hills. The bridge over the Genil was guarded by strong turreted gates.

When he passed through the first of these the watch made no response to his greeting but looked at him with fierce and sinister eyes. On the other side, at the second gate, the customs official ostentatiously turned his back. Cervantes saw that they were expecting him; he was used to receptions of this sort.

There was no one in the narrow, cobbled streets. His animal's tread echoed back from the windowless walls. He came to a square, grillingly hot. The green and blue glazed tiles on the church tower caught the light with blinding effect. He decided to put up.

The *posada* was full of the droning of flies; he got a meal of bread, bacon and cheese, with a good light wine. The inn-keeper's wife sat down beside him, an attractive woman of forty. He asked a few casual questions. She answered by sighs.

They gladly gave all for their King. And they knew about affairs, too, here in Ecija; it was not a backwater.

But the *señor* would see, there was simply nothing left. The town was scraped bare. Such bread as he was now eating she would not have ventured to set before him two years ago. She could see that he himself was different; but his predecessors had stopped at nothing. She knew eight, no, ten families who had been so exploited that they were a burden on the town. He must be very cautious—the people were roused. She was really frightened for him.

She drew her chair closer. This bloodsucker who threatened her home did not seem such a bad fellow. He was dead-tired. He sank back a little and closed his eyes. His head fell against his hostess's ample bosom. He lay pillowed upon those two high cushions, the flies buzzed over the lees in his glass; she looked at his gnarled stump of a hand, at his staff of office leaning against the wall, and shook her head dreamily, she herself knew not why.

Things in Ecija did look hopeless. Stacks and cellars and storehouses were bare, and the peasants, whose last year's coupons had not yet been honoured, were plainly resolved on resistance. This was not the proud and reserved Castilian breed, but a more pliant stock, with something Arabic about the cranial structure, shrewd and lively. They followed him, gesturing, while he went from barn to barn, inspecting, examining. Two policemen stalked in his rear; he had insisted on having them, but they pulled long, dissatisfied faces. The burgomaster was not at home, it was said. Two days before he had ridden to Osuna. It was not known when he would return—perhaps today, perhaps next week.

The crowd that followed in his rear grew denser. He could feel behind him the bitter anger of these exploited folk. Yes, both royalty and religion had here lost their appeal. True, Cervantes felt certain that they were cheating him. It could not be that they were so completely cleaned out as this. But, even so, they were justified. And when he remembered that he had been adjured by the assessors, by the War Office, by the Treasury, by Señor Valdivia in person, to extract from Ecija without fail five hundred *fanegas* of meal and four thousand *arrobas* of oil, he laughed within himself. He even laughed aloud, quite unexpectedly, to the alarm of his surly hangers-on. Had they been sent a crazy commissioner, for a change?

They came to the banks of the Genil. Three storehouses, close together, lay here outside the city wall. Good stout buildings, and all alike. "Open these," ordered Cervantes, thrusting the end of his staff against the first door. Suppressed whispering and laughter answered him. Then he was told: the worshipful Commissioner would probably think twice. To be sure, there was plenty of stuff here, of all sorts; nobody had levied on it. But it was the property of the Church, the provisions of the monastery of La Merced, to which the best land in the whole countryside belonged.

Cervantes had already seen across the river where a priest came hurrying up, his soutane flying, and two monks behind him. As he came he waved and gestured with both arms, and scarcely took time to greet Cervantes when he reached him. Surely the Commissioner understood his instructions better than to lay hand on the property of the Church! If not, he warned him not to encroach.

The crowd had formed a semicircle round them, and waited tensely. Some of the men were grinning maliciously. Of course the Commissioner would not dare do anything. It was all a sham fight, arranged beforehand. State and Church were allies; they were the same. They banded together to skin the peasant alive.

Cervantes explained that there could be no thought of encroachment. These requisitions were made in a holy cause, which God had blessed, the crusade against England. Then who more bound to contribute than the Church itself?

But the priest was forearmed. With a scornful side-glance he submitted that King Philip had actually received his dues of assistance for the crusade. And the tenth of the income of the Church was, of course, always collected. He knew to an *escudo* the exact sum which His Holiness Sixtus the Fifth had himself contributed to the cause. Nothing had been spared. The people must contribute now.

The people had contributed, had sweated and bled, Cervantes replied, with a nervous irritation which surprised even himself. Some of them had not even seed-corn left, and many once well-to-do folk were now in the workhouse. It could not be Christian, or pleasing in the sight of God, if the clergy sat on its full sacks and looked on. He would be obliged for the key.

The priest said that he had not got it.

"Open the doors," Cervantes said to the policemen. They looked irresolutely at each other. It was a bad, a ticklish situation.

Cervantes lifted his right foot and kicked the door with all his strength, so that it cracked. Two more kicks and it sprang open.

"There comes our Burgomaster," cried one of the policemen, drawing a deep breath as though his conscience were relieved.

Cervantes turned round. A little man in dark clothing was advancing from the city gate, waving his hands as he came, like the priest before him.

"The secular arm will admonish you," said the latter, with recovered dignity.

Cervantes leaned on his staff and waited for the Alcalde to come up. He knew quite well that he had exceeded his instructions. But the sense of injustice, numbed by the hateful compulsion of his office, had stirred within him. It was not merely sympathy with the inhabitants of Ecija—to whom he did not particularly take—it was that burning sense of wrong of the old days, the good old days of slavery and rebellion.

The Alcalde came up. He waited to catch his breath, shutting his eyes, which stood like two little pools of water in his wrinkled though not elderly visage. When he opened them again and directed their gaze upon the Commissioner, on whose alarming account he had been summoned, they seemed to start from his head with surprise, which passed swiftly over into rejoicing. Cervantes, the priest, the monks, the policemen, the populace, saw with the uttermost of stupefaction the Alcalde stretch out his arms. A blissful smile overspread his features, he put his head on one side as though ravished with delight. He opened his mouth, and spoke in verse:

> "In him it waxeth, in him it doth come
> To such a height of excellence that he,
> The Licentiate Mosquera, well may claim
> To rival e'en Apollo's self in fame."

The priest frowned. Obviously the Alcalde was wandering in his wits. Most likely a sunstroke. How else explain the fact that he had come up in the clear resolve to do the right thing, but had then embraced this impudent official and begun to prattle verses in which his own name, Mosquera, so ridiculously figured?

"Señor Cervantes! Don Miguel! Your Grace does not know me?" he cried out.

An idea came to Cervantes. It made him red in the face.

"First we must settle our business, Señor Alcalde," he said officially. "My office empowers me with full authority."

"Full authority," Don Bartolomé, the Alcalde, repeated after him, with a shoulder-shrug. "Give him the keys." He could scarcely wait to get to the end of the business.

The priest acquiesced with a wry face. One of the monks produced the keys. Without a word all three faced about and the three black figures presently disappeared through the gate.

The storehouses were opened. The large rooms were filled with bags, boxes and casks extending into the dim background in perfectly ordered rows.

"That will be enough for everybody," Cervantes said. A wave of whispers and murmurs reached his ears. Every man there protested that from the first he had known that this one-handed commissioner was not at all like the others. They could tell by the way he came; by the greeting the burgomaster had given him, by the way he was now pressing him for the honour of his entertainment. He was only a bachelor, he was saying, but he knew how to live.

By this time Cervantes understood what had happened. What an extraordinary joke! This burgomaster was no other than the licentiate Cristobal Mosquera de Figueroa, one of the hundred poets to whom he had burned incense in his *Galatea*. Probably his family had bought him this post here in the south, to give him a living and to get rid of him. Evidently he looked back with longing to the days of literature and the "Liars' Paradise." They had been the great time of his life.

They went back to the mansion house, and Mosquera led his guest into the living-room. "I have held my honour in honour," he said pompously, and pointed to a printed sheet that hung framed against the wall, with a little lamp burning beneath as though before a shrine. Yes, it was the page out of the *Galatea*—page three hundred and twenty-eight. Cervantes read:

> And yet one more behold, summed up in whom
> Apollo's rarest learning ye will see;
> Which doth the semblance of itself assume,
> When spread through countless others it may be.
> In him it waxeth, in him it doth come
> To such a height of excellence that he,
> The Licenciate Mosquera, well may claim
> To rival e'en Apollo's self in fame.

When he had read it, he stood some time without turning round—he did not dare to, for his eyes were full of most unwonted tears. So that was what his poetry served for—to make a village magistrate help him collect his taxes! That was the result of all his pains and humiliations, that was the sum total of his life. And for the little man behind him this printed page represented all that life had vouchsafed him in the way of name and reputation and lovely imperishable youth. He paid homage to that cold-blooded expenditure of printers' ink, it was the best thing in his life.

Well, at all events, thanks to this fact, the citizens of Ecija would still have a little something left to eat.

The provisions levied from the Church went down the Genil to Palma del Rio, from the Guadalquiver to the sea, and by the third day arrived in Lisbon, where a part of the fleet was gathered.

But the day before that, which was a Sunday, Miguel Cervantes was solemnly denounced and excommunicated from the chancel of the cloister church of La Merced.

CHAPTER TWENTY-FIVE

Blood Test

The sentence was given out in the cathedral church at Seville. He hastened thither.

The anathema had not precisely cut him to the heart. Long ago he had given up the literal piety of his youth. He did not cling to formulas and ritual. But this rejection from the community of the faith would ruin his existence. It was impossible for a Spanish official to fall out with the Church.

He took counsel with his friend, mine host of the "Greek Widow," Tomás Gutiérrez, the one-time actor.

How far back lay that evening when Cervantes had first seen him, standing on the empty stage between the producer and Lope! His ambitions had since altered their aim. No longer did he think of playing the slender princelings; his figure was no longer suited even to the bluff army colonels, the swaggerers, the betrayed husbands, the comic fathers. He had become immensely fat and very asthmatic; from early morn to late at night he was on his barrel-like legs; noisy, jolly, vastly good-natured, he presided over kitchen and cellar, tap-room and stall. His tavern was the best in the populous suburb of Triana. The table at the

"Greek Widow" was of the best; and it was Liberty Hall, so long as no blood flowed.

Since the days in the "Liars' Paradise," he had known and loved Miguel Cervantes. Simple, robust men had always loved him—Fumagalli, Rodrigo, Captain Urbina, the men round the inn-table at Esquivias.

There was always a place in the "Greek Widow" for the commissary. And let business be as rushing as it might, with captains and merchants, governors and adventurers, officials and money-changers, ladies of gallantry under honourable escort—Cervantes found a bed and a plate ready for him, whenever he returned, weary and disgusted, from his work. When it came to paying, however, there was trouble. Cervantes threatened to leave. But his host drowned all difficulties in an outburst of wheezy laughter in his mighty bass, and they never came up again. From that day on he paid Cervantes the extra honour of a tablecloth. He took care of his mule; he had his clothes washed, he lent him money, he spoke for him. And in this trouble with the Church he gave him excellent advice.

They called in a certain Fernando de Silva, a *confidente* of the Inquisition, an enigmatic and much-feared individual, who went about in civilian garb with a large shining metal cross on his breast. He knew things known to few, and was at the service of all. On the fifth day he brought word that the sentence against Cervantes had been quashed. But in addition to certain prayers, penances, special fasts and pilgrimages—Gutiérrez shrugged his powerful shoulders—he would of course have to make restitution of the sequestered goods. Miguel burst out laughing: five hundred *fanegas* of wheat and five thousand *arrobas* of oil, of course that was a mere trifle for him! But Señor de Silva made a soothing gesture and produced a receipt. Of course, bribery was a rather expensive business—but, as Gutiérrez remarked, the "Greek Widow" could probably bear the outlay without foundering.

So then all seemed to be in order and Cervantes was about to ride off in the direction of Ronda when he received another communication, even more serious. There was no rest for him; it seemed they would have his blood. He was in fact summoned to the blood test before the "Purity Commission."

Silva was called in again. He shrugged his shoulders. He could do nothing. But even without him it would surely be easy for Señor de Cervantes Saavedra to prove that he came of an old Christian family, into which no Jewish or Moorish blood had flowed for four generations. Such a proof was required of all Spanish officials. And he departed squinting.

It was a filthy piece of chicanery. For such proof was *not* required of every official; otherwise there would have been none. But once the question was raised and satisfaction was not given, there was an end to office-holding.

Of course in the Spain of that day the idea of unmixed race was absurd. Iberians, Basques, Celts, Phœnicians, Romans, Vandals, Jews, Goths, Arabs, Berbers had mingled here. The product was a splendid race that controlled the four quarters of the earth. And, equally of course, there were many who realized the absurdity. The Jews, for instance, had been driven out; but there was not a grandee's family but Jewish blood flowed in its veins. The same was true of the upper orders of the Church. Bishops slunk by night to the graveyards and dug up the bones of their forefathers who had been buried according to Jewish rites.

And again of course the idea of race went contrary to the teaching of the Catholic Church. But the reigning theory was that purity of blood conditioned purity of faith. *Estatutos de limpieza*—"Purity Ordinances"—were issued, chambers of inquiry were set up, and examiners went about in the land, studying pedigrees centuries back. All that cost much money, and the accused had to pay. But since not a man in the kingdom could really prove himself without reproach in this respect—not the examiners, not the clerical judges, not the cardinals, not the royal house itself—they had finally agreed upon certain rules to the game.

Whoever had members of the Inquisition in his family, on his father's and his mother's side, was counted pure. Whoever paid no meat tax, likewise—the upper nobility, for instance, paid none. There was a huge list of such persons, a regular work of reference. And if you did not belong to the upper nobility you paid heavily to be put on the list.

The Cervantes and Cortinas families, certainly, were not on the grace-giving list. They were poor. Their title of nobility had no weight whatever. Miguel was advised to draw the judges' attention to his battles for the faith; to magnify his services at Lepanto and display his mutilated hand. It might help; who knew? He hated the idea —it disgusted him. To boast and to be humble in one breath—and to what end? To retain an office which he equally hated, the office of extortioner and skinner-in-ordinary, behind whom a storm of curses always swelled.

On his way to the court he stopped on the bridge connecting Triana with the old town. The Guadalquiver was covered with shipping far and wide, barks, feluccas and house-barges at anchor. The big sea-going boats that came up with the tide lay to the left, by the Gold Tower. Everything looked gay and brilliant that morning in the summer sunlight, but he saw it all as through a dirty veil. He longed to take his staff, which he had brought with him for the sake of appearances, break it across his knees and throw the pieces in the turbid water.

He went on, however, with lingering tread, along the bank on the other side, and past the great prison. Here, as always, was a lively scene. Visitors streamed through the open gate, among them many prostitutes, recognizable by the short flannel mantle with the prescribed fold. Prisoners stood behind the bars and shouted to the passers-by, yelling and laughing. It was in other ways a curious sort of prison, and Cervantes never passed that way without stopping. But today he morosely avoided it and threaded a maze of Moorish streets to reach the episcopal palace where his judges awaited him.

He was kept waiting a long time in an unfurnished room on the ground floor. The window had a swelling lattice, through which one saw the side of the cathedral and the soaring Giralda, that mighty minaret. Cervantes bent to one side to be able to look out. They had put the figure of a saint on top, holding a banner in its hand. But the whole graceful and magnificent building remained oriental, its every surface enchantingly broken by horseshoe windows, fragile little columns, openwork screens. Everything beautiful in this city came from the East. Moors and Jews brought the best they had to Spain: the one beauty, the other knowledge and wisdom. It would be good to be able to tell the purity commission that, instead of boasting about Lepanto!

At last they summoned him.

The table, with the three judges, stood in the distant shadows of the large and lofty room. But light shone on the accused through two high windows. In the first place that disturbed him; also, it made it possible for them to scrutinize his features for oriental traits.

The hearing began like all other hearings, that was to have so different an end. The middle Capitular, a man with hysterical eyes beneath shiny, stringy black hair, took up his papers.

"I will translate the preliminary proceedings," said he, in ordinary lower-class speech, "as Latin is hard to understand."

"It does not trouble me," said Cervantes.

The Capitular looked at him and went on in a somewhat more courteous tone:

"By order of the competent authorities and in compliance with the regulations, a rigorous investigation is ordered into the ancestry of the Commissioner for Provisions and Taxes in the Royal Service, Miguel de Cervantes Saavedra, son of Rodrigo de Cervantes Saavedra and Leonor Cortinas de Cervantes, born in wedlock in Alcalá de Henares, and baptized there in the Church of Santa Maria La Mayor on the ninth of October 1547 . . ."

A commotion had arisen. The reader paused. One of the Commission, a Dominican, sitting on the left, had given such a violent start as to shake the whole table full of documents. The sallow, puffy-faced man stared at the examinee with wide-open eyes, full of fright and horror.

"Impossible!" cried out Cervantes. "The Stinker!" Everybody jumped at the offensive word.

Obviously the Dominican had not known of the case—there were batches of them at a time. The name of Cervantes, thrice repeated, must have sounded in his ear like the last trump.

"The Stinker!" Cervantes repeated slowly, with relish. "How is Your Odoriferousness? Have you licked up the butter-tub? Spent the ducats in lecherous living? That King of Algiers was a shabby dog!"

"What does all this mean, Dr. Paz?" asked the Capitular with some heat. "What does the man mean? Is he mad? Do you know him?"

But Dr. Juan Blanco de Paz did not let him finish. He simply had to forestall Cervantes. For if the accursed man once opened his mouth, he would tell the story of the Dominican's doings in Algiers, and the sixty Christians delivered over to the knife. And then all would be up with him, career and office and all, and he would himself be spending the rest of his life in the dungeons of the Inquisition.

"Just a little joke, Your Worship," he began, in a voice quaking with fright. "Just a little joke between friends—you know how it is. That about the butter is a very old one between us. The gentleman, that is, is an old friend of mine—we were both in the bagnios of Algiers, and inseparable friends. I could have saved the judges the trouble, if his name had come before me earlier. There is no doubt about you, is there, Don Miguel? He fought for God and the faith, was heroic in battle—show them your hand, that you gave for the holy cause! De Cervantes Saavedra—that is blood of the best and purest, as it existed eight centuries ago in the Pyrenees. I vouch for him personally—I guarantee his claims; I move that the case be quashed at once."

Had he said enough to convince them? His leaden eyes were goggling out of sheer fright, his breath came fast, and its foulness pervaded the air. The other two judges scowled as they listened to the impassioned defence. It was obvious that this was not all the story. But even so, it was unimpeachable evidence; after all, this was one man among ten thousand, and what difference did it make to them?

Cervantes took his time. The moment was his to enjoy. He even felt tempted *not* to be sensible, *not* to accept the good luck the gods provided, but to utter biting words to the traitor sprawling there in the judge's seat and sting him to betray himself.

But he controlled himself and kept still. For all answer he lifted his staff of office and thrust with the gilded tip at the Stinker's belly. The gesture might be interpreted as a rough form of friendliness. But he and the Stinker knew that it was as though he had spat in the man's face.

Without a word of leavetaking he turned and left the hall.

Gutiérrez went wild over the story. He could not hear it enough. "Stuck him in the belly with your staff, eh? Good for you, Miguel!" And he brought out of the cellar his best and fieriest Aledo. But at the third bottle Cervantes fell silent.

"Have you any writing-paper, Tomás? Or a copybook?"

Gutiérrez fetched an old account-book, worn-out and stained, but with the reverse of the pages bare. Cervantes took it and went unsteadily upstairs. He shut himself in, and kept out of sight all day.

In the evening he showed Gutiérrez what he had written. "Read it," he said. "It is about you."

"About me?"

It was still light in the paved court. Gutiérrez put on

his glasses and propped the account-book against an empty cask. Presently his guests heard him roaring with laughter. Tears were coursing down his cheeks.

When he had done, he sought Cervantes with open arms. "Miguel, it is a masterpiece! What wit, what shafts of satire! That will get under their skins! And nothing coarse about it, all done with a delicate touch! I wish you had written it when I was acting; I would have played that slyboots, Chanfalla."

"So you shall!"

"You are joking. How could I? An inn-keeper—with a figure like mine!"

"Why not? A fat rascal? So much the better!"

And there was actually no difficulty about it. The Director, who was just finishing a part in the Corral del Rey, was enthusiastic. The fine satire and comedy of the little piece took him at once. And it would be an added attraction to include Gutiérrez, once so popular an actor, in the cast.

"And the censorship?" Cervantes said conscientiously. "It won't scratch you?"

"They don't need to see it, Don Miguel. They don't trouble about interludes. So long as you do not have it printed."

There was no great delay. *El retablo de las maravillas* was put on with two rehearsals. On Monday it had been written, on Friday it would be played. That was August twelfth.

It was brilliant hot weather. A sailcloth awning was spread over the whole court—a much-criticized innovation, for it only made the court the hotter. The summer performance began at four o'clock.

By way of variety no piece by Lope was given, but a play by Juan de la Cueva, a local celebrity. For years he had been running to the Director with complaints of envy, prejudice, spite and so on, and had even stirred up the authorities on his behalf. Now he was pointed out at a balcony above the ladies' loge: a yellow-faced man with a bitter mouth, constantly wiping the sweat from his brow.

His play *The Death of Ajax* had four acts instead of the usual three. He was proud of the novelty. But unfortunately Cueva was not master of his material. The weak action was hampered by long recitatives, and pathetic rhetoric took the place of the clash of emotions. The public were bored. There were a few hisses. Luckily it was too hot for any violent emotion.

The interludes after the two first acts were crude and silly horseplay, which likewise evoked no enthusiasm. The third act of *Ajax* consisted of nothing but pointless effusions. The audience groaned. There was a strong smell of sweat.

Cervantes was among the crowd near the stage. No one knew of his authorship; the little play was not even mentioned on the notice posted at the entrance, though a line at the bottom announced that Gutiérrez was to appear. Some members of the audience were here on his account.

When he came on, in the patched red smock of a wandering jack-of-all-trades, there was a burst of applause. He smirked ingratiatingly. His vast belly lifted up the smock in front; he looked like a pregnant woman. And out of this enormous body his voice burst with a roar like the bellows of a smithy.

It was the story of a small producer who comes to town with his wife and one hump-backed musician, without a company, without scenery or costumes, and yet bent on fleecing the public. He is after big game. He knows the delusion of the upper classes, their maniac, panic obsession with pure blood. He promises them a performance full of the strangest marvels. And only he can enjoy it who is quite pure-blooded. Descendants of Moors and Jews will see nothing.

And after he has been paid in advance, Chanfalla the producer sets up his theatre. It is quick work. There is no division between his imaginary stage and his august audience. The Burgomaster himself is there. Privy-Councillor Juan Castrado, who looks just like his name. Benito Muttonhead, the town executioner, with pure Christian fat on his ribs three fingers deep. Señor Ragbag, too, the notary. And their wives.

And he shows them things which no one else has ever seen before, displays his marvels on the bare, bald, naked boards, while they all look meekly on. For if they saw nothing, they would come under suspicion.

Gutiérrez's bass voice resounded, he made lively play with grimaces and gestures. He showed them first the biblical Samson, half-naked and giantlike, about to tear down the columns of the temple.

"Magnificent!" cries Señor Muttonhead. "I can see the Samson as though he were my Christian grandfather. That must mean that I am a good, old Christian."

"Take care! Here comes the raging ox. You know, last week in Salamanca he picked up the carrier on his horns. Look out, here he comes!"

They all fling themselves on the ground, as though they were afraid of the ox, though what they really fear is each other.

"Here comes an army of mice—white, spotted, sky-blue, chequered—a hundred thousand mice!"

The pure-blood dames in the audience shrink back screaming.

"Jordan-water, Jordan-water! A shower of Jordan-water." Gutiérrez spread out his hands and looked up at the sky. "Makes all the ladies beautiful but the men get red beards."

They all make as though the water were running down their backs and into their trousers. Everybody shivers with doubt as to his racial purity, squinting at his neighbour and trying to make more noise than he.

Gutiérrez quickened the pace. "A Hercules," he thunders. "Hercules with his sword in his fist. A few dozen honey-bears. Lions too, and tigers. Two fire-belching dragons. All of them make-believe, of course, but pretty dangerous all the same. You'd better hide, all of you—crawl under your chairs!"

And the whole company, twittering with fear on the score of its pure-bloodedness, and making a tremendous to-do with squawking and bleating, flee before these terrors of the empty air.

At the end a real person comes in, an official with a billet for his company—and the Burgomaster will not believe that he is real. At last he is seeing something. They are all seeing something. Perhaps they have not got Jewish blood after all. And they joke with the officer, quite beside themselves with relief over their racial irreproachableness, until he loses patience at last and the whole pure-blooded company gets a beating. For that is the way an interlude has got to end.

There were shouting and applause and cries of "Bravo!" Noisy discussion arose in the pit. This was something for the "musketeers"—they were not in the meat-tax catalogue. The audience would have liked to hear the whole little piece over again; it was a long time before they were quiet enough for the *Ajax* to proceed.

The more elegant part of the audience showed reserve and even displeasure. Cueva was visible at his window, gesticulating in obvious exasperation.

Cervantes did not wait for the end of the *Ajax*. He left the court unheeded and waited outside for Gutiérrez, who soon appeared, sweating and smeared with paint. He embraced Cervantes and gave him a sounding kiss on the brow.

Then they strolled together arm in arm through the streets full of the usual nightly crowds; across the bridge and homewards. They were radiant with delight, almost drunk with it indeed, and they sang:

> *"Limpieza, limpieza—*
> *Gran burrada y torpeza!"*

A poor song, invented of late, the burden of which, more or less, was:

> "Today every ass
> For pure-blooded would pass."

They sang it over and over.

But when they got to the "Greek Widow" the taproom was in a state of tremendous excitement. A ship-owner was there from Lisbon and had brought news of the great Armada. Under the leadership of its pure-blooded but unfortunately not seaworthy admiral, it had suffered frightful shipwreck.

CHAPTER TWENTY-SIX

2,557,029 Maravedis

In large part, the catastrophe might have been foreseen: the unwieldiness of the huge galleys was known, and the lack of a safe base in Holland, the difficulty of effecting a junction with the Flemish army. Also Philip's floating fortresses were attacked by gales. But the decisive blow came from the English fleet. In full consciousness of the combat as a struggle for civil and religious liberty, under daring and skilful command, it struck at the fighting power of the ancient faith and reduced it to ruins.

Admiral Medina-Sidonia had confessed to being incapable. But he had proved a coward as well. Before all was by any means lost, he lost his head and fled northwards in the grip of fear. He gave himself no more concern for the fleet. With half of it sunk and the rest leaking, the Spanish colossus drifted helpless along the coasts of Ireland, Scotland and Norway.

King Philip scarcely raised his head from his papers, when they brought the crushing news to him in the Escorial. And he continued in the same bearing. His was the guilt. He did not shift it on to others. He received the Admiral graciously when he returned. And had a thanksgiving held in the churches as though there had been a victory. "It does not matter," he calmly said, "that they have cut off our boughs, so long as the trunk remains, so that new can shoot."

But it was not true. The trunk had been struck. All was over with the sea-power of Spain, for ever—and with the Catholic hegemony of the world.

King Philip had staked his all upon one infallible card. He had sacrificed the material and military strength of his people.

Twenty thousand of his best, most experienced soldiers lay at the bottom of the Channel. There too lay the noble gentlemen who had fleeted the time with such pomp and splendour before they set out. And there, finally, lay the little army of Spanish wet-nurses, who had embarked in the galleons in order that English infants might no longer be suckled on heretical milk, but draw orthodox nourishment at once from Catholic breasts.

Twenty million ducats had been spent. There was not a *real* in the Treasury. Philip sent to his Viceroy in Peru, for money to be hurried to Spain. But pirates ruled the seas, bandits the roads—and nothing came. Then new loans were applied for, from European bankers, no matter at what rates. But the ruler of the Roman Catholic world no longer possessed credit. He had to turn to his own, his folk whom already he had bled white.

All taxes, direct and indirect, were increased, and the officers ordered to redouble their severity.

Like one accursed, Miguel Cervantes went his unholy way. It seemed to him that he had been doing it since time was. From Málaga to Jaen, between Granada and Jerez, there was not one stony road unknown to the hoof of his mule. For ever the same roads. . . . He seemed to be riding to meet himself, like a ghost.

He levied on cash, requisitioned produce, fought with the town authorities, came to blows with the peasants, then yielded suddenly, overcome by weariness or pity or disgust. He had the corn ground, himself stood on the scales, hid away cash, watched out the nights for fear of treachery. To Seville he only came at intervals and did not stay long. Gutiérrez was depressed to see his merry moods give way by degrees. The man lived in a welter of bills and receipts, abstracts, lists, reports, appeals, denunciations, protocols. He was never supported by his superiors. He was in perpetual conflict with the bureaucracy of Seville. The elegant Guevara, secluded in the Residency, was hostile to the executors of his orders. He was careful and troubled about one thing only: there must be no scandal. He died; his successor, Isunza, was no better. Isunza's private affairs were involved; he always knew how to divert suspicion upon his tax-gatherers. When the population rose against the latter, he rejoiced to leave them in the lurch. On a certain September day—the twentieth, it was—Miguel Cervantes was thrust into the debtors' prison at Castro del Rio, at somebody's instance; nobody knew quite why. After a few days he was set free, again no one knew why. To the avaricious Isunza succeeded a Señor de Oviedo, an intolerable pedant. Sheaves of documents passed between Madrid and Seville on account of some petty sum. The most skilled accountant could hardly find his way through the complicated columns of figures; and Cervantes had no head for figures at all. He simply shut his eyes. Then he was given notice of a deficit of seventy *thaler*. He sent in his vouchers. On a sudden the seventy *thaler* became four hundred and fifty, with no reason given. He went his unholy way, making no answer. And heard no more; the thing seemed forgotten. And he himself was in the dark as to whether his accounts were in order or no.

How could he know? He never got his pay promptly; often it was months behind. He was not supposed to lay out his takings for his own expenses, but everybody did it, Cervantes like the rest. How else could he have lived? But gradually he became wholly involved in the net. Could no longer think of giving up his office—he would have been convicted of embezzlement at once. He would just have to go on, and on, until death overtook him in some village tavern.

However, there were people who thought great things of him still. One of them was his brother Rodrigo, a letter from whom followed him about and eventually reached him. Rodrigo was still ensign—a fifty-year-old ensign—still serving with the Villars regiment in Flanders. And as much as ever convinced of his adored brother's power and influence. Timidly he asked if Miguel would do him a favour: he would surely find no great difficulty in it. "Thou, Miguel, as General-Intendant. . . ."

On one single occasion the tormented man tried to escape from the treadmill.

The members of the Council of the Indies were probably astonished or even amused to find in their correspondence the petition of a certain Cervantes that he, an unknown person, might be considered for an important colonial office.

It had cost Cervantes untold trouble to find out about the four vacant posts which he mentioned. They were very various: Governor of the Province of Soconusco in Guatemala, Paymaster of the Fleet in New Cartagena, Judge of the city of La Paz, Finance Minister of the kingdom of New Granada. He copied it all out like copper-plate, beautifully spaced; folded it neatly and addressed it to the President of the Council.

He was prepared to wait months for an answer. Naturally business dragged in the chancelleries. If only the four posts did not get filled in the meantime! He dreamed of renewing his youth, of a brighter, cleaner world.

But an answer came in a very few days: it was brief and it was insolent. "Should look for some other office, nearer home. Dr. Nuñez Morquecho, Assessor." That was all, scribbled in the lower margin of the petition.

Some other office! Among the seventy thousand which King Philip had in his gift there was for Miguel Cervantes no other than the one he loathed. And even in it he was dependent upon the arbitrary ill-will of his superiors. Returning to the "Greek Widow" from his latest tour he found a letter to the effect that his pay had been reduced from twelve to ten *reales*. In the sacred name of economy.

In these days his mother died, not in Alcalá, but in Madrid, in the house of strangers, a tanner and rag-picker.

It was not sensible for Miguel to connect this death with his own reduction of income, but he did. He could not rid himself of the idea that his mother wished no longer to be a burden to her sore-tried son. The sixty *reales* which he had sent her monthly was the exact amount he had been reduced.

Miguel began to suffer from notions and whimsies, almost obsessions. Gutiérrez looked sadly at his friend, shaking his head.

The contract, for instance, which he signed with Ossorio the producer, could hardly be considered the work of a sensible and practical man.

This was the Ossorio who had married Lope de Vega's mistress, the handsome Elena Velásquez. He had a reputation in the stage world, and the piece in which he was playing the title role was sold out every day. He had taken up his quarters in the "Greek Widow," accompanied by Elena, who sat beside him sleek and silent, and was now grown very ample, her beautiful eyes always gazing dreamily into vacancy.

With Ossorio then, Miguel Cervantes, the tax-gatherer, signed a contract. It must be admitted that there had been a good deal of drinking when it happened. Gutiérrez watched them mistrustfully as they sat in a corner together.

Cervantes was to write six comedies for Ossorio. Ossorio bound himself to produce all six, each time within twenty days from the delivery of the manuscript. Cervantes was to receive fifty ducats apiece for them. But the payment was only to be made as each piece was produced and proved itself to be "one of the best that was ever played in Spain."

Full of pride Cervantes showed the contract to Gutiérrez, who looked first at the paper and then at Cervantes' face, where self-deception and a sort of defiance were mingled.

"My poor Miguel!" was all he said. Did his friend believe that this was worth anything, this contract? "One of the best"—who was to be the judge? The public? Or Ossorio himself? The man was sitting there in the corner with his wine, his fine, fat, speechless wife beside him. Was he not laughing? Yes, of course he was: laughing at poor Miguel.

The six comedies would never be written.

Had Miguel then quite turned his back on poetry? No. For instance, there had been a competition at Saragossa, in honour of Saint Hyacinth. He had sent verses and won three silver spoons. He wrote other things: an introductory poem for Dr. Diaz's book on diseases of the kidneys, canzonets for lovers unvisited by the afflatus, that they might serenade their loves. The charge for these was two *reales* a strophe. And for the love of Our Lady romances for street beggars.

Once, one single time, the beaten man lifted his voice in another key.

An English-Dutch fleet fell upon Spanish ships before Cadiz, destroyed them and entered the port. The defence was lamentable: the cannons burst of old age as they had done in Oran, the bullets did not fit the guns, the wealthy city was left exposed to the foe, who landed and plundered. But when it was all over, Cadiz evacuated, the English gone, there entered as in triumph, with banners and foot-soldiers in gala array, the man who should have defended her, His Grace the Duke of Medina-Sidonia, Captain-General of the Ocean and the Andalusian coasts, still the favoured and fêted of the King.

The sonnet which celebrated these events—a well-turned sonnet with a subtle ring of irony—was not at once printed. It was passed round among the taverns of Cadiz and Seville on hand-written fly-sheets. It was not signed, but some people knew that its author was a certain Cervantes, apparently an official of the Crown.

Of course it did anything but make him beloved. The

upper classes stuck together, they were friends and connexions, they feasted and hunted together. In the suitable places an occasion was sought to trip up this disloyal subordinate. Occasion was found.

Once more he was summoned to the capital for an accounting. As the roads were unsafe, he deposited the sums to be delivered with the banking house of Freire de Lima, against a draft on Madrid. When he reached that city, he found no money. Freire de Lima had failed, and levanted. Certain assets were left. Cervantes managed, with difficulty, to arrange that his claim, which had to do with public moneys, should have priority. He breathed again.

But in the seat of authority they took upon themselves to act as though he had had something to do with the failure. He was suspended from his office.

Gutiérrez consoled him. Bed and board were his for the asking; he need have no worry as to that. And indeed he was almost glad. He slept himself out, felt easier in his mind, could enjoy himself and divert others, warmed his ageing bones in the good sun of Seville.

But in Madrid they did not rest. Out of a blue sky the Upper Chamber of Finance ordered an examination of all his accounts from the year 1594 onwards. That was four years back.

He ought to have been on the alert, have taken pains to be exact. He should have looked through the papers and vouchers that were yellowing in his cupboard. What had happened in Salobrena? In Baeza? In Loja, in Almuñecar?

But he could not. He was weary unto death. It must be all in order; after all, there were all the vouchers. It would have been sensible to go at once to Madrid. He behaved as though he were deaf. He stopped in Seville.

Then came the catastrophe. A royal decree arrived, through the hand of Don Gaspar de Vallejo, Counsellor of the Superior Court.

The man called Cervantes Saavedra was called upon to give evidence concerning the receipt of money amounting to 2,557,029 *maravedis*. A shortage of 79,804 *maravedis* was already proven. Cervantes was to present himself within three weeks before the financial chamber. Sureties were to be taken both for his appearance there and for the sums due. In default of sufficient sureties he was to be arrested at once.

The entries looked larger than they were. The whole sureties represented six thousand, the deficit not even two hundred.

Gutiérrez hastened to Señor de Vallejo. He was ready to pay the two hundred *thaler* at once.

Señor Vallejo looked venomous. It was not a matter of two hundred *thaler* at all, but of the whole sum, of 2,557,-029 *maravedis*.

This was sheer nonsense, a deliberately malicious interpretation of the royal edict. For the delivery of the principal had never been called in question.

Gutiérrez came back to his inn. "They want security for six thousand *thaler*, Miguel. That is—it isn't more than four thousand ducats and a half. Not so bad, really. If I just put a little mortgage on the 'Widow'—"

Miguel was already packing. He did not get up, perhaps on account of the tears in his eyes. Bent over his chest, he muttered:

"You might send me something to eat now and again, and a quart of wine. They say the food is terrible in that famous prison of yours."

CHAPTER TWENTY-SEVEN

Singular Prison

The city of Seville was full of knaves and thieves; but nowhere else did such systematic and ruthless thieving go on as in the King's prison. And here too King Philip's enterprises were to blame for the state of things.

In his zeal to raise money for the Armada, he had rented the prison to a rich Andalusian grandee, the Duke of Alcalá. The Duke was far too fine a gentleman to soil his hands by direct contact with the ugly business; he sub-let his rights to the highest bidder. And this bidder was now Director of the prison, and exploited his two thousand criminals to the top of his bent. There were never less than two thousand. And for years and years these two thousand were mulcted and fleeced so as to pay for a couple of Philip's state galleons, which ended up at the bottom of the English Channel.

Nothing in the prison was gratis. Whoever wanted anything to eat, beyond the villainous bread, must pay for it. There were four canteens in the big building; the Director supplied wine and victuals. Several shops sold greenstuffs and fruit, oil and vinegar, candles, ink, paper. On every onion, every goose-quill, the Director made his profit. Goods entering from outside had to pay duty. There was a tariff for everything. Sweeping the floors, de-lousing the beds, extermination of vermin, permission to burn a light —for all these there was a fixed charge. The warders made no bones of it; whoever did not pay of his own accord had his property taken from him. A prisoner's clothes would be taken off and auctioned in the "Old-Clothes Fair," quite simply so called.

In fact, most things here were unblushingly called by their right names. The prison had three gates, one behind the other: the gold, the silver and the copper, with reference to the amount of the bribe deposited on entrance. The accommodation depended on the size of the sum. You could live very well in this prison, in a comfortable room to yourself in the upper story; and you could endure the torments of the damned, herded two or three hundred together in foul-smelling enclosures.

Cervantes knew little of these arrangements and was badly provided with money; he found himself in the "iron room," a large, low chamber in the first story, with windows, much too small, looking out on the Posamenta.

The straw sacks lay close together on the floor. There was never an intermission to the quarrelling, screaming, laughing. A wild, incredible gaiety reigned. Constant games of chance went on. The most poverty-stricken would rake in his threepenny-pieces or accept the "word of honour" of his opponent; the game cost only money, for the Director lent cards and dice.

Miguel Cervantes, in the first few days, scarcely stirred from his bed. For if you did not die of hunger here, or get eaten up by lice, you had enough entertainment to last you for weeks. His fellow-prisoners were a medley of men beyond his dreams.

There was no classification according to the cause of imprisonment. Debtor, criminal and prisoner on trial were all lumped together. The merchant who could not take up a bill lay next to the condemned bandit. The dandy who was there on the suit of his tailor had to lie with the matricide for whom the gallows was being set up in the court. Burglars and brawlers, forgers and counterfeiters, perverts of every kind lived in fantastic association with people who had done nothing whatever and were only waiting to prove their innocence. A shaft with a grating over it gave a view from here into the women's quarters. The opening always had a crowd round it. In ten hours Cervantes learned more picturesque indecency of phrase than in all his roving existence until then.

The door to the "iron room" stood open. The inmates went to and fro. Visitors from the town were constantly being announced and received with uproarious acclaim. But when Cervantes got up for a breath of fresh air, he was met at the door by crossed halberds. He had to pay, once and for all. Nobody in the room was so poor as not to have done that. For the right to go to the latrine. And this was why so many ran about half-naked, with a shred of rag or half a bed-cover as clothing.

He made acquaintances in these days. They stole up about him, sat down beside him, breathed their all-too-fragrant breaths in his face and formally told him their cant names. They looked with respect at his stump, obviously in the belief that he had lost his hand on the executioner's block. "Bad job," said one. "He must have been a novice to chew it up that way." Miguel did not feel bound to enlighten them—he had told the story of Lepanto too often already. Another introduced himself as

Gambalon—"also nicknamed the Ham, since the day before yesterday His Majesty's slave." Which meant that on that day he had been condemned to the galleys.

"On what ground?" Cervantes politely asked.

"Street theft."

"Ah!"

There was a commotion at the door. A man was carried in, to all appearance dead. His friends hastily damped a sheet in wine and wrapped it round him.

Gambalon got up, excusing himself with formality. The man, he said, was Polarte, a very good chap, condemned to the lash twice a week. They had unfortunately not been able to raise the money to buy off the executioner. "What had Señor Polarte been guilty of?" "He had sinned with what you use." And as Cervantes looked inquiringly at him he paraphrased curtly "With what you use up," and took his leave, somewhat put off by so much ignorance.

Night came, and time to sleep, but no quiet with it. The shout of the guards echoed through the huge building: "Gates closing! Gates closing! For the third time: Gates closing!" Trampling, laughter, shouts. A flourish of trumpets. With a crash the gates fell to.

People crowded into the room. Many of them Cervantes had not seen during the day. Everybody pressed towards a rude little altar, with a picture of the Madonna done in saffron-colour, an oil lamp beneath it. A thick-set man who had draped his *capa* to make it look like a soutane, lighted two wax candles. Cervantes was astonished to see that he carried a short whip in his hand. Whoever lingered on his straw sack or did not interrupt his game was roused up. They all sang the *Salve* together, with the responses. Then the man with the whip ordered an *Ave Maria* and three *Pater Nosters.* And the whole extraordinary performance ended with a chorus roared full-throated by the assemblage: "Lord Jesus Christ, Who hast poured out Thy dear blood for me, have mercy on me, a sinner!"

There was a tremendous echo, the words seemed to come back from all the walls at once. In fact, they did so; for the several other similar rooms were the scene at the same moment of the same ceremony. Then the choir leader snapped his whip, and in the same moment the door opened and gave entrance, heralded by a cloud of musk, to thirty or forty women, the choicest product of the "Compas" and the Calle del Agua. It was plain that they were regularly admitted here, to offer their brief consolations.

Impossible for the new-comer to sleep. There was not the smallest concern. Everybody did what pleased him, publicly, ostentatiously. Light came from the altar and from the two images of saints to right and left of the door. Every half-hour the warders' cries resounded, like those of a ship's watch: "Vela! Vela! Ahao!" as they made their halberds ring on the stone floor.

But at last he did drop off. Then a glaring light pained his eyelids. By a weird torchlight he saw a group of masked people before him: the executioner in red clothes, two policemen and a monk. They were swinging a filthy doll that had a rope round its neck. "So shall the sinner die the death!" they cried all four in high, theatrical voices, and then stretched out their hands to beg. This happened every night, so Cervantes learned from his neighbour Gambalon, who scarcely interrupted his snoring to explain. The people who were responsible for it paid a monthly sum to the Director.

In the morning he saw no chance of washing. He

handed the turnkey half of his money and received free entrance to the court, where a fountain played between two permanent gallows.

Some hours later bread was given out. Always for three people a big, black, ill-baked slab. But prisoners were not allowed to have knives; so in a file they proceeded to the official cutter, who divided the loaf into four, one of the pieces being his to sell again. His fee to the Director for the privilege must have been quite a sizeable sum.

Cervantes sat on his straw and chewed, following with his sleep-weary eyes the painful progress of two bugs across his ticking. Then suddenly Gutiérrez stood before him. His friend was red in the face and gasping for breath, from either exertion or excitement. A thin-necked, fat-bellied flask of red wine hung down from his left hand. He looked about the wretched room, looked at one of the bugs—the other had disappeared—and made a sympathetic clucking sound with his tongue. "Come on, old man," he said then; that was all. Miguel got up obediently. His bundle was not yet unpacked. Gutiérrez put his arm about him and led him out of the "iron room" and through passages and up stairs alive with human kind. Miguel thought nothing else than that he was free; there was nothing Gutiérrez could not do. But before they reached the copper door they turned off and mounted higher. He followed where he was led.

In the top story a door stood open. It led into a good-sized, unoccupied room that was clean and sunny.

"Board and lodging paid for a month, Miguel mine! But you will be out before then. Write your petition as soon as you've the head for it. Then we shall pay them their two hundred *thaler* and you will be free."

Gutiérrez had set down his fat-bellied flask on the table; the September sun, pouring in, broke the crimson colour into a thousand flashing rubies. Cervantes looked at it dully.

He sat there, idle, in the middle of the room, after his friend had gone. Only the hum of voices came up to him from the madhouse below.

The Director lived in this top story, and let out the other rooms. They were but few, and the inmates were attentively served. They lived as in a good inn.

After a little while, a warder appeared with paper and writing materials. "By order of the gentleman who has just left. For the petition to the authorities. Your Grace was to be sure not to forget."

Cervantes nodded.

"If you have other wants, you have only to stand at your door and clap your hands. For supper there are eels and then ox-tongue with *sauce piquante*. But you could change it if you liked."

Cervantes sat submissively down in front of the sheaf of paper and dipped his pen. Of course, this imprisonment could not last. The case was so clear. But what then? What would he have gained when the three doors lay behind him and he stood in the streets of Seville once more?

He wrote slowly, with scribal flourishes, the superscription:

"To the Lord President of the Royal Finance Chamber, in Madrid."

But there he stuck. He could not get on. He happened to glance into the mirror which hung on the wall behind the table: a cheap affair, of polished tin instead of glass, three-cornered, with the point below, in a red wooden frame. Cervantes looked at himself. Good God, did he look like that? His chin-beard, and the long, drooping moustaches—had they not been golden but a little while ago? Now they were a dingy silver. And the long, deep, flabby folds beside the nose . . . and the mouth—he showed himself his teeth. Certainly there were not more than eight or ten, and no two of them met, sticking up in obstinate isolation. Only the eyes were unchanged. Otherwise . . . It was a bad glass and made all the features look long-drawn-out and quaintly melancholy. It was months since he had looked at himself—he took a melancholy pleasure in observing what life had left of him. Idly he began to scratch a picture of himself on the paper intended for his petition. The long lean visage went down, extravagantly long, with ridiculously hooked nose. To send the President of the Chamber a picture like that—it would be more impressive than any words. Suppose he drew himself on his mule, riding the stony roads on that accursed errand of his, his staff of office under his arm?

He made the sketch, and it pleased him. But he did not draw the well-fed, fiery-eyed Arabian mule. He drew a wretched, worn-out skeleton of a horse, and himself perched upon it, dry and seared of body, his legs hanging down without end. The staff of office he drew not round-topped, but pointed like a lance.

And, besides the lance, armour. He gave himself a coat of mail and a thing like a helmet, without a visor. And on the feet huge wheels for spurs. This, my lords and gentlemen of the Finance Ministry, was the knight who in the name and for the behoof of the Treasury plundered the already plundered land.

But the knight had come off his horse, and now sat

comfortably in jail. Leisure at last. A strange sort of satisfaction overtook him . . . that good Gutiérrez, who had helped him to this!

A man must look at himself some time, before he falls into his not far distant grave! He began walking up and down in the large room. He tried to think of and to clarify the past.

But it was too much. A confusion, an indistinguishable mingling of hope, resolve, and disillusionment, new attempt and new discouragement. "Church, or sea or court of Kings"—all illusion and disappointment. As King's bailiff, cursed and stoned by the peasantry! So it had ever been. Sometimes he had thought he held gold in his hand; opened it and found it filth. The Venetian Gina stood in the middle of the room, with a malicious smile on her white face. Don John of Austria's letter, hope of his youth —and his sentence to long imprisonment. Illusion, illusion! Drawn out till one was old and stiff, spreading chimeras before one's eyes, chimeras of happiness, chimeras of freedom. Once he had held freedom actually in his arms, and naught but disappointment ensued. For ah, her face was not lovely! What a trail of commonness lay, like a judgment, over all that the dreamer did!

Dusk had come in the room. He did not notice. The warder had brought his supper. He did not eat it. To and fro, across and across, he traversed his past. Always he followed the same roads, the rider seemed to meet himself, ghostlike. Illusion and dream! Dream of an India office, judgeship, governorship. Dream of immortal fame! Dream of country peace in the village in La Mancha . . .

But again he stopped. Always it filled him with an obscure sense of shame to recall that time. For long he had not thought of Catalina, although his child was growing up beside her. His child . . . a dream, too. He saw Catalina with her books. She sat on the floor, with all those dog-eared volumes of romantic rubbish about her, in which she believed. Hundreds of thousands of Catalinas there were in the broad lands of Spain, nourishing themselves on cobwebs, filling their ears with the last, foolish, dying echo of a great past, dreaming of all these Olivantes and Clarians, with shining weapons smiting giants and wicked spirits to earth. Far other was his hero.

His hero. . . . He went up to the table. By the candle that burned there he gazed at his primitive sketch. No, his knight was no beautiful youth, no rosy cherub. A rickety old man, grown a little queer in the head through reading all that bombastic tripe. Would it not be gorgeous to make such a one set out in the faith that the days of chivalry were still living? What a mad and bitter jest, to make him ride his bony nag through modern Spain, Spain as it was today—through La Mancha, where the peasants anguished over the price of eggs! To make him see in everything the honour of battle and the rescue of innocence—a touching foolishness, which thinks to grasp that which for ever escapes him and dissolves! And everywhere he draws down blows upon his head, is beaten, gets up again, goes on, for ever unconquerably deluded, with his ancient gaze fixed upon the light of his delusion, to him unquenchable!

From below came up the shout that heralded the closing of the doors. The babble of prayers began, it came up through floors and walls, the house shivered with the thousand-voiced chant of those outcast men. But already he had forgotten it. He seized his pen. On the page where he had set his superscription to the President, below his scribbled sketch, he began to write:

"In a village of La Mancha, the name of which I have no desire to call to mind, there lived not long since one of those gentlemen that keep a lance in the lance-rack, an old buckler, a lean hack, and a greyhound for coursing. . . ."

CHAPTER TWENTY-EIGHT

El Escorial

The chamber smelt of decay. And it was hot.

The window stood open to the September day, and incense was burning. But the smell of death persisted. For weeks King Philip had been dwindling and decaying as he lay, still drawing breath.

He was a skeleton. But in some places dropsy had puffed him out, which was gruesome to see. His open, festering sores exuded pus every day. They had long given up washing, bandaging or even moving him an inch in bed. He was sinking down motionless into his slough.

His mind was clear. And he was sick with loathing of himself. All his life he had been meticulously clean, morbidly fastidious. To drink from an unpolished cup was always impossible to him. Now the flies left him no peace.

He suffered for his attendants. He saw that doctors and priests, ministers and servants found it hard to be near him. He could scarcely summon courage to ask for service. If he needed something he spoke with a deprecating politeness, which was in itself an apology. Frightful it was to hear such words from that cold and distant man.

God was sending him sore trial. His whole body a seething and welling mass, he had a raging headache, sickness and oppression, no sleep, and a scorching thirst which the doctors forbade him to quench—and indeed there was no longer anything that could quench it.

He had regarded his whole existence as a forecourt of death. He had lived, so to speak, for his dying hour. But that it would stretch itself out like this, so endless, in this horrible, disgusting torment, he had not dreamed.

He endured it. Forty years of fantasy, in rigid and solitary majesty, bore now their sublime fruit: not one word of complaint issued from his cracked lips. In the midst of this rotting and dissolution, in this fetid atmosphere of the grave, he remained a king. It was still possible to address this remnant of a human being as "Your Majesty."

He was still able to think that this last affliction was God's pledge and promise of heavenly bliss. He who was most sorely tried would be most greatly exalted. From suffering and bodily humiliation he deduced the triumphal confirmation of his faith, to which he had sacrificed his happiness and the happiness of his domains.

In such a trial how insufficient must be the consolations which a human being could find within himself! One's own judgment, the untrammelled examination of one's own conscience, what frail reeds those were, upon which the northern heresy rested! What a pitiable wretch must a heretic be, in this frightful moment of passing over!

But all the saints, all the hosts of the blest encompassed him, King Philip, in this, his heavy hour. The thirty thousand masses for the dead had years ago been provided for down to the last detail; now from high to low the priesthood of Spain was safeguarding his road to bliss. From his pillows he could look through the adjoining room to the high altar of Capilla Mayor. In jasper, agate and porphyry the tabernacle glittered there like a foretaste of eternity. Beneath that altar lay the sarcophagus of his father the Emperor. About him the dead of their house. There, only a few paces away, their bodies waited upon his. And above in glory their purified souls were waiting for his to join them.

He was surrounded, encompassed, by the symbols of redemption. Wherever his dying eyes might rest, they fell upon some consoling sight. The whitewashed walls of his chamber were almost covered by pious pictures. There were reliquaries upon tables and tabourets, containing his greatest treasures, a splinter of the True Cross, the arm of blessed Saint Vincent, the knee of Saint Sebastian. The costly receptacles were lined with velvet, bound with gold, studded with bright jewels. In his bed hangings was suspended the small crucifix which the Emperor had held in his dying hands at Yuste.

Three times already had he confessed and taken communion. He listened greedily to the reading of the sacred texts. But tomorrow would be his greatest day, when he should receive the last unction, the crowning ceremony of his austere and ceremonial life.

He was prepared. He had had his hair and nails cut, to be more worthy to receive the sacrament. He had had indicated to him the parts of the body which the priest would anoint. He knew the very silver receptacle, containing the oil blest by the Pope. The new Archbishop of Toledo was to administer the unction, his assistants were most carefully designated, confessor, prior, house chaplain, majordomo, minister, members of the royal household. The Crown Prince was also to be present, that sole and half-foolish, weak-blooded heir who alone had survived from the King's four marriages; upon him it had pleased God to lay the burden of the crumbling state.

Today, for the last time, he had administered the affairs of his kingdom. There had been documents from the four quarters of the earth. But his arms hurt him too much; the fingers of the right hand were all one bleeding wound. So his confessor, Fray Diego, and his valet, Mora, read the papers to him, holding various ones before his eyes. He dictated marginal comments. All that had been done; there was an end now to all his earthly tasks. From tomorrow onwards the rest of his suffering earthly course should be devoted to prayer alone.

He lay alone. The two others waited, silently, near by.

One single paper was left. He had listened unmoved to the reading of it, then ordered it to be laid face down on the cover of his bed.

He had kept his eyes closed. There were faint clinking and rattling sounds from the church, the sacristan was probably setting things in order for evensong. The King let his gaze travel thither, and then back.

He was passing in affliction. He was a defeated man. His kingdom was split and furrowed by dissensions. For the third time, a few months ago, he had been declared bankrupt. The hegemony of the world, the dominion of the seas, the strength of his own nation, had all been staked on one single idea.

And God had not willed that this idea should triumph. Spain, indeed, and Italy, were preserved from infection. In Germany and Poland the disease had been checked. But Orange ruled in Holland and in England that abominable Jezebel. . . .

With all this he had come to terms. But one wound still smarted. With his ulcerous fingers he turned over the sheet of paper on his coverlet. It was a printed announcement, which had come yesterday from Paris with the embassy post. At the top was the coat of arms with the lilies, and another. The text was French, and began:

"On fait à savoir à tous que bonne, ferme, stable et perpetuelle Paix, Amitié et Réconciliation est faite et accordée entre Très-haut, Très-excellent et Très-puissant Prince, Henry par la grâce de Dieu Roy Très-chrétien de France et de Navarre, notre souverain seigneur et Très-haut, Très-excellent et Très-puissant Prince, Philippe Roy Catholique des Espagnes. . . ."

Peace, friendship, reconciliation—he had had to grant them to France, now before his death. To declare himself beaten. To give back Calais and Blavet. To yield all that he had gained in his frenzied struggles of forty years. And to recognize the sovereignty of this fourth Henri, who was all that he hated.

He had been converted, this King. Yes. He had been the chief of the heretic powers, now he was Catholic. He changed his faith like a coat. He was a thousand times worse than those who paid for their error at the stake. Unthinkable—yet quite obvious: this King believed in nothing at all. That which in his seventy years of life had filled Philip's heart and mind, to Henri was less than nothing. What counted was the sovereignty, the unity of his land, the well-being of his people. For these he would have become a Turk, a fire-worshipper. His famous edict, promulgating religious toleration and the equality of all the confessions before the law—what was that but the indifference of an impious man, to whom earthly happiness was all?

And God granted it to him. Philip was well informed. God had crowned with all the gifts of sovereignty the head of this blasphemous prince. He was an indefatigable worker; his memory was unerring, his judgment clear and independent, his intelligence like a flash of lightning. And his courage was like steel.

He routed the arrogant nobility with successive, stunning blows; selected his ministers with genius, and gave to his people a sense of being led and protected by an enlightened will. He did not govern France from a monk's cell, through sheaves of documents; he travelled throughout the land, went among the people, made himself accessible to his poorest subject, spoke to each in his own language and asked him what he wanted. France blossomed as under the rains of May. He took the same lively interest in agriculture, in business and in trade. With unerring touch he cleansed the financial and judicial administration of the country. No privilege availed, no questions were asked as to coats of arms or purity of blood—and a vast wave of confidence and trust went out towards this altogether earthly king.

Paix, Amitié, Réconciliation—no greater lie had ever been printed! How often had not Philip tried to have him killed!

A few weeks before, in the watches of the night, he had studied for a long time the portrait of his rival. Then put it away for ever. But it was a face not to forget, he saw it clearly. The small, sturdy, robust man, with his powerful face, the dashing crop of curly hair combed high above his forehead, the enormous, sensual nose, the wide, pleasure-loving mouth, the square-cut beard. And then the eyes, sparkling with life and irony, "hellishly clever and heavenly friendly eyes," as a tactless spy had described them, surrounded by playful wrinkles.

The portrait showed him in gala dress. But even so it betrayed that he wore it negligently, mockingly. The man was a Gascon: facile, rough and ready, without a shred of elegance or pomp; it was nothing to him that he smelt of sweat or garlic, he did not care. All the embassy mailbags were stuffed with shocking scandals about him: he had had three hundred love-affairs and not a ray of shame. When a woman had given him pleasure, he did not shut her up in a cloister after his mood had changed; he openly honoured her and loaded her with gifts. He was grateful for the joy she gave him. Harshness and cruelty were complete strangers to him—even treachery he scarcely punished.

How Philip hated him! Henri's very existence made a mockery of his own seventy years, of his stern, sombre life of renunciation in the service of the one, the exalted, the only true ideal. How could God let such impious unbelief triumph? Thy will be done, O Lord; but this will was incomprehensible, frightful. This hatred it was which still divided him from the peace of final parting. Not prayer, not confession and not the Sacrament had washed this hatred from his soul, this deep, mysterious, frightful doubt. O God, help me! Let me not be lost in my last hour! Incline unto me, O my God, give me strength, give me strength!

The two in the antechamber, confessor and valet, heard a rending shriek. They rushed to him.

The King, who for weeks had not been able to move an inch in bed, sat upright now, with tears streaming down his face. He had wrenched the Emperor's crucifix from the curtains and with his ulcerous hands was pressing it frantically to his lips.

CHAPTER TWENTY-NINE

The Knight

There was a timid knock. It came thrice before he lifted his head from his manuscript. Gambalon and Polarte entered.

"His Majesty's slave," still waiting on his transport, advanced bowing and scraping. Behind him, Señor Polarte —"sinner with that which one needs"—entirely beardless and hairless, his body somewhat awry from his frequent beatings. They had come with a request.

It concerned a certain Boffy, hanged today in the courtyard below. They were collecting money for his grave.

"Your Grace understands," explained Gambalon, choosing his language with care, "men set their hearts on all sorts of different things. This one was keen on his own funeral. He is unfortunately refused Christian burial; but he wanted to have a stone outside the wall, with a proper inscription. He would have liked Filabres marble, but it costs so much."

Cervantes reached in his drawer and gave them from the money which Gutiérrez had left.

But they did not leave upon that. They felt the need of justifying their efforts.

"It is a pity," Señor Polarte remarked in a falsetto voice,

"that Your Grace did not see him hanged. It would have been worth your while. His penitential shift fitted as though it had been made for him, and his hair was curled something beautiful. He spoke to the Father most politely and asked him to speak out and then praised what he had said. Then he went up the ladder in fine style, not in leaps and bounds nor yet too lingeringly; drew back the folds of his shift and put the rope round his own neck. What more could one ask?"

"That's enough," Gambalon interrupted him. "Don't talk any more. You'll make His Grace forget all his inspirations." Then, by the door: "But it is all right about tonight, after the Ave?"

"Yes, come along," Cervantes said.

But now that he had been interrupted, he drew his chair up to the open window and rested a while. He could see both shores, the river and beyond. The sky above Triana glowed with the purple and emerald hues of sunset.

Forty or fifty times he had seen from his window the sun go down. His imprisonment could not last much longer. To be sure, he had never sent off his petition. But Gutiérrez had gone to Madrid, it was not hard to guess on what errand.

Cervantes was grateful. What a friend to have! But when he asked himself, he found that he was in no hurry. He would not have been horrified at the idea of being shut up in this room for a year—or even three—and finishing his work.

In art everything depends on the point of departure. His was good. His journey was blest.

Don Quixote was now no longer, nor had been for some time, the simpleton whose head had been turned by the romances of chivalry. He was one possessed, but thereby exalted. He committed the follies of a dozen madmen, but his speech was wisdom.

And for some time now he had had a companion. Sancho Panza trotted beside him on his little ass! Sancho Panza the platitudinous, baked out of very coarse meal. Half credulous, half doubting, half out of love of gain and half in a dumb sense of reverence for the nobility of the delusion, the future lieutenant followed his master, and his heavy peasant back got used to blows.

Long ago, too, the Captain of the castle—who was the landlord of a tavern—had dubbed Don Quixote knight; the frightful, unheard-of battle with the windmills had taken place, the noble Rosinante been avenged, the painful adventures in the enchanted castle been blamelessly withstood, and Don Quixote wore, instead of his cardboard head-gear, the enchanted golden helmet of Mambrinus, a shiny barber's basin.

The fount had been tapped, and it gushed forth—a perfect flood of stories and characters. All that he had perceived and felt, in all his thirty years of wandering, now saw the light. There was room, in the frame set up in his first happy attack on his theme, for everything—slave stories, love stories, travel stories—everything fitted as into a happy dream.

And as in happy dreams there is a certainty without words, so without words he knew all the faces that hid behind Don Quixote's lean visage. They peered out, but he did not summon them. Not himself, though after all it was he who had come down out of the looking-glass into this book. Not Don John of Austria, that last brilliant knight who in his folly had clutched after crowns like a frantic boy. And not that monkish mute in the Escorial, whose life had ended in these autumn days and for whose mighty, lifelong illusion the prisoners downstairs were still paying.

He was simply writing a funny book, to make a mock of the romance of chivalry. Would anyone inquire further? Would anyone see behind his hidalgo the spirit of Spain, in blind enthusiasm seeking the past, while all about her the world was rousing to new realities? He shrugged his shoulders. There was nothing to explain. Fable and meaning were one, like a fruit and its smell.

Cervantes was happy. He knew what had been vouchsafed him. Before him, this had not been in the world.

The name and fame of his knight had already reached beyond his prison cell. The first confirmation had come in, the first priceless premonitory gleam of future renown.

It was probably his warder who had reported abroad that there was a gentleman sitting in the top story who wrote day and night on a romance of chivalry. Visitors came. Not the most innocent in the world. The worst gallows-birds from the "iron room" and the "pestilence" mounted the stair to learn what the one-handed man up there was doing.

And he did not let himself be asked twice. He did not hold off. He gave of his best. His fame spread through the house. All these ruffians, procurers, bandits appreciated his jokes. They came in groups, in crowds. Three weeks before, for the first time, his public had assembled *en masse*, with their ladies. He read aloud the tilting at the windmills. Next day half Seville had heard of him. The Director of the prison appeared in person, more like a refined and drooping little scholar than the exploiter he really was, and asked the loan of the manuscript for a few hours. Irreproachable gentlemen of the city let themselves be locked in of an evening to be present at a reading.

But today they were among themselves, no visitors from the city. Hardly had the bawling of the evening prayer ceased to ring through the house than Cervantes' room was full. They squeezed against the wall, they squatted on the floor, the door had to be left open, for there were more in the corridor. Cervantes sat beside two candles, with the smallest of free space about him.

He was glad, on certain grounds, that he had not a mixed public today.

He waited good-naturedly until all was quiet, scanning his audience by the flickering, dancing light. Bald heads, barbaric beards, astonishing heads of hair. Legs stretched out towards him in torn hempen shoes, yellow drawers, huge red knee-ribbons, slashed jerkins, coarse bed-covers that disclosed the naked flesh, frayed Walloon collars. The women's faces were rouged a garish red, their uncovered breasts a bluish white.

"How Don Quixote conferred freedom on several unfortunates who against their will were being carried where they had no wish to go."

It was the story of the twelve galley-slaves whom Don Quixote meets, chained neck to neck and under heavy escort, on their way to the harbour. He learns of their plight and decides to free them. "Here is a case for the exercise of my office, to put down force and to succour and help the wretched. . . . For, dear Brethren, it may be that perhaps this one's want of courage under torture, that one's want of money, the other's want of advocacy, and lastly the perverted judgment of the judge may have been the cause of your ruin and of your failure to obtain the justice you had on your side." And as of course the escort is not at all minded to surrender, he lays his lance in rest and brings the King's officer to the ground. This is the signal for a general confusion, the guards are overpowered and the slaves set free.

Applause was about to burst forth, when Cervantes raised his mangled hand for silence. His tale was not yet done.

He read the conclusion. Read how the freed slaves do not thank their deliverer; how they mock him and throw stones at him, beat him about the body with his golden helmet, steal his and Sancho's mantles and run off. . . .

"The ass and Rosinante, Sancho and Don Quixote, were all that were left upon the field; the ass with drooping head, serious, shaking his ears from time to time as if he thought the storm of stones that assailed them was not yet over; Rosinante stretched beside his master, for he too had been brought to the ground by a stone; Sancho stripped, trembling with fear of the Holy Brotherhood; and Don Quixote fuming to find himself so served by the very persons for whom he had done so much."

Shrieks of delight broke out before he had done. The roars of laughter made the candles flicker. They howled. They slapped their thighs. All the women were beside themselves; screaming in their enthusiasm they flung their arms about their neighbours' necks and slobbered kisses on them. Truly this was fame!

Not quite that which Cervantes had expected. He could hardly believe it. He had shown them their own lot, their own misery—and one, in crumbling armour, who had taken it upon himself. But they had for him nothing but jeers. They agreed with their companions in misery, who stoned him. Cervantes had not exaggerated—here was the proof. It froze him to the marrow.

He got up, held his candle high and let its light flicker over the assemblage. On the floor in the front row sat Gambalon, His Majesty's slave, awaiting as he had done for weeks for transport and the chain round his neck. He had flung himself back in merriment till he lay in a woman's lap, his mouth was so wide open with laughter that you could see deep into his gullet.

They broke up unwillingly. The echo of their voices died away. The atmosphere they left behind dissipated slowly through the open window.

The autumn sky was glorious with sparkling stars. Above Triana the heavens were still bright from the departed day.

He smiled at himself. What was his grievance against them? That they laughed? But Don Quixote was made to be laughed at. Why should he complain?

But he took a resolve: there should be one place, one single place in his book where the naked truth should be expressed, for all to see. Just once, he would speak. At the very end, after a thousand pages, a hundred adventures, the magic word should be spoken. Upon the further threshold of his mighty edifice he would lay the tiny key which should open its innermost chamber.

Don Quixote's end has come. His friends are about him. Sancho talks amid sobs of new expeditions and new adventures. But the long dream is slowly dissolving from the view of that obstinately deluded man, and he says:

"Slowly, my friends, very slowly. There are no birds in last year's nest. I am no longer Don Quixote of La

Mancha. I am Alonzo Quijano, whom folk once called *the Good.*"

Yes, so at last should his book end, with the simple key-word: Good.

Above Triana the sky was still a little bright. Against it he saw his knight's gaunt form riding, always after the Gleam, through space and centuries; his horse's hoofs stumbling across Spanish soil, but that noble and fantastic head of his among the stars.